Of Shadows, Sins, & Saviors
Red Death
An Elven Shadow Warrior Tome

B.G. Ridge

OS3 Publications—Okmulgee, Oklahoma
Paperback ISBN: 979-8-9912608-0-0
eBook ISBN: 979-8-3303-5452-8
Library of Congress Control Number: 2024916354
Title: *Of Shadows, Sins, & Saviors: Red Death: An Elven Shadow Warrior Tome*
Author: B.G. Ridge
Digital distribution | 2024
Paperback | 2024

This is a work of fiction. The characters, names, incidents, places, and dialogue are products of the author's imagination, and are not to be construed as real.

Published in the United States by New Book Authors Publishing

Dedication

This book is dedicated to my beautiful wife. You have put up with my long hours spent creating, cursing, and changing this fictional work into the beautiful world it has become. This world and its inhabitants would not be possible without your loving spirit and beautiful soul guiding my thoughts and hands.

From the moment I saw you, you have been and will always be my inspiration in life. This book is also dedicated to my six kids. You all have enriched my life beyond measure. Your unique qualities are instilled into my characters bringing them to life and enriching the world they create for themselves.

MLR & HDR Sr. Embrace eternity with HDR Jr. and SPU. Tell them we miss them down here in the realm of Terra.

Prologue

A female shrouded within a red misty haze watched the crimson haired dwarf enter the building a floor below her. Strapped to his back was a massive war hammer covered in red stains. She didn't need to question the nature of the red stains. The splatter pattern more than explained that in detail. "He and his mercenaries will do. Show him to the office." She felt a small breeze behind her as the wraith vanished.

The red haired dwarf paced impatiently back and forth in the large open foyer that was two stories tall. He hated being kept waiting for whoever he was to meet to show up. Just as he was about to walk out, an elven female walked into the foyer and bowed.

"Right this way sir. I'll lead you to the office." The elf led him to an oversized thick door. After opening it she gestured for him to enter. "They will be along shortly. Help yourself to some alcohol while you wait."

He didn't bother acknowledging her as he entered the large office. Opposite the doorway, sat a wall-to-wall dark stained wooden book shelf loaded with books, small paintings, and other odd trinkets displayed as trophy finds. He figured they were more likely just purchases displayed as treasure hunter finds. Sitting in front of the book case facing the door was a large akora wood desk with a large leather chair. Sitting in front of the desk were two smaller chairs turned in slightly so whoever sat there would see the person behind the desk and the person beside them.

He knew this arrangement well. The size of the desk and main chair were scare tactics used to intimidate the one or two sitting in the smaller chairs. Lord of the manor looking at the lesser people. He scoffed. He'd seen the matriarchs in the dwarven districts use this tactic all the time. Including his mother who used to be matriarch of their district before she died.

"Big hammers intimidate people more than large desks and chairs.

One is all show, the other is all action." He patted his war hammer as he looked around the rest of the room waiting once again. Which he also knew, having to wait was another intimidation tactic all on its own. It was meant to tell him whoever he was waiting on was more important than he will ever be. In their own mind anyway.

He faced away from the desk and looked up at a framed painting of a male orc dressed in noble clothes wearing an uppity-I'm-better-than-you grin. Sticking out of the painting was an arrow that had been shot through the forehead of the man. "Did they not like the painting or the man?" Crimson pondered.

"Neither." He spun around at the sudden sound of a male's husky voice. A large beefy orc the color of the evergreen trees that covered the Southern Isles sat in the chair behind the desk. It was as if he'd just appeared. Crimson looked towards the door and back at the orc. He wondered how such a massive figure snuck in and sat down without him hearing any noise or noticing any movement. He also noticed the orc's strong resemblance to the man in the painting. The large orc's voice drew him out of his thoughts.

"He would have been lucky to die that way instead of in the manner he did. He was ripped apart by a shadow magic user while his heart still pumped traitorous blood through his veins. But we aren't here to discuss my brother and the manner in which he died. We are here to discuss other individuals and the manner in which they are going to die."

"Red death here will smash their heads to a pulpy mess," the dwarf said, reaching his hand up to pat his beloved war hammer. "But you look important enough and massive enough to have your own mercenary army. Why bring me and my Legion of Red Death in to do the work? Your way, you control the slaughter and pay only your hired mercenaries. My way, I control the slaughter and it becomes quite expensive for you. My legions services are not cheap."

"Why, doesn't matter and neither does the gold you get paid up front and after you complete the task." The massive orc grinned at the dwarf. "If you survive to come see me again and collect the rest." He threw three large bags of coins onto the desk as well as a note with a list of names.

"The names on this list must die, however you see fit. Most of the order doesn't matter. The only one that matters is that the last name on that list. They are your top priority. You will need to be smart in order to accomplish this task. Meaning you won't be able to just ramble through the kingdom killing at random as you normally do. Quiet and discretion over loud and obnoxious. If the dominion knows you're coming, you will lose the battle and your life. I pay you. You pay your legionnaires. The top priority name is last on that list to die. Do you understand my terms?"

The dwarf looked at the names on the list then the three bags of coins. He smiled wide and nodded. "They are as good as dead. Your top priority name is a dangerous individual. This will be fun."

"Don't get cocky. They're a hard target to cage."

The red headed dwarf smiled. "There's your mistake. Don't cage what you can pulverize."

"Leave and get to work. Come find me after you've had your fun." He watched the dwarf load up and walk out.

Twenty minutes later a wraith appeared in front of the large orc and bowed. "The dwarf has left the estate."

The orc slumped to the desk, his head landing hard face down. A red ghostly figure rose up out of the large unconscious orc and floated to his side. "Good. I didn't want to be that big oaf's puppeteer any longer than I had to. He reeks of months' worth of sweat, dirt, grime, and alcohol. Too much time invested in hunting down his brother's killer, who was on that list of names, and not enough time invested in personal hygiene. If the damned dwarf didn't have severe mommy issues, I wouldn't have had to use him. Luckily, the orc won't remember any of this but he will wake up with a splitting headache. Watch the dwarf from a distance. Do not approach him or his mercenaries. If he starts straying from his task alert me."

The ghostly red figure watched the black wraith bow then vanish. She smiled at the unconscious orc.

"Thanks for being a narrow minded and simple fool." She pulled the arrow from the picture and placed it on the desk by his head. "Ponder that when you wake up somewhere different from where you went to sleep."

A red smoke ring appeared then rose up as both vanished.

Chapter One

"There will come a time when you must embrace the darkness and use it to your advantage," Luthias Blackridge whispered into the night breeze as he peered deeper into the dark forest around him. The same words his grandfather would always say when they would begin their night hunts and training sessions. As a kid, Luthias hated and feared the darkness, so his grandfather began training him in the ways of the ancient elven shadow warriors. Warriors who take the disadvantages the darkness provides and uses them to their advantage.

"If you can't see, use your other senses to help you see. Listen for their footsteps. Sniff the air and see if you can catch your enemy's scent. Always imagine you are hunting yourself. If you can hear your footsteps, so can they. If you can smell your own scent, so can they. Also don't distract yourself by thinking too much."

Luthias laughed at the last point and pushed the thoughts of his grandfather to the back of his mind as he continued searching for his prey.

He knew she was nearby, because unlike most people, he had an uncanny sense that told him when his prey was nearby. *"Trust your gut. Trust your instincts."* He shook the thought of more of his grandfather's wise words away as he stalked through the darkness crossbow in hand, loaded and ready to shoot.

He searched the forest floor for any sign that his prey had walked the same path. But the clutter of the forest floor hid any such signs, so he stopped and knelt onto one knee. As he looked around it occurred to him where she was. "Nakira, you clever fox," he whispered with a chuckle. "You're getting better at hiding your trail."

Nakira sat on a large branch, up against the trunk of the tree she sat in. Bow in hand with an arrow notched, she watched Luthias walk into view then stop and look around. "Perfect spot, prey. Gotta love our version of hide and seek," she whispered as she pulled the string of her carved oak recurve bow back to take her shot. But as she lined up her shot, she got lost in the sight of his broad muscular body, his high cheekbones, and angled elven jawline partially covered by his long light brown goatee.

She watched him spot the branch she accidentally cracked when she climbed up into the tree. She knew he would notice it if he walked down the same path she did, which he always had the uncanny knack to do somehow. So, that's why she moved to another tree, two trees over.

"Even if you crack it accidentally, use it as a diversion. Move to another tree leaving your enemies to look in that tree while you shoot them from another angle." She chuckled when she heard his voice in her mind repeating the words for the millionth time.

She watched him remove his broad-brimmed black hat revealing his long light brown hair when he started looking up into the trees for her. The thing that stuck out most to her was his angled deep-set purple eyes. She got lost gazing into his bright glowing purple eyes as he searched for her knowing she was nearby and in one of the trees.

Before she could take the shot, he replaced his hat and walked out of her line of sight. "Damn it, don't get distracted. You're so close to winning this round," she said, cursing herself quietly in the hot night air. She pushed her hood off her head to keep the sweat from running down her face and getting into her eyes. She hated wearing the hood on hot nights, but he always made her wear it. "I got the shot this time," she whispered as she waited for him to walk into sight again.

Luthias walked a couple of steps, looking up into the trees. A noise on the ground grabbed his attention. He crouched low and smiled as he changed directions and walked towards the sound.

When he arrived close to where he thought he had heard the sound, he dropped to a knee and raised his crossbow as he watched for movement up in the trees. He heard another noise on the ground a little west of him but stayed put, keeping his eyes focused on the trees.

He smiled when he caught a glimpse of movement in a large akora tree that was two trees right of the tree with the cracked limb. He aimed his crossbow when he caught a glimpse of her lavender-colored hair shimmering in the faint moonlight. "I always warn you to keep your hood up. Even if you have the shot. Someone else might have a better shot." He squeezed the trigger on his crossbow sending the cross-bolt towards his target. "That lavender hair will get you killed."

"Ouch!" Nakira said, feeling the sting of his cross-bolt striking her just above the left breast. "Damn you, Luthias Blackridge."

He burst into laughter when he heard her cursing from her treetop perch. He let his crossbow fall beneath his black gambeson jacket then sat down on a nearby fallen log. After she climbed down she walked out into a small patch of moonlight that had made its way through the thick forest canopy. The first part of her he saw was the dark skin of her beautiful heart-shaped face glistening from the sweat of the unseasonably humid night. As she walked closer, his eyes followed her lavender-colored bangs hanging down over the right side of her face. Her narrowed almond-shaped emerald eyes glowed in the darkness.

He continued to scan over her femininely muscled human figure hugged beneath her form-fitting dark leather armor. "The tailor did an excellent job on that armor."

"Yes, it fits tight how I like, yet still gives me the freedom to move naturally." He watched her unfasten the top of her armor, then pull it open to reveal everything from the waist up, including the whelp developing just above her left breast. "Damn it, Luthias, how do you keep taking the first shot? On our last hide and seek session, I stayed on the ground and you went up into the trees. Once I figured out you were up there, I figured balancing and moving up high would hinder you, giving me a chance to see you. But you tagged me before I spotted you. This time I decided to go up into the treetops. I wanted to see if I could settle in and get the height advantage, which I did. But you disappeared behind a tree and shrubs before I could take the shot. Again, a little bit after you disappeared, you shot me before I could find you again. I heard you off to the west, yet you shot me from here."

Luthias whistled loudly. They watched a majestic midnight-blue wolf trot out of the darkness.

"Luthias, you used Nera as bait?" she asked as she tossed his cross bolt to him.

He laughed as he caught the cross bolt. "Embrace the disadvantages the darkness gives you and use them to your advantage. Don't let my devilish good looks distract you next time."

She dropped to her knee as Nera walked up and laid her head on Nakira's foot. "Nera, how could you do this to me? I could have shot you." Nera sighed then panted as Nakira petted the soft fur on her head and neck.

Luthias laughed, "I'm not even that good a shot with my crossbow, so the chance of you shooting her with your bow is purely accidental."

Nakira stuck her tongue out making him laugh as he dug a vial out of his jacket pocket and tossed it to her.

"Looks like my cross-bolt broke the skin, rub some of that on before it gets infected. Knight Captain Clive Brasscoat won't be too pleased if I send his scout back too injured to report for duty tomorrow."

She smiled flirtatiously, "I'd just have to heal up at your place making you take care of me all night and all day." Nakira held up the vial and watched the thick red slimy salve slowly ooze back and forth. "What is this?"

He laughed at the face she made as her eyes followed the slime.

"It's a salve a traveling merchant makes for me. I've been out since we left Tros'mura and haven't seen him until recently. It smells like dragon dung but works quickly. Come on, we need to get back to Traemorra and get some rest. Your Knight Captain knows you're out with me and will have you up early to put you to the test."

Nakira looked down at the growing lump above her breast. "This is going to hurt for a while." Her nose wrinkled up after she pulled the cork out of the vial. "This stuff does smell like dragon dung."

She looked up as Luthias laughed and stood. She rubbed the salve on the lump as she watched him adjust his hat. She loved his long light brown hair and how his bright, round purple eyes glowed in the darkness. As she sat and stared at the rest of him, she realized he and Nera were now walking away leaving her alone. She closed the vial then ran to catch up.

He groaned and laughed when she jumped and landed on his back wrapping her arms and legs around him. He looked back over his shoulder at her.

"You did a lot right but still made one critical mistake, tonight. You did well keeping your tracks hidden in the clutter of the underbrush and forest floor. You also moved two trees away from the tree with the cracked limb. Even if you crack it accidentally, use it as a diversion. Move to another tree leaving your enemies to look in that tree while you shoot them from another angle. You did well there. But you didn't leave your hood up like I keep reminding you. You also could've used your cloaking spell. Remember, just because you have a shot on your prey, doesn't mean someone else doesn't have a better shot on you. I caught a glimpse of your hair in the moonlight as you adjusted to take your shot. If you had your hood up or your cloak spell up, you would've gotten your shot off and won this round of hide and seek. Had I been a bandit or a mercenary, you would be dead right now. I would be hunting someone down and dragging their ass away to become live bait for hellions down in the Lava Flats."

Before she could defend herself, Luthias dropped to his knee causing his wolf to crouch, look around, and let out a low, guttural growl.

Nakira looked around as she slid off his back and quickly refastened her armor. She watched him point at what had caught his eye. When she saw his target, she knew what he had planned to do. They notched their bows and aimed. When Luthias nodded his head, they both fired their weapons. In the distance, a rugged-looking husky dwarf with a long, scruffy black beard and long scraggly hair, let out a holler as he and his tipped-back chair fell to the ground.

"What in blazes?" the confused dwarf hollered out then shook his head and straightened his beard. As he stood up, he reached over, picked up a blunt-tip arrow and cross bolt off the ground. He looked out into the darkness but didn't see anyone moving around.

"Come on out so I can kick your asses. Pritchett, Shamus, if this was you two, I'm gonna shove these so far up your asses you're gonna cough up these blunt tips. Then I'm putting you two on latrine duty for the rest of the year."

The dwarf had just finished speaking when Luthias, Nera, and Nakira walked out of the darkness. The dwarf kept an angry look on his face. "Shadow Knight Blackridge, don't believe yourself too high and mighty to have my boot upside your ass."

With a stern look, Luthias stared down at the young dwarf. "Gate Captain Borgroff, there is no way you're kicking my ass without standing on that chair first." They busted out laughing. "Sorry Borgroff, we saw you tipped back in the chair and couldn't help but take advantage."

Borgroff rolled his eyes. "Yeah, yeah." He turned to Nakira. "Don't let this ornery bastard get you into trouble with the knight captain."

Nakira giggled, "Nor with my Gate Captain."

Borgroff chuckled as he nodded then looked up into the night sky for a minute then back at them.

"I finished my guard patrol then sat out here and gazed up at the stars for a little while. Kind of hard to do with my eyes shut, I guess. I'm going to head off to the barracks and finish my nap in my bed where I am hopefully safe from arrows and bolts."

Borgroff smiled as he tossed the arrow and bolt to Luthias. "Goodnight." He reached down and petted Nera. "Goodnight to you as well my lady." He bowed and laughed when the wolf wagged her tail and barked at him.

Luthias, Nera, and Nakira followed him into Traemorra. "We better get some sleep as well. Clive will be getting you up early."

After walking through the city gates, she watched him head off towards his house.

"He can't wake me up early, if he can't find me right away. You do have room for one more in that lonely full-sized bed, don't you?"

He kept walking as he answered her, "why Ms. Karvina, are you suggesting a sleepover at my place? What will my girlfriend think?"

"I personally know that she loves the idea. I figure it will take the knight captain a while to find me." She watched him stop then turn and smile at her as she continued talking, "More sleep for me."

"It might not take him as long as you think. He already knows we were training tonight and he knows we are together." Luthias looked her over and smiled as she began unfastening her leather armor again. "Come on, demon spawn. I knew those two Rein sisters would corrupt you."

They watched Nera lie down on the front porch as they entered the wood framed stucco house. Luthias laid his crossbow and Nakira's bow onto his worktable then hung the two quivers up on the wall above the workbench.

Nakira smirked, "I should make you swap places with Nera for shooting me and using her as bait."

Luthias chuckled and shook his head, "Every trap needs bait." He watched her until she disappeared into his bedroom.

He was checking her bow over when he heard quiet footsteps behind him making him smile. "There comes a time when you must embrace the darkness and use it to your advantage," he said without turning around. He chuckled when he heard her sigh.

"My grandfather repeated those words every time he trained me in the ways of the ancient elven shadow warriors. Once I was far enough along in my training, he blindfolded me in the woods. Through that training, I developed a heightened awareness of my surroundings by using all my senses to see what my eyes couldn't."

He turned to see her standing in the middle of the room wearing nothing but a beautiful pouty smile upon her rose-colored full lips.

"I heard the shuffle of your footsteps and smelled your rose petal and lilac perfume. These are the lessons I'm passing on to you. Besides, it defeats the purpose of trying to sneak up on me when you and I are the only two people in this small two-room house."

She ran her hand through her short lavender hair and pulled the bangs away from her face, revealing her beautiful, sparkling, emerald eyes. He followed the feminine muscled curves of her nude dark-skinned human figure down to her beautiful long legs. "But, I see you did pick the best outfit to do it in at least."

"Would you rather work on the curves of my bow?" she asked smiling as she walked over to him, pressed her body against his, and wrapped her arms around his neck. "Or the curves of my body? Also, you only mentioned three of the five senses. What you heard and smelled, then saw after you turned around. What happened to what you feel and taste?"

He leaned in, kissed her, and pulled her soft, supple body tighter. "I'll tell you about those two in the bedroom." Luthias lifted her off her feet, walked into the bedroom, and threw her onto the bed. Luthias stripped and lay down beside her, wrapping her in his arms. "We're not getting much sleep tonight, are we?" He laughed when she bit her lip, grinned, and shook her head.

"Pure demon is what you are."

She smiled and laughed, "Etherika and Syn Rein trained me right, I guess. Good thing I'm dating a demon hunter."

Chapter Two

Luthias felt like he hadn't been asleep for long when he heard someone knocking on the door. "I'm asleep, come back later." He lay there listening but didn't hear anything so he rolled over and snuggled against Nakira.

A minute later, he heard a knock again, but this time it was a little louder. He huffed as he rolled over, "Fine, I'm coming." He climbed out of bed and slid his britches on as he watched her lying nude and uncovered in his bed. He smiled when he saw her hair had formed a set of horns upon her pillow. "Definitely worthy of demon horns."

Once again, he heard an even louder knock on the door. "Yes, patience please, I'm on my way." Just as he reached the door they knocked again. "This had better be life and death…" He opened the door to see a young, short, light-skinned, Traemorra guard looking up at him with tired squinting eyes as he finished talking. "Because if it's not a life-or-death matter, it will be for you."

Luthias looked past him and saw it was still dark outside. "What's wrong, soldier? Why are you disturbing me in the middle of the night?"

The guard bowed. "I apologize for disturbing you this early Shadow Knight Blackridge, but Knight Captain Brasscoat sent me to retrieve you."

"Good morning," Nakira said in a tired voice behind him.

Luthias turned and saw Nakira walk into the room wearing nothing, but Luthias's black tunic shirt which only half covered her naked ass as she stretched and yawned. He turned back to see the young guard grinning ear to ear, his tired squinting eyes now wide open. Luthias laughed as he heard her speak again. "Sounds important, did Knight Captain Brasscoat say what he needed?"

The guard stood quiet for a second before answering her, "Some men are causing trouble over at the Red Dog Saloon."

Luthias watched the soldier's eyes follow her as she walked up to them. He heard her snicker at his attention before she replied, "Isn't that a task more suited to Traemorra guards, like yourself, than a Shadow Knight and a rogue scout?"

The young guard stood red-faced and embarrassed by her appearance as he stuttered his answer, "Ye, yes, ma'am, my lady. But Knight Captain Brasscoat said it was someone Lord Blackridge and the Council of Kings had a bounty on."

Luthias stood there waiting for the young guard to continue but all he could do was stare at Nakira. "Soldier, who would that be?" Luthias heard Nakira giggle quietly in his ear again.

"Oh! Sorry, a mercenary named Cut-throat."

"Okay, wait out here with Nera." Luthias laughed as the guard stumbled backward unable to turn away from the sight of Nakira walking away.

"That is what I mean when I say Syneris and Etherika Rein have corrupted you. You enjoy doing that way too much."

Nakira laughed as he shut the door. "I have no idea what you're talking about. Your former girlfriends, Etherika Rein and her sister Syneris Rein only showed me how to handle this world and make it work to my whims. Besides, all I did was walk out to see who disturbed our sleep. I didn't expect Clive's wake-up call to be this damn early."

"Work to your whims? When I see them again, we are going to see whose whims are best served." He heard her laughing. "This time it was that poor young guard, the last time it was the young man delivering my order from the General Store. Both times you walked out with your naked ass peeking out from underneath my tunic and your hair looking like you just wrestled a demon."

Nakira smirked, "I believe I had just wrestled a demon slayer both times and if I heard you right, you did say I'm worthy of demon horns."

Luthias laughed as he walked past her and slapped her bare ass. He shook his head when he heard her laughing behind him. "Come on demon spawn, let's get dressed. We have a bounty to collect."

As they approached the main road Luthias stopped and looked at Nakira. "You, Nera, and the guardsman grab some men and have them set up an ambush just west of the southwest gate. I want three archers hidden up in the trees and the rest hidden on the ground. Nera no one escapes the perimeter." He petted the wolf as she barked. "Clive and I will lead Cut-throat and his crew into the ambush. I don't want any citizens getting caught up in the fight."

After he kissed Nakira and watched them hurry off, Luthias felt an odd sensation come over him in the dark early morning cool air. He searched his surroundings carefully. He watched a dark red female orc vagrant disappear into a darkened alleyway. He saw a large black raven sitting on the corner of a building, and a young female walking a dog down a side street. Seeing nothing suspicious, he shook the feeling away and hurried to the Red Dog Saloon.

As he approached the front entrance, he saw a tall, rugged-looking human with a long gray, blonde mixed goatee waiting with a group of soldiers. Luthias waved the soldiers over to him. "You men head out to the west side of the southwestern gate. Another soldier's gathering men to form an ambush." He watched the guards run off. "Clive, I was sleeping peacefully."

"I'm guessing this other soldier is my scout, Nakira Karvina. The one you were training with last night," Clive said, smiling wide. "I bet your training completely wore you out. Did you two even leave your bedroom during this training session?"

Luthias laughed rolling his eyes.

Clive laughed as he patted his shoulder, "I will say though, an ambush is a clever idea though. Draw them away from the townspeople. The only bad part about your plan, we are the bait."

Luthias shrugged and chuckled. "Every trap needs bait, old friend."

They walked in and saw several broken tables and a bunch of chairs turned over with shards of glass shattered throughout the mess. The mercenaries were all bellied up to the bar being rowdy and causing trouble as Luthias yelled over their loud voices. "What's the matter Cut-throat? Is the ale not as terrible as you're used to so you decided to throw a tantrum?"

He watched a brutish-looking red orc with a single braid of black hair extending from the top of his head down to his shoulders turn to look at him. He also saw the long scar leading from right to left across his neck which was the orc's namesake. Luthias looked around at the others.

"The Red Dog's ale is probably colder and fresher than you fellows are used to. I bet the bartender has some old, warm, rotten ale out back that'll be more to your liking."

The orc, a head shorter but twice Luthias' mass, walked towards him and the knight captain with an evil grin. Behind Cut-throat and the rest of the mercenaries, Luthias saw a fiery-haired olive-skinned female orc with upturned, rounded, ruby eyes glaring. He noticed she had a flame spell ready in both hands. Luthias slyly shook his head and watched the saloon owner drop her hands and the flame spells.

Cut-throat laughed when he saw only two people standing in front of him. "Well, look here boys. The heroes have finally come to save the day. But you seem to be shorthanded. Where's the rest of your crew at Blackridge? Is the Traemorra guards too afraid to fight us?"

Luthias laughed, "No, we told them to sit this one out. They would all just be standing around bored while the knight captain and I kill your men leaving you to rot in the dungeons alone."

"Big talk for someone who hasn't made his move yet." As Cut-throat finished talking, Luthias shot a cross bolt right past his head causing Cut-throat to duck to the side quickly. "You missed. You're getting sloppy Blackridge."

A large, ruthless-looking, blue-skinned orc two heads taller than Luthias crashed hard onto the floor, interrupting Cut-throat.

Luthias smiled, "The dead large blue orc lying on the ground with my cross-bolt sticking out of his eye might argue your point…" He shrugged. "…if he wasn't dead."

"Futuo!" Cut-throat shouted at his men as he pointed. "Get them but I need Blackridge alive."

Luthias and Brasscoat ran out leading the mercenaries through town and out the front gate. As Luthias and Brasscoat ran through the ambush, arrows rained down behind them from the trees as men jumped out surrounding the orcish mercenaries and preventing their exit. Luthias and Brasscoat watched as the Traemorra guards cut down Cut-throat and the other bandits. Luthias ran up to Cut-throat seeing him still moving. "Who hired you?" But his body went limp before he could answer. Luthias dropped his body to the ground. "Damn it! No help."

Clive walked over beside Luthias. "Why did you choose to kill the large orc that Cut-throat called Futuo? If you take the leader out, the rest will be undisciplined."

"Did you see the size difference? Take the biggest guy out first, the rest will be more fearful and hesitant to attack you. Besides, Cut-throat only brought the blue brute into a fight when he wanted terrible things to happen to someone." Luthias smiled, "And futuo wasn't his name. In the ancient orc language, futuo is the vulgar word for what I did to your scout last night." He held up two fingers. "Twice."

Clive chuckled shaking his head, "Best five minutes of her life, I'm sure. You think the someone he wanted to do terrible things to was you?"

"Not when I killed him, no. But then he told his men he needed me alive."

Brasscoat looked at the large orc with the scar cut across his neck lying dead. "So, Cut-throat was here to draw you out?"

Luthias nodded his head. "He knew I wouldn't involve that many guards while we were in town. He also knew I wouldn't risk collateral damage to city residents, which is why he chose the Red Dog to start trouble in. He felt they could handle any guards I brought with me and with the big blue brutish orc, they could sneak me out of town."

"Wait, what did you just say?" They both turned and watched Nakira walk up sliding her bow onto her back. "Why in the hell is anyone but me trying to sneak you anywhere?"

Luthias shrugged as he looked over the dead mercenaries. "Cut-throat died before he could answer me. So, he was of no help."

Clive watched his guards start cleaning up the mess. "What information could you have that would be of any use to him? Are you currently working on a case for the Council of Kings?"

Luthias shook his head. "No, my last job ended a half month ago and with Cut-throat dead, I won't be able to get answers from him. Not that he would have given me any more than he already did. All he would have done is spew more orc profanity at us. Well, not unless I let him question me his way."

He knew he'd messed up and said that in Nakira's presence. He knew the slap to his arm was coming when he heard Nera bark.

Clive laughed at him, "I don't think your girlfriend or your wolf approved of that plan."

Luthias laughed, "I want to go check something out before we head back to my place." He looked at Nakira. "Are you coming?"

Nakira could tell something else was bothering him, but she would get answers from him in bed. "Let me help here first then

Nera and I will be along."

She watched him walk towards the city gates. She knew by his determined walk that something else had happened that no one else had witnessed. She turned and looked at the wolf. "Nera, make sure they are all dead for me girl." Nera barked and began sniffing the bodies as Nakira started helping the other guards strip the bodies of armor and weapons. They were almost done when Nera suddenly began growling and ran off toward the city gates.

Clive watched the wolf run at full speed towards the gates. "What's up with Nera?"

Nakira looked at Brasscoat as she quickly ran after the wolf. "I don't know but we better follow her. You four finish up, the rest of you with us." They took off following Nera.

When they got into town, they saw Nera tugging on the legs of Luthias's britches. "Nera, what the hell is wrong with you?"

At the same time Luthias asked, a ball of flames lit up the city and the dark early morning sky.

Nakira and the rest ran toward the flames. When they arrived Luthias was lifting himself up off the ground horrified to see his house fully engulfed in flames. As Luthias sat and hugged Nera, the flames darkened his purple eyes. Clive and Nakira knew someone just started a fight they couldn't win.

Chapter Three

Luthias hated being away from Nakira for the last month and knew she was worried about him since the fire had burned his house down. They both knew if Nera had been a second or two slower, he would have made it inside and died in the fire. He was angry because not only did someone try to kill him, but they would have killed her as well if Cut-throat hadn't started trouble. Despite searching the area and the burnt wreckage of his house they turned up no clues. So, he followed the only clue he had, Cut-throat. He traveled everywhere Cut-throat had been spotted in the last couple of months according to Dominion guards.

He knew Nakira wanted to come with him, knew she also wanted revenge. Although she witnessed him magically rip a mercenary apart in Tros'mura during the mission with Etherika and Syneris several years earlier, he didn't want her to continue to witness him doing things like that to people. The more brutality a person is subjected to, the more likely they were to start doing the same thing. That wasn't what he wanted for her.

But he also knew that she was stubborn and wasn't letting him go alone. So, he agreed to take his best friend, Gate Captain, Volf Borgroff with him. But only if she kept his wolf, Nera with her for extra protection considering she could have also been a target if someone had watched her walk into his house. Although Borgroff was usually a jovial dwarf, if you crossed him, his friends, or family, he would head down a dark path and develop a nasty dwarven temper. That dwarven temper and his twin battle hammers made him the perfect company for this type of mission. Torturing mercenaries for information about Cut-throat and who hired him.

The information he and Borgroff had collected so far during their investigation led them to a tiny village called Hells Canyon. It was a mercenary town along the Ellehcim kingdom's southern border. It was squeezed in among the Ziamicawl Mountains and the Hellion

Lava Flats.

They'd been in Hells Canyon for a week posing as mercenaries looking for Cut-throat and his gang but hadn't ran across any information. He and Borgroff had gotten halfway through a bottle of whiskey when three mercenaries wearing dirty, ratty clothes walked into the saloon.

"Wench, bring us three bottles of your best whiskey. We're celebrating our friend's good luck and good fortune."

The bartender looked at Luthias and rolled her eyes. "Never any respect from these filthy assholes. I don't know why I stay in this hell hole town."

Luthias tipped the bottle of whiskey up, pouring him and Borgroff another shot.

She smiled, "I'd join you two in a toast if I could, but then I wouldn't be able to handle these assholes when they try to paw at my ass and tits." She bent down and brought up three bottles of watered-down, bottom-shelf whiskey. She winked and smiled. "They'll never know it's cheap ass watered-down whiskey." She walked away and headed to the mercenaries' table. "Here you fellas go. Best whiskey in the house."

Luthias watched the group in the mirror as a young elven mercenary with a long scar cutting down his right cheek, chin, and neck reached out for her ass while a middle-aged human wearing an eye patch reached out for one of the bottles. She quickly side-stepped the elven mercenary's clumsy attempt and pulled the bottles away from the human mercenary. Luthias chuckled knowing she'd done that move enough to become an expert at it.

"You keep your hands to yourself or I'll cut them off. Also, none of you touch a drop of whiskey until I have the money for them in hand."

The mercenary who tried to grab her ass smiled with broken and missing teeth. "Start us a tab wench, we're good for it." Luthias watched in the mirror as she turned and walked back towards the bar with the tray of three bottles.

"Okay, okay, fine." He watched the only other mercenary she hadn't interacted with pull a large bag of coins out of his pack and toss it onto the table.

She smiled as she picked the bag of coins up. "Just enough to pay for three of the best bottles in the house, but not a drop more."

Luthias knew she had just cheated them, but they were mercenaries, so he didn't care. He usually did a lot worse than that to them. He continued to watch the mercenary with the pack as the scarred elf pointed at him. "Who paid you that much coin, anyway? Mercenary work don't pay that damn well."

To Luthias, the mercenary with the pack looked to be of orc blood but because his skin was so pale, Luthias figured him to only be half-orc. Judging from the coloration and other minor features, Luthias guessed the other half was human.

"You all hear about the death of Cut-throat and his men?"

Luthias and Borgroff slyly smiled at each other knowing their lead had just walked in. They watched the older human slam his fist against the table looking at the half-breed orc. "Bullshit! If you are about to try and sell us on the fact you killed them all, I'll call you a liar to your face right now, right here."

The half-orc laughed at him, "Hell no. I'm not stupid enough to take them on. His big blue brute alone would smash all three of our heads in at once. Another man paid me all this coin to lure the knight captain of Traemorra and the Traemorra guard into following me out of town until we lost them. I was to use the coin to enlist and pay men to help me do the job. A little after I accepted the job, the huge ass blue-skinned orc walked up to me. I knew who he was immediately. He told me that he had heard what the man said. He told me he and his men would take the job instead and I could keep the coin because they wasn't in it for the pay. Sucker was massive, I wasn't arguing with him."

Luthias spun quickly and threw two daggers. The human and elf fell to the floor, dead. The half-breed orc stood up and circled the table towards him. Luthias lifted his crossbow that was hanging hidden underneath his large black leather gambeson jacket. He pointed it at the mercenary and fired. The bolt hit his shoulder, pinning him against the wall. Luthias quickly loaded another bolt and pinned his other shoulder against the wall locking him in place.

Borgroff looked from the mercenary to Luthias. "Remind me to never piss you off."

Luthias walked up to the half-breed orc and leaned on the bolt in his right shoulder causing the mercenary to scream out in pain. Luthias leaned in close to his face. "I'm going to ask you some important questions. The length of time you live depends on how quickly and truthfully you answer. If you answer quickly and sound truthful, you walk out of here with only these two wounds. Nod your head if you understand."

The mercenary groaned and then spit on the floor at Luthias's feet. Luthias loaded another bolt then took a step back and fired it at the mercenary.

The mercenary laughed when he heard it hit but didn't feel any more pain from it hitting him. "You missed."

Borgroff walked up to the mercenary. "Idjit, he just nailed your shoulders to the wall while you were moving. Do you think he's going to miss you while you're standing here still nailed to the wall? It was a warning shot, fucking idjit. He's letting you know where the fourth cross bolt is gonna hit."

The mercenary followed the dwarf's line of sight and noticed the bolt rested in the wall between his legs. He also noticed the crotch of his raggedy britches were bolted to the wall.

Luthias leaned in close to the mercenary's face again. "Now, let's try the first question again. Nod your head if you understand."

The mercenary nodded his head quickly, not looking away from the bolt between his legs.

"Good." Luthias looked over at the auburn-haired bartender. "That bottle you sold me is yours to finish if you close up now." Luthias looked back at the mercenary. "You can also have the coin this asshole collected and put the unopened bottles he bought back in stock to resale."

The mercenary started to argue but shut up quickly when Borgroff pulled one of his battle hammers out of its holster.

"You have a deal, but I'm hanging around to watch the show." Luthias noticed she was missing a couple of teeth in her smile. Most likely from bouts with whiskey-loaded clumsy handed patrons no doubt. Despite that, she had a certain beauty hidden underneath her dirty appearance.

"Your bar, your rules." Luthias watched her walk over and lock the doors then flip the open, closed sign over.

Borgroff looked at her and chuckled, "I like her. If she wishes, she's getting out of this hell hole town when we leave."

Luthias let the crossbow fall and disappear back under his jacket. He reached over and pulled a falchion-style sword with a red leather handle out of its sheath. "For every answer, I don't believe, you'll lose a finger. After I'm done with your fingers, I will move on to another small worthless appendage on your body." He leaned in close to the mercenary. "My bolt might have missed…" The mercenary squirmed when Luthias tapped his crotch with the end of the blade. "But my sword won't. Who hired you?"

"The nasty whore behind you."

Borgroff turned towards the bartender and gave her his dagger. "Choose an extremity but we need him to still be alive after you're done cutting."

She walked up smiling and shoved the dagger into the leg of his britches at the knee. She slid it upwards, cutting his britches and the skin of his leg with the tip as she slid the blade upwards. He tried not to scream but the higher she got with the blade the more he had to let it out.

"Okay, okay!"

She stopped the dagger just below her intended target. "Damn it! If you'd been an inch longer." The bartender looked up at the mercenary, smiling.

Luthias looked down at her. "I bet he hears that every time a female sees him naked. Keep the blade where you have it. If I don't like the next words out of his mouth. You get to finish cutting while he wails like a banshee."

Luthias looked back up at the mercenary who was staring at the bartender's smile and the edge of the dagger that was still dug into his leg. Luthias's voice brought the half-breed's attention to him. "Now, one more chance. A wrong answer means the nasty whore cuts it off. Who hired you to lure knight captain and his guards away from Traemorra?"

"A pompous ass elven nobleman in Ridgewood told me to lure the guards away from Traemorra. He said that it had something to do with some special sword he needed."

"What else?" Luthias asked, letting the bartender keep the blade in place.

"That is all he said I swear," the mercenary said before Luthias looked down at the bartender and nodded.

"Okay, okay. That is all he said but I noticed a wolf's head tattoo on his right forearm. I remember it because the old psychic lady in Ridgewood described that wolf's head to me in detail. She told me not to have anything to do with it because it would only lead to my death."

The bartender looked up dejected as Borgroff reached down and removed the dagger from her hand. She glared at the half breed mercenary. "If you'd only been an inch longer."

Luthias chuckled as he looked at Borgroff, "Let's take our new friend for a ride to see some of the nightlife around here." He pulled the bolts out of the mercenary's shoulders and knocked him out cold. Luthias turned towards the bartender. "We will be back to help you clean up my mess after we feed him to the hellions."

A little while later on the edge of the Lava Flats, Luthias sat on a black igneous rock watching the hellions gather and circle overhead. He looked over when he heard the mercenary waking up.

"I was wondering if you were going to wake up before the hellions forced us to leave." He smiled at the mercenary hanging upside down from a large tree limb. His hands and feet bound. The mercenary looked up at the circling beasts and started struggling to get loose. "They're looking mighty hungry."

Borgroff laughed watching the mercenary trying to get loose. "Save your strength lad, there's no way you're getting out of the knots I tie. Ah hell, on second thought, go ahead. Here in a few minutes, you won't be alive to need any strength."

Luthias looked from Borgroff to the upside-down mercenary. "Those hellions are going to tear you apart fighting over your body parts to feed themselves and their young. You should have listened to that old psychic in Ridgewood when she warned you about the wolf's head leading to your death."

Luthias and Borgroff walked away while the mercenary struggled to get free.

Borgroff looked up and yelled, "Feeding time!"

They listened to the mercenary scream and plead for his life as they climbed onto their horses and rode away. The screeches of the hellions grew louder and drowned out his screams as they fought over who got the first bite of dinner.

Chapter Four

Luthias, Borgroff, and the young bartender rode north out of the mountains passed the villages of Kallinstyne and Pantreus. Then through the village of Shadow Pass to reach Ridgewood. Once they reached Ridgewood, Borgroff and the bartender went to the tavern to secure rooms and find out if the tavern needed bartender help. Borgroff knew Luthias needed to use his skills as a shadow warrior and he would only be in the way.

First, Luthias needed to pay a visit to the old psychic's shop to find out more about this elven nobleman. Luthias entered the front of the shop and heard a bell ring above him as the door hit it alerting the old psychic to a visitor. "Come in young one. You are right on time. Come sit, sit."

Luthias noticed the old woman was blind, frail, and ghost-white. He walked forward and sat down. She reached her hand out towards his, so he placed his hand into hers.

She smiled at Luthias, "The half-breed orc in Hells Canyon mentioned me to you. Then as I warned him, he met his death via hungry hellions. You do have a way with the dramatic, don't you?"

"I guess so." Luthias noticed someone wearing a white cloak facing away working in the corner of the shop.

The old blind psychic smiled, "That's just an assistant who works for me from time to time. Pay them no mind. You're here about the wolf-branded elven nobleman. I need you to find the brown-haired elf carrying the dangerous sword out in the open. He has no idea the danger it will bring down onto him. Retrieve the sword from him, a bounty for its retrieval and possession will be paid to you. This elf was not responsible for the fire, but the sword he carries will lead you further into your investigation. The elf will be walking down Port Street in an hour. Happy and perhaps even whistling as he sometimes does when he is particularly proud of himself. Afterall, he just received the boon he longed for most of his adult life. I told him to be careful of the things you wish for. You might just get it."

He watched a grin appear on her thin pale pink dry lips as he stood up. "When you return with the blade, enter through the back door. Be wary of watchful eyes."

The mercenary who told him about the nobleman and the old psychic was believable as he pleaded for his life. Luthias wasn't sure what the sword had to do with the fire that destroyed his house, but the old psychic told him it would lead him further into his investigation.

Luthias's path after the fire had been dark, twisted, and deadly but thankfully Borgroff hadn't let him stray too far. He tortured, mutilated, and killed the mercenary for his part, this nobleman's fate would end the same. He hid within the darkness of the dancing shadows to the side of the streetlamp. He watched people walk by him, sometimes within inches of him unaware of his presence. Suddenly the sound of whistling filled the air. Luthias smiled.

The brown-haired elf walked towards him wearing a red velvet cloak over a white, ruffled, silk shirt. But Luthias's eyes were on the sword hanging proudly at his side. He watched the elf nod and smile at everyone he passed.

Luthias took advantage when the elf stepped into a darkened alleyway to allow a couple to pass by him. He crept forward, grabbed the nobleman, and dragged him deeper into the dark alleyway.

He shoved the side of his face against the rough rock wall, then leaned in and whispered into his ear. "I'm going to remove my hand from your mouth. If you scream, the dagger against the back of your skull will sever your spine." Luthias pressed the tip of the dagger against his skin. "Nod your head if you understand?"

The nobleman nodded his head nervously.

Luthias removed his hand then reached down and drew the sword in question from the sheath tied to the elf's side. "Tell me about this sword and don't lie to me because an old blind psychic and a dead half-breed orc mercenary set me on your trail." He leaned and put his lips against the elf's ear. "The half-breed you hired was fed to a group of hellions down in the Lava Flats because he didn't answer quickly and honestly."

The elven nobleman stood quiet and shaking against the building's wall. Luthias pushed the tip of the dagger enough to break the skin to make his point. As the elf felt blood trickle down the skin of his neck, he quickly started talking. "Okay, okay! It's called Fijandsvarg's blade. Don't ask me what it means because I don't have a clue."

Luthias's mouth was still next to the elf's unusually large, pointed ears. "Fijandsvarg is an ancient elven dialect that translates to Wolfiend."

"Then you know more than I do and you can let me go?" the elf asked nervously.

Luthias pushed the tip farther into his neck as he leaned away from the elf. "If that is true then you are of no use to me. I can kill you now." He pushed the blade deeper to prove his point. "How did you come to possess the blade?" Luthias released a little pressure.

"I hired the mercenary you mentioned. As a reward for doing so, I was given the blade. I walked into my house after hiring him and it was lying on my table inside the scabbard." Luthias reapplied the pressure of the blade to his neck urging him to continue. "The job was for the mercenary to lead the knight captain of the guard in Traemorra and the Traemorra guards away from the city."

Luthias leaned into his ear as he put more pressure on the target's neck. "Listen to me carefully as this next question is important. How the guards find you in the morning depends on how you answer it. Lie to me or don't answer, they find you lying here dead, the victim of a street urchin who killed and robbed you."

The nobleman nodded vigorously and could feel the blade cutting into his neck.

"Who promised you the sword in return for hiring the mercenary?"

"Please don't kill me, I don't know." Luthias pushed the tip of the blade deeper. "My pocket, a note with a wax seal is in my pocket. That is the only communication I had with them."

Luthias reached in and pulled out the note. The wax seal resembled the wolf's head on the handle of the sword he took from the nobleman. "Why did you want the sword and what does it have to do with a fire that burnt a house down in Traemorra?"

"I, I don't know anything about a house fire in Traemorra but I needed the blade so I could find someone to translate the carvings and runes on it. It is rumored to be ancient and responsible for the death of a powerful demon. If you let me go, I will get the blade translated. I will give you the blade and the information."

"Show me your right forearm." The nobleman lifted his arm quickly. Luthias pulled the sleeve of the white silk shirt up. "Tell me about this tattoo."

The elf stood still and remained quiet, shaking in fear.

"You choose to speak of everything else incriminating, but grow quiet when I ask about a simple tattoo. Why is this wolf's head tattoo worth dying over?"

The elf shivered and cried. Luthias knew the elf realized he was dead either way, dying by his dagger must have been the less painful option. Luthias shoved the dagger in severing his spine and breaking some of the bones in his neck. Luthias let go of the dagger watching his body drop to the ground as if it was a child's lifeless stuffed rag doll. Luthias removed the elf's coin, jewelry, scabbard, and other personal items to make it appear like a robbery. He pulled the dagger and shoved everything into his pack, disappearing into the darkness.

Luthias watched the back entrance of the psychic's shop from a rooftop ledge but didn't see anyone in the area. He climbed down and slipped through the back door. As soon as he entered, he heard her start talking. "I sense success and death upon you, my dear. A blade through the back of the neck will do it every time."

The old blind psychic's voice from the darkness surprised him, so did her knowledge of the elf's death. Luthias looked around the room as he pulled the sword and scabbard out of his pack and placed it on the table in front of the blind old woman. "I sent my assistant home for the evening. You are my last customer."

He watched her push the sword back towards him with her ghost-white crippled, arthritic hand.

"I do not need this item. As I said, it will help you in your investigation. I only needed to know he did not possess it anymore. Keep it as your gift from me for performing the job." He saw an eerie smile form on her lips. "Seems the bloody reputation that precedes you is more truth than lie. A fact the three people you ripped apart would attest to, if they could."

Luthias tilted his head a bit but before he could speak, she placed a large bag of coins beside the sword.

"Danger lies deep within you, but all is not what it appears to be. Your payment and a bonus as well."

Luthias picked up the bag and the sword. As he placed both in his pack, he tried to speak again but she interrupted him once again.

"Young one."

Luthias watched as she extended her ghost-white arthritic hand out. He grabbed a hold of it and was surprised by her strength when she pulled him into a hug.

The old woman whispered into his ear, "Run child, quickly up the stairs and through the open window. Deception is upon us. Death is here for your soul, but it will only get mine today. Run!"

Luthias pulled out of the hug, ran up the stairs, and jumped out the open window. He caught hold of the window ledge on the building next to it. He quickly scaled the building and jumped to another. He scrambled into an open window. He turned and watched as the psychic's building went up in a tower of flames and smoke. Images of Traemorra and the night he lost his house and Nakira almost died came to the forefront of his mind. Just as the flames broke through the roof, Luthias noticed a couple of men running away. He climbed out jumping from roof to roof, following them. He listened to them brag about setting the flames. He followed them until they turned into a dark alleyway.

He quickly climbed down and followed them into the darkness where he heard a female's voice. "Is the job done?"

Luthias could hear the fear in the man's voice as he quickly replied, "Yes, yes dark mistress. We waited until after he entered then set fire to the building as you instructed."

Luthias watched a ball of fire hit the ground in front of the men's feet causing them to jump backwards.

"You two better pray he died in that fire. I burnt the last being alive when she failed. Get out of town quickly before anyone sees you." As the female spoke, she threw a pile of clothes onto the ground in front of the two men. "Here are some clothes for you. Burn those guard uniforms once you get far enough away from town. Again, if he is alive, I will have my birds of prey track you down so I can burn you alive as well."

Both men bowed their heads as the female turned and then instantly disappeared into the darkness.

Luthias walked up quietly behind the two guards as they undressed. He then pulled the wolf's head sword, slit one man's throat, and stabbed the other in the chest before either one knew he was there. He pushed the man he stabbed against the wall.

"Who were you just talking to?"

The man squirmed against Luthias and the sword but remained quiet. He lifted the right forearm covered in tattoos, but none matched the wolf's head worn by the noble elf.

"What do you know about this blade?"

The man looked down at the sword sticking out of his chest and shook his head.

"Then I ask again, who were you just talking to?"

Before he could answer, he smiled then his body went limp. Luthias and the blade were the only things holding his corpse up. He pulled the blade out of his chest and put it back in his pack. He left the bodies and uniforms there for real guards to find. He quickly slipped into the darkness to try and find the person these two were just talking to.

Chapter Five

As Luthias hid in the shadows watching the lamp lit streets of Ridgewood, he felt the same eerie sensation that he felt on the morning his house burned. But all he saw out on the streets of Ridgewood was a female in a long coat walking a dog, an orc vagrant sitting beside an alleyway entrance, and a couple of guards walking their rounds. Luthias hit the wall of the stone building beside him and watched a large startled black raven take off in flight, squawking into the night. "Damn it! I need to see if Amunique knows about this sword or the tattoo. It's time to get back to Traemorra."

By the time he had returned to the tavern, Borgroff was already in his room. In the morning they would head back to Traemorra. Luthias drank a couple of ales then went into his room and lay down. Everything that had happened over the last month was replaying in his mind as he stared up at the water stains sprawled across the ceiling. He noticed the stain looked like the outlines of an aged map sprawled out above him. Someone had gone to great lengths to remain anonymous in their attempt to kill him. They used a sword to lure the greedy elf into hiring and paying a mercenary to lure the guards out of Traemorra. All so a third individual could set fire to his house the way the two fake guards set fire to the psychic's shop tonight. This made it impossible to track the crimes back to individual behind the attempts on his life. If anyone else was investigating the crimes, Luthias made their job harder by killing both leads. Then the two men posing as Ridgewood guards burnt the psychic's shop down killing the last known lead he knew of. The second fire aimed at killing him.

"Two fires. Two attempts on my life."

At first, he suspected the two fake guards might be behind his house fire as well, but the female they called dark mistress spoke of killing the previous person for failing to kill him. Although he didn't want to go back to Traemorra without solving this case, to help protect Nakira and Nera from harm, he knew he needed help from his friends. Plus, he wanted to see Nakira and Nera. He needed to know they were still okay.

The morning sun slipped through the shutters to shine perfectly on Luthias's left eye, waking him up. "Damn it, how did this shutter get opened?"

Luthias lifted his hand and slammed it shut causing it to bounce back and blind both eyes. He could only laugh at the situation. He reached up and gently closed it, so it stayed shut. As he brought his hand down and rested it on the side table beside the bed, his hand landed on cold metal. He looked over then jumped out of bed in a panic looking around the room. Lying on the bedside table was the sword he'd taken from the elf. Underneath it, laid the note he took from the elf's pocket. Before he went to sleep, he packed the blade into its sheath and inside his pack with the note. But now, somehow the blade was lying on the table on top of the nobleman's note that he had forgotten to read. Luthias quickly checked his pack, everything including his coin bags was still inside.

Relieved he wasn't robbed, he let out a sigh as he sat back down. But he was also disturbed at the thought that someone was able to enter his room without waking him up. He reached over and lifted the sword then removed the note from the table. He laid the sword back onto the nightstand as he inspected the note. In the center of the wax seal was a wolf's head identical to the one carved into the handle of the sword and the tattoo on the elf's right arm.

"Funny how one second can change your entire world. Those were the words you used when she opened the door and froze not knowing you were sitting in the dark. In that second, her world shifted from making sense to complete chaos. As far as she knew, you should be dead from the poison she laced into your drink. The second that familiar taste touched your tongue, your world also went from making sense to complete chaos. You knew it was her because you watched her make the drink before leaving you alone in your own house. How could she have known you built up a tolerance to it as a child while your mom slowly poisoned you? Your mom needed to know that you'd always have to depend on her? I guess some mothers do have a tough time letting go. In the second your secret lover chose the tiny action of betraying you and trying to poison you,

her entire world changed, and she knew it. But not how she hoped. Funny how one second can change our entire world. As for your lover, we arranged it to look like a thief killed her during a robbery.

"Now to our deal with you. You are to hire a mercenary and give him the coin accompanying this letter. He is to hire a crew and then head to Traemorra. Once there, he and his men need to lead the captain and his men out of town. Once we know you hired the mercenary, we will present you with the sword in question. If you fail at any part of this request, we will kill you with the sword you so badly desire."

On the bottom of the note was a message addressed to Luthias. *"Luthias Blackridge, chaos is a funny thing, don't you think? As the note above says, it's funny how one second can change your entire world. One second, you are in Traemorra creating chaos for Cutthroat and his gang, who, in turn, created chaos by messing up well-laid plans. Then it only took a second for someone to create chaos by burning down the house you were just in. We're glad Nakira wasn't still in there, by the way. Now here you are in Ridgewood causing chaos by killing a noble elf. Then it only took a second for two mercenaries posing as guards to set fire to a second building you were once again just in. Flames have way of following you. Fire seems to be the embodiment of chaos, wouldn't you say? Chaos is indeed a funny thing. It only took you a second to kill the two fake guards as well. But you did the world a favor when you killed those two. They were murderers, rapists, thieves, and arsonists. The bartender downstairs has the reward for their apprehension. We find the nobleman's apparent robbery and death quite ironic. We couldn't have produced a better ending to his story than for him to die in the same manner as his secret lover. Ridgewood seems to have a serial thief and murderer on the loose. There will be an antique dealer downstairs in the saloon when you get up. He rushed to get here when he heard a rumor this infamous sword showed up in Ridgewood. Its history is quite entertaining. But do not sell it for any amount of money to him. We do not want to have to redeliver this sword to you thereby killing this nice scholar. We look forward to watching your progress in your investigation. Go forth and create beautiful chaos, Shadow Warrior."*

Luthias sat on the bed staring at the blood on the rune-engraved saber-style sword. The mysterious note hanging from his fingers. He grabbed the handle of the sword and cleaned all traces of the blood from the blade before putting the sword and note back into his pack. He then hurried downstairs.

"Morning friend, I hope your night was restful." Luthias looked up to see a white-haired balding bartender with an overlapping gut pick up an empty tankard and smile. "Would you like a drink this morning?"

Luthias approached the bar but didn't take a seat. "No, but I need to know if you saw anyone acting strange last night after I went upstairs. Did anyone else go upstairs after me?" Luthias watched as the bartender thought for a minute then shook his head. "Damn it, okay."

"Did you have a night visitor and not catch her name?" Borgroff chuckled as he walked up to stand beside Luthias. "Ah, don't worry I won't tell Nakira. I'll just hold it over your head when I need you to do things you don't want to."

"Good sir, if you pardon my interruption," came a voice from behind them.

Luthias and Borgroff turned to see an older gentleman standing behind them. He was human but barely taller than Borgroff. Luthias noticed how the gray suit jacket he wore swallowed his slim frame. The older gentleman pushed his mended round glasses back up onto the bridge of his nose as Luthias pulled the sword from the pack and laid it in the man's hands.

"Are you the antiquities dealer?" He watched as the man nodded his head not taking his eyes from the sword in his hands.

"I need to know everything you know about this blade and its rune engravings." Luthias turned to the bartender. "Give him anything he wants on my tab. Give us two an ale." He didn't bother waiting for a reply. They led the man to a table at the back corner of the saloon.

After Luthias, Borgroff, and the dealer sat down at the table, the bartender walked up and sat the drinks down along with a large bag of coins.

"A soldier dropped off this warrant and the coin for the capture of the Bagswell brothers. The soldier said thank you on behalf of the citizens of Ridgewood, the guard, and the town magistrate." The bartender read over the warrant before continuing. "These were two of the worst mercenaries I've ever heard of. Murder, arson, rape, theft, and he said you killed them without either brother drawing a weapon. I added the rest of your tab money into the bag as well, so you won't have to settle later."

The bartender looked at Borgroff. "And thanks to you as well sir. That young lady you brought with you will help tremendously here. Hell, I might even get a night off here and there now."

Luthias watched as the bartender laid the warrant on the table and turned to head back to the bar. As he did, he signaled the bouncers to stand guard and keep people from getting anywhere close to the table they were sitting at. Luthias placed the coin bag and warrant in his pack and turned his attention back to the dealer.

"What can you tell us about this blade? We want to know about the runes, who engraved them, the blade's history, and who made the blade. Whatever you know about this blade we want to know it as well. Whatever you don't know I want you to investigate and find out, you now work for me."

Luthias and Borgroff listened as the dealer told him what he knew about it while throwing out several extremely generous offers to purchase the blade for his museum's collection. Borgroff looked at Luthias like he was crazy for not accepting the offers, so he handed Borgroff the note. Borgroff read the note then tucked it away, and nodded his head understanding why. As the dealer walked away disappointed that he couldn't purchase such a rare piece for his museum, Luthias looked over the runes engraved into the blade and the several interesting points that he hadn't noticed yet. The bartender walked over and sat down in the antique dealer's chair. "So, he was quite a chatty fella." Luthias didn't look up from the blade as the bartender continued. "A messenger told me to wait until the old man left before I gave you this note." The bartender laid the note on the table.

Luthias looked up from the blade. "What did the messenger look like?"

"Hood covering her face, long black cloak and armor covered her body, black gloves covering her hands. Hell, if she hadn't spoken, I would've sworn it was a man. Sorry, that's all I can tell ya." The bartender shrugged and then headed back to the bar.

Luthias wasn't sure he wanted to look at the note considering the one he woke up to. But he removed the same wolf's head wax seal and opened it anyway.

"By now you have talked to the dealer and saved his life by

Luthias gathered his pack and ran out of the saloon to catch up with the dealer. He looked all around, then spotted the man talking to a burly silver bearded human with long hair and a patch over his left eye.

"Wait, I have one more question for you. Borgroff, show him the seal." Borgroff pulled the first note from his pack and showed the wax seal to the dealer.

"What do you know about this wax seal? Does it have any connection to the sword itself?"

As the dealer looked over the wax seal, Luthias looked around for the messenger but didn't see anyone acting strange or matching the description.

The dealer looked over the wax seal closely. "The wolf's head in the middle of the wax seal does resemble the wolf on the sword's handle. I am heading back to my shop in Traemorra, may I take an impression of the wax seal with me so that I can investigate it further?" Luthias nodded as the dealer took out some paper and some of his charcoal to make an impression of the wax seal. "Give me some time and I might have something for you."

"We are heading to Traemorra as well." Luthias looked at the burly one-eyed man. "I'm guessing he was trying to book passage aboard the stagecoach to Traemorra."

He watched the man nod his head.

"Good, all three of us need a ride to Traemorra." He tossed the man a bag of coins. "Three for Traemorra with no stops. Let us grab our horses and tie them to the back of your stagecoach."

He didn't wait for a response and just walked off towards the stables with Borgroff.

Chapter Six

The stagecoach pulled up to the front gate of Traemorra later that evening. The guard at the gate addressed the antiquities dealer who exited the stagecoach first. "Welcome back to Traemorra. Did you find anything new and interesting on this trip?"

"Young man, how many times do I have to tell you, 'New' is not the business I'm in? It must be old to be interesting. But your answer is yes, however," The antiquities dealer looked back at Luthias and Borgroff. "I was not able to obtain them all."

The young elven guard smiled, "And how many times do we have to tell you, your old crap is new to us. The only old thing we have around here isn't that interesting unless he has some new junk for us to look at."

The guard heard Borgroff laugh.

Luthias watched the young elf smile as the dealer stomped off. The elf turned and bowed. "Welcome to Traemorra, gentlemen. Is this your first visit?"

Before either one could reply, someone spoke up from behind the guard. "Only their first visit in just over a month." Luthias looked up to see Knight Captain Brasscoat walk up beside the guard.

"The large orc-sized elf is Luthias Blackridge, Knight of the famed Elven Shadow Warriors and knight hunter employed by the Council of Kings. His house is the blackened bonfire pile in the center of the residential area. The dwarf beside him is Volf Borgroff, your gate captain. He is on temporary assignment with Blackridge. Luthias, Borgroff, it is good to see you two alive. We thought you might be dead by now, although no way in hell would I have ever said that in front of Nakira or Nera. Those two have been inseparable since you left. Every patrol she goes on, Nera is nearby hidden among the shadows as well."

Luthias walked up and hugged him. "Clive, it is good to see you too, and thank you. As far as death is concerned, we took a dark and twisted path, but this ornery dwarf kept me on task and alive. You and the guards got my house rebuilt yet?" Brasscoat laughed and shook his head. "You had a little over a month. I figured I'd come back to a house fit for a lord."

Borgroff chuckled, "Luthias, I'm going to go clean up and change. I will meet you at the Red Dog. Assuming my other boss has no objection and hasn't thrown my stuff out." He turned to look at Knight-Captain Brasscoat.

"Borgroff, sir your stuff is safe where you left it. I kept Pritchett and Shamus out of it while you were gone." Borgroff walked off doubting the last part of his statement, those two were constantly trying to prank him.

Luthias decided to follow suit as well. "Clive, I'm going to go get settled in at the Red Dog."

Clive nodded his head and began to speak before he walked off, "I wanted to tell you, we found the body of a young female who'd been burnt to a crisp the morning after you and Borgroff headed off. The mortician said it happened within hours of your house fire. Though since she was found a few blocks away we aren't sure she was connected. Also, I'd be careful when you walk into the Red Dog. Although Amunique is sad you lost your house, she still has not forgiven you for disappearing without talking to her first. Nera and Nakira should already be there."

"She was connected. I'll explain how I know later," Luthias said as he grabbed his pack and headed into the city.

Luthias walked down the main street of Traemorra taking in the familiar sights and enjoying the chilly night air. After he walked a few blocks, the chilly night air developed the same familiar eerie sensation to it once again. The same eerie feeling from the night his house burnt and in Ridgewood just after he killed the two fake guards. Luthias was already walking in the shadows beyond the streetlights. The habit he developed during his training in the ways of the shadow warriors. He stopped and looked out from the darkness watching his surroundings.

"Never ignore your instincts. Your gut is your compass when things go wrong. Always follow your gut," Luthias whispered the words his grandfather taught him into the eerie night air. All he saw was a raven perched on a building. He watched it but after a few seconds, it flew off squawking into the night. "I guess you felt it as well."

Just as he was about to start walking again, a young light-skinned human female with long dark hair walked out from a side street. In her hand was a leash leading to a small breed of dog. When he noticed her, the eerie sensation chilled him to his bones. Luthias followed his gut which was telling him to follow her. A falcon squawked in a tree nearby adding to the eeriness of the moment. "You felt it as well."

He followed her through the streets of Traemorra. He watched her long black hair sway back and forth matching the swing of her hips stride for stride. Her dress barely hung below her ass. It was form-fitting and made from expensive material. This told Luthias she was of high social status but also rebelled against it. A brightly colored dragon-fairy tattoo extending from just below her ass down to the calf of her right leg drew his attention.

"Definitely rebellious."

He knew she was completely unaware of the danger that lurked just a few paces away. As he watched her, he thought back to the other times he felt the same feelings. He remembered seeing a young female with long black hair walking a small brown dog all three times. She was wearing a different outfit every time but the gut feeling he got all three times told him it was the same female.

He brought his focus back to his surroundings. He noticed the feeling remained strong while he remained close to her. He looked around at the few other people out and about. An unkempt rotund guardsman walked his rounds on the other side of the street. Luthias noticed he kept one hand resting on the hilt of his sword and his head in constant movement taking in his surroundings. It made him wonder if the guard felt the strange sensation in the chilly night air. Up the road on the same side heading towards the guard was a street peddler pushing her cart home for the night. Just ahead of his young target, an older couple walked slowly hand in hand. Luthias smiled because it brought back memories of his father and mother walking the same way around Gatesboro during his teen years. Just ahead of them sat a young dark red female orc begging for change and scraps of food. While he had been following the young female, he hadn't noticed anyone appearing out of place or paying her much attention. Yet the night air had taken on the same eerie sensation as just before she crossed his path. It could be a coincidence, but he didn't believe in them.

"Everything happens for a reason." Luthias looked around as he whispered another of his grandfather's quips of wisdom into the night.

He continued to follow the young female as she aimlessly wandered through the streets of Traemorra. He felt she could be simply walking her dog before putting it to bed since it stopped her every so often to relieve itself on a bush or in the grass. The rest of the people he saw earlier had all taken different paths. The guard continued his rounds turning down a dimly lit side street. The older couple went into a house, while the street vendor went into a house across the street from them. When he passed by the young vagrant, Luthias looked down at her, smiled, and tossed her a small bag of coins. The young vagrant stood up and ran off into a nearby dark alleyway to hide her new found fortune from the other homeless. Just ahead of him, his young target slowed down and stopped at a corner that led onto a darkened side street. He watched as she leaned against a lamp pole and looked around. Luthias noticed how the streetlight highlighted her hair with a bit of a dark blue tint. She looked to be just taking in the night air with her dog, but his gut told him something else was up. Then as Luthias suspected, she quickly stepped into the darkness of the side street and disappeared. Luthias knew this side street led to Traemorra's scarlet district. An area of the city he knew to be unfit for a young high-society female just out for a late-night stroll with her dog. As he walked up to the corner to follow her, a faint sound in the distance caught his attention. He turned and quickly caught an arrow just before it struck his right shoulder.

"Jage Brannpil," Luthias whispered, setting the arrow on a fiery path back towards the individual who had shot it.

He watched as the arrow shot across the street and flew by an old tree before disappearing over the city wall. All three times this young female and her dog crossed his path someone tried to kill him. First was his house fire, then the store fire, and now with an arrow. He took off into the night to follow the fiery path of the arrow. He would just have to cross her path another time or hope Amunique knew who she was.

Outside the city, he saw a middle-aged elven male pinned to a tree by the blackened arrow. Luthias walked up hoping to get information, but someone had slit his throat from right to left making sure he didn't talk. He searched the body but the only clue he discovered was the same wolf's head tattoo on the dead elf's right forearm.

"A tattoo worth dying for. Damn it! Why do my leads keep dying without answering the questions I need answered?"

He hit the tree sending a raven flying off and squawking into the night. He left the body pinned to the tree and hurried back to Traemorra. As he passed through the gates, he informed the gate guards of his discovery. Now he needed to see if he could find the young female and hope she knew anything or had the same tattoo. If not, he knew someone who would or could find out more information.

Luthias returned to the spot where he lost the female then hurried off down the side street. As he walked farther away from the gas lamps, the sound of laughter, music, and the smell of ale and lust filled the air. All luring him back home. He hadn't been back to the scarlet district since the night he led Cut-throat and his goons to their deaths. The same night he lost his house and almost lost Nakira. Just like the nobleman's note said, it only took a second for his world to go from making sense to complete chaos. His world hasn't made sense to him since that night. He noticed not much had changed during the last month. Trash still littered the dark side streets. Vagrants and criminal elements hid in the shadows while the occasional drunk slept off a bender wherever they landed. The bars and bordellos were the same, most of which one bouncer or another had tossed him out of when he had too much to drink. Once again, he shook the old thoughts from his mind and brought his attention back to the task at hand.

"With the gas lamps of the main street behind me, I need to be more aware of my surroundings."

He checked every bar and bordello on Scarlet Street for his young target, but he had not found her. He was now standing outside the last business on the block, the Red Dog Saloon.

Luthias knew the area behind the Red Dog was strictly off-limits to customers so he knew his approach would go unseen except for the usual guards that patrolled the grounds.

"Halt friend, you've wandered too far off the main path. This is private property, if you wish to enter the Red Dog you will need to do so from the front entrance on Scarlet Street."

Standing in the shadows Luthias smiled at the sound of the guard's voice. "Just who do you think you are to try and tell me where to go and what to do?"

"I know that gravelly voice. Luthias Blackridge you old whore's son, we thought you were dead. It's about time you come back to town. Amunique is still mad as hell that you disappeared without telling her. She's been taking it out on everyone around her." He watched as the guard walked up close and put his hand on his shoulder. "Sorry to hear about your house. Did you ever find out who did it and exact vengeance?"

"Thanks, not yet. Vengeance is a long, dark, twisted path that needs to be walked carefully. Lest you lose your mind." He shook the dark thoughts of his actions from his mind. "Is she in her office or out-front entertaining?" The guard just gave him a big smile and let him in the back door. "Out front, it is then."

Chapter Seven

As soon as he entered the Red Dog Saloon, Luthias knew he was home again. Walking through the back hallway, he noticed Amunique had removed the curtains covering the private rooms and replaced them with doors. But even with the new doors, he could still hear the many different sounds of pleasure and pain coming from behind the doors. Luthias shook his head, chuckled, and kept walking.

When he entered the main room, he noticed the Red Dog Saloon was busy. Customers packed the old akora wood bar. Every table in the business had at least two patrons drinking, talking, and watching the show on the main stage. As he looked around, he searched for any sign of the young woman, Nakira, or Amunique. Hopefully, he would see them before they spotted him.

About the time he gave up looking, someone slapped him across the back of the head. "You, low-down rotten son of a bitch. I give you years of upstanding business and you choose to repay me by sneaking off and disappearing without a single word. Now you decide to snake your way in through my back door. I hope you don't think that groveling will get you back into my good graces anytime soon?"

Luthias turned around to see the fiery-haired, olive-skinned female orc staring up at him trying to maintain her look of anger. He smiled down at her, "First of all, only some of the business conducted here is upstanding, most of it is done lying down in one position or another. Second, I didn't snake my way in your back door, I simply strolled through lover's lane. The doors were a nice addition though. Third, you know I don't grovel. Lastly, if you ever slap me from behind again, I will swing first and ask questions after you wake your ass back up."

Amunique laughed as she wrapped her arms around him giving him a tight hug. "I sure missed your dumb ass." She squeezed him tight as she whispered into his ear, "I'm sorry to hear what happened to your house. They are lucky you and Nakira weren't in there. I hope you tracked those bastards down and killed them painfully." She released her grip. "I will meet you up in your usual spot after I get us a couple of drinks."

Luthias made his way to the corner on the upper floor balcony overlooking the main bar area and facing the stage. From that spot in the darkness, he could watch the bar and had lots of times while following a bounty. He watched the crowd for the young female but so far, he hadn't seen her. Unfortunately, he hadn't seen Nakira and Nera either.

"So, who are you stalking tonight? Hopefully, it's one of the bastards responsible so I get to help set their ass on fire."

She knew he wouldn't answer. She noticed he was already in what she calls his shadow mind.

"By the way, Nakira and Nera have spent every single night while you were gone in your room here."

"Good. Hopefully she kept Nera off the bed though. I still don't have a clue who the bastards were that were responsible but the burnt body the guards found after I left was the person hired to do the job. Someone only known as the dark mistress is the one who hired her. As for who I'm tracking, I don't have a clue about her either. I arrived at the front gate and started walking here when the night air developed an eerie feeling. I stopped and looked around then saw a young female walk out from a side street with a small dog. I've felt this sensation three times and all three times I've spotted a female with a small dog. The first two times someone tried to kill me with fire, so when I saw her this time, I followed her. As we approached the corner leading onto Scarlet Street and into the scarlet district, someone fired an arrow at me for attempt number three."

Amunique smirked, "I see they missed."

"Only because I caught the arrow then placed a chasing fire arrow spell on it and sent it back after them."

"No feeling like having the arrow you just fired hunting you back down, and on fire even. I love your grasp of shadow magic, no one can use it as well as you do," Amunique said, smiling at him.

Luthias chuckled, "When I found the arrow, there was a dead elven male pinned to a tree. But the arrow isn't what killed him.

Someone else slit his throat. Right to left. The only thing I found as a clue was a wolf's head tattoo on his right forearm. I don't know if it means anything or not, but I've seen this same tattoo twice now and both men died without telling me anything about it. I figured you could check into it for me."

"Only back for a few hours and already barking orders."

Luthias turned and stared at her.

"What? It was just a small doggy joke."

He shook his head and returned to watching the floor below.

Amunique laughed, "I need to get with some of my contacts about the tattoo. I will let you know more if you don't disappear again. So, what did this female and her eerie little doggy look like?"

"She is a young light-skinned human female with long black hair and a dragon fairy tattoo extending from below her ass down to the calf of her right leg. The dog is a small terrier breed of some sort, medium brown in color. I have checked every other dive on Scarlet Street but haven't found her yet."

"You own a large midnight blue dire wolf but it's the little brown terriers that give you the eerie feelings?" Amunique asked catching the napkin Luthias threw at her. "She doesn't sound familiar and neither does the dog. But Luthias, you know there are a few side streets that she could have turned onto."

Luthias nodded. "Yeah, I know, but her dress screamed high society. High society females don't walk their dogs down Scarlet Street."

Luthias continued looking out over the bar and watched Nakira walk in with his wolf, Nera. He looked over at Amunique who was laughing when they had seen the same sight. "Not a word, that's Nera and Nakira."

Amunique continued laughing at Nakira's perfect timing. "I'll go remind her you don't think highly of her."

Luthias shook his head, smiling, "Borgroff should be along shortly as well."

"Will he be walking a dog as well?" Amunique asked while laughing. "Head into my office. We can discuss everything, once we are all together. I will go down and send both in to see you. I will also make sure my bouncers know to watch for your mysterious female and her little, vicious, eerie doggy."

Luthias ignored her last bit of banter as he walked to the staircase.

He had to trust that her men would inform him if they saw her. He needed to talk to this female and see what all she knew.

Luthias had just walked into the office when Nakira barged in behind him and jumped up, forcing him to catch her as she wrapped her arms and legs around him. "I'm so glad you're back," she said, squeezing him as tight as she could. "I was scared you were not going to come back or if you did, you would be a dark, twisted version I wouldn't recognize." She never wanted to let him go again.

He squeezed and held on to her as if she were trying to slip away. "I will honestly say if you hadn't talked me into taking Borgroff then one of those two outcomes would have been likely. I still walked down a dark, twisted pathway, but Borgroff always pulled me back when he knew I was close to going over the edge."

Luthias pulled back and stared into her bright, beautiful, emerald eyes as he smiled. "You and I can continue our reunion in private. Amunique told me you and Nera have been staying here in my room."

She leaned in and kissed him then dropped her feet to the floor. "Yeah, it was the only place I could feel close to you." She looked down as Nera whimpered. "Sorry girl, it was the only place, we could feel close to you while you were gone. She laid on the floor by your side of the bed."

Nakira reached down and petted the wolf. "I will say though, Nera here just cornered and caught a thief for Knight Captain Brasscoat."

Luthias bent down and petted Nera. "I missed you too. I'm glad you were here to keep Nakira safe for me. And to capture the thieves she is supposed to catch."

Nera barked and wagged her tail as Amunique and Borgroff walked in.

Nakira slapped his arm playfully. "Hey, I was up on a roof trying to get a shot at him when she cornered him forcing him to give up."

Amunique and Borgroff chuckled at Luthias getting slapped. Amunique smiled, "Hell, I figured we would walk in and see you two all hot and heavy on my desk with Nera's paws covering her eyes. But I'm sure plenty of skin slapping will happen upstairs later." Amunique watched Nakira blush a bit.

Luthias ignored the banter as he walked over and opened his pack. Luthias pulled out the sword he'd obtained from the elf and laid it on the desk in front of Amunique as she sat in her chair.

"Our investigation led us to this sword. A nobleman in Ridgewood said he received it as payment when he hired a mercenary to lure Clive and his guards out of the city. The nobleman also received this wax-sealed letter."

Luthias took the letter out and handed it to Amunique. "Look at the center of the seal. The wolf's head imprinted in the wax seal looks exactly like the wolf's head engraved into the handle. The nobleman in Ridgewood and the dead elven male who shot the arrow at me had tattoos on their right forearm that matched the wolf's head as well. Do you recognize any of this?"

Before Amunique could respond, Borgroff interrupted. "A third attempt? Damn someone doesn't like you."

Luthias glared at Borgroff shaking his head as Nakira walked up and slapped Luthias's arm again but this time not playfully. "A third attempt? When in the hell did the second attempt happen? When were you going to say something?"

Amunique laughed as she carefully looked over the sword and the wax seal. She lifted the letter up off the desk looking at Luthias. "May I hold onto the letter?"

Luthias nodded as he picked up the sword and put it back into its scabbard.

Amunique continued looking at the seal. "I need to investigate the seal and the tattoo but I will let you know as soon as I know anything. What did the nobleman say about the tattoo?"

"Nothing, that was strange part. He told me damning evidence linking him to my attempted assassination. He was a fountain of information feeling the dagger cut into the back of his skull. But then he clammed up when asked about the tattoo. He chose to die by dagger instead talking about a wolf's head tattoo. I guess it would've led to a more painful death somehow. I need to know why this tattoo is worth dying over. Is this dark mistress connected to the tattoo? Cut-throat and his gang talked the mercenary that the nobleman hired into letting them do the job instead. Somehow, they learned it had to do with me. They even let the half-breed mercenary keep the pay he received. I took half to fund my investigation while a bartender Borgroff rescued from Hells Canyon received the other half to start over."

"Where is this mercenary now?" Amunique asked, "He may know more."

Borgroff chuckled. "He doesn't know anything now. He ended up feeding some hungry hellions down in the Lava Flats of the Ziamicawl Mountains."

Luthias noticed Nakira still glaring at him as Amunique talked again. "You have been busy! A dead nobleman and a dead mercenary. Anymore we need to know about?"

"A couple of arsonists in Ridgewood who tried to torch me but ended up killing an old blind psychic instead." He looked at Nakira to see her still glaring at him. "The second of the three attempts. When I tracked the arsonists down, they were talking to a female shrouded in darkness, but I lost track of her. She is one of the people behind my two brushes with fire. The only thing I know about the sword is its name, Fijandsvarg's Blade. In the ancient elven dialect, Fijandsvarg means wolfiend. According to the legend, Koraegin forged the sword in the eternal fires of the demon realm. I don't recognize any of the runes along the blade. As I said before, the nobleman in Ridgewood and the assassin tonight bore the tattoo of the wolf's head matching the handle and the seal. The mercenary in Hells Canyon was supposed to lure Clive and the guard out of town but Cut-throat's brute orc took the job and messed up the plans for me to die in the fire."

Amunique looked up from the note. "The blue brute you killed here in my bar?"

Luthias nodded as he continued, "The nobleman in Ridgewood received the wax-sealed note you hold in your hands. It talks about a secret lover he killed after she tried to poison him. But the strange part is, I put the note and the sword in my pack before lying down for the night last night. This morning, both were on my side table with a new message written for me at the bottom of the old note."

Amunique looked the letter over and read the portion addressed to him out loud.

"Luthias Blackridge, chaos is a funny thing, don't you think? As the note above says, it's funny how one second can change your entire world. One second, you are in Traemorra creating chaos for Cut-throat and his gang, who, in turn, created chaos by messing up well-laid plans. Then it only took a second for someone to create chaos by burning down the house you were just in. We're glad Nakira wasn't still in there, by the way. Now here you are in Ridgewood causing chaos by killing a noble elf. Then it only took a

second for two mercenaries posing as guards to set fire to a second building you were once again just in. Flames have way of following you. Fire seems to be the embodiment of chaos, wouldn't you say? Chaos is indeed a funny thing. It only took you a second to kill the two fake guards as well. But you did the world a favor when you killed those two. They were murderers, rapists, thieves, and arsonists. The bartender downstairs has the reward for their apprehension. We find the nobleman's apparent robbery and death quite ironic. We couldn't have produced a better ending to his story than for him to die in the same manner as his secret lover. Ridgewood seems to have a serial thief and murderer on the loose. There will be an antique dealer downstairs in the saloon when you get up. He rushed to get here when he heard a rumor this infamous sword showed up in Ridgewood. Its history is quite entertaining. But do not sell it for any amount of money to him. We do not want to have to redeliver this sword to you thereby killing this nice old scholar. We look forward to watching your progress in your investigation. Go forth and create beautiful chaos, Shadow Warrior."

Luthias opened his eyes and looked up to see Amunique looking at him. "What makes you lower your head and close your eyes? You are a trained rogue assassin with the Elven Shadow Warrior. A knight hunter employed the Council of Kings. Hell, you've probably killed more men than all of Traemorra's guards combined. You used your shadow magic to rip two people apart in Tros'mura a few years back."

"I stood there and watched my house go up in flames. I could see and hear Nakira burning, screaming, and dying inside, even though I know you weren't in there."

He looked at Nakira, grabbed her hand, then took a deep breath.

"I headed down a dark and twisted vengeful path. I didn't need to kill the mercenary. He didn't even do the job the nobleman paid him to do. The nobleman didn't even know anything about the fire or even why he hired the mercenary to lure guards out of the city. Neither of these men deserved death as their punishment for these crimes. Neither of their deeds led to the death of others. Cut-throat led himself and his crew to their death."

Amunique reached over and squeezed his other hand.

"As I said. You are a trained rogue assassin with the Elven

Shadow Warriors. Death is the punishment you hand out. The word mercenary speaks for itself on why he deserved death. There is no telling how many people he killed over a few simple coins and trinkets. As for the nobleman, the first part of this letter explains why he deserves death. The infamous Bagswell brothers you killed were notorious for their crimes and deserved death as well."

Luthias looked down. "The brothers tried to burn me alive. I wasn't including them in my feelings of guilt. I don't have an issue with killing when it's justified. I know the other two deserved their deaths for other reasons, but I didn't witness these crimes. I didn't kill them for those crimes. I killed them out of rage over what didn't happen to Nakira in any other place than my mind."

Amunique decided to lead the conversation away from the dark, twisted path his mind was heading down. "I will reach out to the antiquities dealer here in town and have him look into all this also."

Borgroff answered, "He rode in on the stagecoach with Luthias and me. He knows about it already, but it would be good to have you two comparing notes and working together."

Nakira followed their lead distracting Luthias from his dark thoughts. "Luthias, you've seen the crossing dagger tattoo on my lower back. The artist I use is here in town. I will see what he knows." She smiled, "It's about time to get another." She looked over at Nera who was lying on the floor beside Luthias's feet. "Maybe a majestic wolf of my own."

Luthias chuckled halfheartedly when Nera barked. He reached down and petted her. "Don't let it go to your head, girl. I'm going to check with your bouncers to see if she showed up. If she didn't, Nakira and I are going up to my room and retiring for the night. Nera, patrol the bar for Amunique." Nera stood and barked.

Borgroff perked up. "Wait, who showed up?"

Luthias and Nakira got up and walked towards the door.

Amunique bent down as Nera trotted up to her. "Well girl, you have the run of the place. Keep everyone in line." Nera's tail wagged as she petted her.

"Hello, who showed up?" Borgroff watched Luthias and Nakira walk out without answering. He got up and followed Amunique out as he talked. "Damn it. I keep the boy alive. I keep the boy in touch with reality. I even drag the boy back to a civilized nature from a dark, twisted path, and still, they all ignore the dwarf."

"Bartender, Borgroff here gets his drinks on the house tonight for his heroism. He feels we are all ignoring him." Borgroff smiled and winked at the bartender as he sat down.

Amunique mingled as she listened to Luthias talking to one of the bouncers about the young female, but no one saw anyone fitting the description.

Amunique slyly followed Luthias and Nakira up the stairs. After he shut the door behind them, she walked up, pulled the do not disturb sign down, and hung it on the center of the door. As she turned around, she started speaking.

"Is there anything I need to know?" She watched as a wraith appeared out of thin air staying in mist form.

"No mistress. But I am worried about the effect this will have on him when he discovers the truth. Do I continue to watch over him?"

Amunique turned to stare at the door. "Yes, but be careful, I also worry about what will happen when he uncovers the truth. My oracle powers show him revealing the truth, but everything grows dark afterward, and I see nothing. Once fate reveals the truth to him, he will be a powerful force."

The figure within the mist turned towards the door as well. "A force of good or of evil?"

"That is a question only fate has an answer for. And it's not revealing any clues." Amunique watched the figure hidden beneath the black mist bow. She then felt a gentle breeze as the wraith vanished out of sight.

She turned and took one last look at the door. "An answer we may not wish to know. Rest dark prince, you will need all the energy you can muster for the coming darkness."

Chapter Eight

Luthias woke up to the sun shining in his eyes once again. He looked up and noticed the shutter above him was open just enough to shine directly onto his left eye. "Not again. Did you open this damn shutter?" Luthias lifted his hand and slammed the shutter closed but it bounced back, allowing the sun to blind him completely again. Luthias could only laugh as he reached up and gently closed the shutter once again.

He sat up leaning against the wall and rubbed his hands across his face. He looked over to see that Nakira wasn't in bed. When he looked around, he saw her sitting naked on top of the dresser, laughing at him. "What are you doing on the dresser? Why aren't you here in bed with me?"

"This position gives me a better view to watch you sleep." Nakira had one leg bent, resting her foot on top of the dresser, and the other leg hanging off the front spread slightly apart from the other one.

He smiled and winked at her. "And me a better view to wake up to."

She laughed as she nodded her head towards the side table beside him. "Seems someone snuck in and watched us sleep last night. Do you think it was your mystery girlfriend? Is she the jealous type?" She smiled at him. "You think Etherika's trying to win you back from me?"

He smiled and shook his head as he replied, "You mean the female connected to three attempts on my life? If she is the jealous type, she's trying to kill me not you. That means she has her eyes on you as a love interest and is trying to eliminate the competition."

He looked up and tapped his bottom lip as if he was thinking. "You and Etherika did get along quite well during that mission a few years back. I remember you two getting naked together quite a bit to swim in mountain streams."

Nakira giggled at his comment as he looked over at the wax-sealed letter on his side table lying underneath the sword.

"Just like he or she left the last note, digging this sword out of my pack and placing it on top of the letter."

He grabbed the letter and examined the wax seal. Inside the seal was the impression of a wolf's head resembling the tattoos, the sword, and the other wax seals.

He looked up at her and smiled. "Not from your girlfriend though. It's another letter from the not-so-friendly wolf cult. You think Nera is behind this? Maybe she is trying to pick you as her new best friend. Clive did say you two were inseparable while I was gone."

Nakira laughed as she climbed down and walked over to sit beside him on the bed. "Hmm, maybe Nera is leaving them for you, or maybe she is their deity. Maybe they are mad at you for keeping her as your domesticated pet. She is an animal of the wild you know."

He looked at her and shook his head then opened the letter, reading it aloud.

"*Luthias Blackridge, nice catch with the arrow. Also, that was an impressive shadow magic trick with the flame spell on the arrow. That assassin didn't stand a chance. I guess someone else knew that and slit his throat before you arrived. Funny, one second, he thought you were dead, the next second, he was being chased by his own arrow. The arrow he fired at you. Funny how one second can change the course of everything around you. One second, you're following a young female and her dog while the world starts to slowly make sense once again. The next second, someone is trying to kill you a third time and your world slips back into complete and beautiful chaos. We are watching, Shadow Warrior.*"

Luthias turned the paper over and inspected it front and back. "No other words or clues?"

They dressed and headed downstairs to an empty bar. Luthias looked over to see Borgroff sitting on a bar stool drinking. Amunique was standing behind the bar drying and putting mugs away. Luthias then looked over to see Nera lying up on stage napping. "Wench, poor me a tankard of ale."

"Call me that again and I will burn your hide to ashes, completing what that assassin and the two fires failed to accomplish." The smirk never left her lips as she slid a full tankard of ale toward him. But Nakira caught it before it could get to him.

Luthias chuckled and sat down beside Nakira. "Cranky this morning, isn't she?" Borgroff shook his head as Nakira just smiled at

Luthias. Luthias looked over at Amunique and Borgroff,

"I'm assuming I already know the answer to the question I'm about to ask, but I will ask it anyway. Did either of you see anyone walk upstairs or downstairs last night or this morning?" He watched Amunique and Borgroff shake their heads. He looked over at Nera who just groaned and rolled to face away from him.

"So much for my majestic wolf on the prowl. But, I didn't think so. Last night when we went up to our room, I kept the sword in its sheath inside my pack. Then this morning we woke up to this letter laying on my bedside table with the sword on top of it just like the last time."

He tossed the note to Amunique then picked up the ale she slid in front of him and drank it down.

Amunique chuckled as she read the last line of the letter. "We are watching, Shadow Warrior." Amunique scoffed and started inspecting the wax seal and the letter. "What is funny though." Amunique felt the lower right corner of the letter. Luthias watched her grab a candle and hold the flame below the paper. As if by magic, a picture of a wolf's head appeared.

Borgroff sat forward more awake and paying more attention. "How did you know it would do that?"

"A hunch. Leave this with me as well. I want to examine it more thoroughly."

"Yes, mam," Luthias replied smiling at her.

"Lofte," Amunique suddenly said magically lifting two of Luthias's daggers out of his belt. "Trykk." The daggers flew across the room and landed on either side of the doorway.

They followed the dagger's path and saw a thin, pale, old, elven man who didn't flinch at all when the daggers landed. A couple of large, heavily armored elven soldiers stood behind him. "Is this how you welcome patrons into your establishment?"

Luthias heard Nera growl from on top of the stage. "Nera, easy girl but stay alert."

Amunique glared at the older man. "Only the guests who show up and enter without knocking before we are open. But I see by the company you keep that you are here on business from Chief Justice Travon and the Council of Kings. I will forgive you this time."

She reached her hand out towards the door. "Dra." She startled the two elven guards when the daggers flew back to her hands. She smiled as she handed them back to Luthias. "We will continue our conversation after our uninvited guests leave."

"That won't be possible. Chief Justice Travon has requested Lord Blackridge accompany me back to her country estate. She needs the Shadow Warrior's services."

"I appreciate the Chief Justice's request, but I am currently tracking down leads for another case I'm investigating. I will attend to any council business she has for me after I complete this case."

"Yes, she did mention your current case and says she might have information to help. An assassin tried to kill her and will try again." The old elf smiled, "I assure you I do not go anywhere unprepared nor without the knowledge I need."

The old elf snapped his fingers and the two guards stepped back out the door and faced away. "There is a council coach at the main gate. We will be waiting for you."

They watched him raise his hand. "Lofte." As he did, Luthias rose off the stool. "Dra." At the old elf's next word, Luthias floated over to land on his feet in front of the old elf. "Also, please do not make the Chief Justice wait or think cheap parlor tricks will get you out of the meeting. You will go by choice or by force."

The old man looked him over. "By choice is a lot more comfortable." The old elf smiled and bowed before turning to walk out.

"Okay, but I have two conditions of my own before I agree."

The old elf stopped and turned back around looking at him. Luthias lifted his arm. "Lofte." The old elf looked over both of his shoulders to see his elven guards suspended in the air kicking their feet and waving their arms.

"One, don't bring your own brand of cheap parlor tricks thinking they are going to intimidate a shadow warrior trained by one of the best. Two, I won't be going alone. The dwarf, the human, and the wolf behind me will be traveling with us as well."

Luthias lowered his hands, sitting the guards down as he watched the old man grin then turn and walk away. He turned to face Nakira and the others. "Well, I guess we're going to go meet with the Chief Justice by choice. I hear it is a lot more comfortable than by force."

Amunique smiled at him as he walked back over and drank down another ale that she placed in front of him. "Ditching me for an old elven man huh? Just be careful and make sure this is on the level, something feels wrong."

Luthias placed the empty mug on the bar. "I'm never careful.

There's no fun in it. But I'm always cautious, that's why they are all coming with me." He winked at her before he turned and led the others out of the Red Dog.

They stopped in Shadow Pass to stretch, grab a bite to eat and some ale before traveling on to the estate that sat at the foot of the Ziamicawl Mountains. The stagecoach pulled into the estate during the middle of the night.

The next morning, Luthias stretched his arms and yawned as he stood on a balcony looking out over the land below. He looked towards the sun rising over the horizon and watched a small dragon fly in between some trees.

"The dragon's emerald coloration is gorgeous." He heard Nakira's voice behind him.

He looked back to see Nakira walking up behind him once again dressed only in his tunic. He shook his head at the sight as he replied, "The color matches your beautiful eyes."

She walked over and embraced him from behind as two more dragons flew into view joining the first one. They brought his attention back to the beautiful landscape in front of him. One of the two small new dragons was white with turquoise scales while the second was a black dragon with dark maroon scales. They flew in to join the emerald dragon. They watched them fly in a v-formation with the emerald dragon in the lead. The dragons separated and flew low over a small lake. Each one caught and devoured a fish then flew back up into the v-formation but this time the black dragon took the lead.

Nakira leaned up to his ear. "I can hardly believe we got to wake up to such a gorgeous view. Dragons flying and diving for fish out of a clear blue mountain lake. The bright sun peering above the horizon. Trees standing three times as high as our second-floor balcony. How does one get so lucky to wake up to such a view?"

Luthias turned towards her and lifted her. As she wrapped her legs around him, he kissed her.

He stared into her eyes. "I get to see a better view every morning I wake to your beautiful face."

"You two are gonna make me hurl." Luthias put her down onto her feet as they both turned to see Borgroff standing in the doorway petting Nera.

Luthias smiled, "I was wondering where Nera wandered off to."

Borgroff walked out onto the balcony to stand beside Luthias and

Nakira. "I woke up to her trying to take over my bed. But I agree, how does one get so lucky to wake up to such a view?"

"By birth, by privilege, or in your case, by invitation." A voice made them turn from the beautiful view outside. When they did Luthias saw a mysterious black-haired female holding a small brown terrier. "You all can admire the view later. The Chief Justice is ready to see you all."

Nakira took Luthias's tunic off and tossed it back to him as she spoke. "Sorry, we're just not used to such beautiful scenery when we wake up. We're more used to waking up to the view of the sun rising above dirty Traemorra cobblestone walls."

Borgroff spun away from the sight of Nakira naked. "You were right, Luthias. She has been around both of your ex-girlfriends way too much."

The mysterious female smiled as her sapphire blue eyes watched Nakira quickly dress into her clothes. Nakira smiled as she asked the mysterious female the same question. "By birth, by privilege, or by invitation?"

"By bags of coin," she answered with a smile. "Since the Chief Justice is of elven descent and I am human, that tells you it's not by birth. You could say by privilege but that would be saying she brought me here because of who I'm related to or who I know. But the truth for me boils down to sheer bags of coins. I'm her mage protector brought here because of what I know and can do."

She smiled as she watched Luthias fasten his last bit of armor. "If you follow me, I will lead you to her," Luthias watched as she turned and walked off. "Eyes up and don't fall behind."

Borgroff quickly lifted his head causing Luthias and Nakira to laugh. Luthias spoke as they caught up to her. "What do you know about this attempt on her life? I take it you are the reason she is still alive?"

She turned to look at Luthias for a brief second as she continued walking. "I only know it was an elven male. But it was her husband and his magic that saved her."

"Why? Did the attempt happen while you were walking your dog down Scarlet Street in Traemorra? No, that's not it because the assassin was there trying to kill me at that time. Were you busy walking your dog in Ridgewood during the attempted assassination? No, I know! You were walking your dog down the main street in

Traemorra just before my house burnt." Nakira and Borgroff turned to look at Luthias. "This is the mysterious female I kept seeing before my three failed assassination attempts."

53

Chapter Nine

She smiled at him, "You are as perceptive as the Chief Justice said you were. She told me the dog would give me away. I was in Ridgewood during her assassination attempt and before you ask, no, I'm not involved in the attempts on your life."

Luthias shook his head at Borgroff as he watched him slowly slide his hand down toward one of his hammers. "Oh, I know you weren't. You were there making sure I survived the attempts." Luthias watched Borgroff's hand move away from his hammer.

Nakira looked at Luthias and then at the mysterious female. "Okay. How did she know about the attempts before they happened? More importantly, why didn't she warn you? I would've died in the first fire if I didn't leave with you.

She turned her head around and smirked at Nakira. "As for how the Chief Justice knew, I remind you, I'm here by bags of coin not by privilege or by invitation. So I only know what she allows me to know. As for you dying in the fire, I knew you were in his house with him. I would have never let you die. I would have gotten you out of the house using my magic."

Nakira looked at Luthias. "Well, now I want to hurry up and talk to the Chief Justice. I want to know how she knew."

"Same," Borgroff added as they walked outside.

Luthias looked over to see his guide standing on a path to his right, gesturing for them to follow her. "Then let's go talk to her because I have a clue where this is going already."

"Eyes up, lass, and lead on," Luthias laughed as she rolled her eyes at Borgroff and walked away. Despite the news they just learned, they still found it hard to keep their eyes on the path and off the natural beauty around them.

"Hard to keep your mind on business out here, isn't it?" The counselor's voice brought their attention away from the surroundings and towards the voice. Luthias looked over and saw an elven female sitting on a stone bench in the middle of a group of lavender flowers. He watched her take a deep breath, inhaling the relaxing lavender scent.

"I come out to this estate and my beautiful garden area to relax my tense body and clear my muddled mind as much as I can. That and my love of books written by Zjenica Robleus get me away from the masses of whiny asses I deal with. I'm not speaking of the public that comes seeking guidance. The council itself is full of child-like adults and their temper tantrums when votes don't go their way." She chuckled looking at her mage protector and spoke again. "Thank you, Jadai. I will send them to you when I'm done."

Luthias watched their guide bow then turn and walk off. He turned back around and watched the Chief Justice taking a few deep breaths while keeping her eyes closed.

She looked over and smiled, "Sorry. This is my place of Zen. I need my Zen after dealing with the whiny asses."

She stood up and stuck her hand out towards Luthias. He took it and helped her back to the path where they stood. She was careful not to step on her flowers.

"Thank you for meeting me out here at my estate instead of in the council building, Luthias. The fewer eavesdroppers that hear our conversation the better. I'm guessing old and ornery told you why I had him and the twins fetch you and bring you here."

"Yes, he and the armored twins were quite insistent that I make the trip by choice rather than force. He said the trip would be more comfortable. That of course was after he sat me back down on my feet, proving his prowess with magic was more powerful than simple parlor tricks."

"He does like to show off his magical parlor tricks from time to time but only with those he likes. If he doesn't like you or respect you, he just has one of his brutes pick you up and carry you to the coach. He has the manners of a hellion, sometimes. My question for you is how did you get him to let the others come along with you. He is precise with my instructions. Usually, if I tell him to get one person, he only shows up with one person."

She looked at Nera and petted her then up at Nakira and Borgroff. "Not that you all are not welcome. I wanted to meet you, but didn't figure it my place to unleash the brutish twins on you if neither of you wished to come. And you dear lady wolf, you are free to roam as you wish."

Nera looked at Luthias who nodded his head. They watched her run away wagging her tail.

"Justice Travon, this young lady beside me is Nakira Karvina, the dwarf is Volf Borgroff, and Nera, who is now lost in her own personal paradise, you know well." He smiled, "As for your husband, he happily agreed to my terms, when I sat the twins down behind him in my attempt to prove my magic powers were as strong as his parlor tricks."

Justice Travon turned and walked towards the crystal blue lake. "That explains the whistling when he got back last night, also why he was so happy. He finally met someone to play his game. He knows of your shadow magic skills. He is a huge fan of shadow magic and an even bigger fan of yours. He asks of your adventures as a Shadow Warrior and Knight Hunter every time I return home."

She looked back at him, smiling, "I have seen you both in action with your magic, you are far more powerful than he."

"He mentioned you had an attempt on your life. He also mentioned you might have information about the case you pulled me away from."

Chief Justice smiled and continued walking towards the lake. "Yes, an assassin tried to kill me and I believe he will try again."

"Your mage protector mentioned it was an elven male. What else can you tell me about him since she was in Ridgewood at the time spying on me and walking her dog?"

Chief Justice chuckled, "I told her that dog would give her away."

Luthias looked up at the dragons flying overhead then looked back toward her as she turned around.

Before either could speak Borgroff interrupted. "Yes, let's get this out of the way finally. How in blazes did you know about the attempts before they happened and why didn't you warn him?"

Luthias was about to speak when she held up her hand stopping him.

"It's okay, I anticipated his outburst. You are an impatient yet enthusiastic dwarf when it comes to protecting your friends and loved ones. Your outbursts and forthrightness are why I wanted to meet you. Stay by his side throughout the rest of this journey, he will need you for more than your expertise with your famed twin hammers."

She turned to face Nakira as she addressed her. "And you my dear, are the anchor these two men need throughout this ordeal. Although they will need your skills as a rogue and scout, it will be your love for Luthias and your ability to out think them both that will truly help them."

Chief Justice Travon turned back to face Luthias. "As for the assassin, the elven male was about a head shorter than you and used a longbow. He had an interesting tattoo on his forearm."

"A tattoo of a wolf's head," Luthias said interrupting her as he brought the sword out and handed it to her. "Are you familiar with this sword?"

"Yes, his tattoo was of a wolf's head and I'm only familiar with this sword through rumors and supposed fairy tales. Until now, I didn't even believe it was real. I thought it was just a legendary tale made up to give the wolfiend tale a bit of spice." She looked it over carefully and then handed it back to him.

Luthias slid it into his pack as he spoke. "The sword is real. But the assassin won't be making a second attempt on your life. He died trying to kill me. Another shadow magic parlor trick, old and ornery would love to learn. But as I continue through my investigation, I'm learning it is not the assassins who are the real problem because they all end up dead."

"But the organization behind them." Chief Justice Travon finished his sentence as she followed his train of thought. "Jegere av Fijandsvarg."

"Which, in the ancient elven dialect means, hunters of the wolfiend."

He smiled as he in turn finished her sentence. "Great minds think alike. Whoever is behind our assassination attempts keeps themselves separated from the crimes via several layers. They hired a nobleman in Ridgewood via a wax sealed note to hire a mercenary to hire a crew to lure the Knight Captain of Traemorra and his guards out of the city so someone else could burn my house down while I slept."

"Only," Justice Travon added, "Cut-throat and his goons screwed that up and lured you out."

Borgroff stepped forward. "Okay. Should Nakira and I give you two a room and a couple of hours to get whatever this is out of your system?"

Nakira chuckled at Borgroff as he continued, "What? You can't tell me you weren't getting sick of hearing these two finishing each other's sentences."

Nakira shook her head and laughed. "If I may. I'd like to ask how you knew about the attempts before they happened. Why didn't you warn him before any of them?"

"Yes. I apologize to you all, but she only told me about one attempt on Luthias and one on myself along with the fact of people with royal descent was in danger. It wasn't until a vision that I had an inclination about what days for Luthias. The only thing the vision revealed was your image along with three days on the calendar, and the image of the calendar burning up from a fire. The four previous attempts were all I knew anything about."

Luthias and the others followed Travon towards the lake's edge as she continued talking. "A demon visited me. She gave me the warning. Then I had the vision which wasn't specifically saying anything about death only that you would have interactions with fire on those three days. I had no information to give you or warn you about. She gave me no motive, weapon, or even who. I would have just seemed like an old crazy woman pretending to be an all-powerful elven druid. I am a druid but most certainly not all-powerful or all-knowing."

Luthias watched the dragons performing their aerial dance overhead as he listened to her, but he turned quickly towards her at the mention of a demon. "Wait, did you just say a demon showed up and was the entity that warned you?"

Borgroff looked from Luthias back to her. "Who conjured a demon from the demon realm on your estate and for the love of the divine why?"

"I don't think anyone conjured this demon. It didn't show the usual limitations that a wizard, warlock, or sorceress was controlling it. This demon showed up in wraith form concealing its true form. But it didn't hide the fact it was a demon once I called it out.

Borgroff huffed, "All wraiths look alike to me. There are no good wraiths. I'd prefer to let my battle hammers talk to them."

"But there are good wraiths, dear dwarf. We call them angel wraiths. They reside with the divine spirits in the spirit realm. We rarely see them within the earthly realm. I attended the Mage College branch in the Zukovia Kingdom, but as a druid not as a mage. My primary area of study was demonology."

She smiled at Luthias, "In fact, I chose demonology because of the legendary shadow hunters. My grandfather spoke of their tales and adventures every time I visited. My dad would tell me more tales every night when he tucked me into bed."

They watched her smile and shake her head. "Sorry, I wandered off-topic. The point is I know a lot about demonology. Even though it looked like a simple wraith appeared in front of me, I could tell that hidden beneath the dark red mist was a powerful demon. I don't know how the demon came to be within this realm, but it is here on its own accord, somehow. I also know why it came to me. She chose me because of my position as Chief Justice within the Council of Kings. She said this news needed to get to every mortal as quickly as possible."

They watched her still her nerves before continuing. "Someone is trying to kill anyone with present or past ties to any royal bloodlines. Whoever it is, they want all royalty and their heirs eliminated."

Borgroff shook his head. "Why would a demon warn you about someone trying to kill mortals, royal or otherwise? Fewer mortals give them more of a hold on this realm. It just seems to me this demon would help them out and make this realm easier to take over."

Luthias looked back up to watch a fish jump out of the lake as he thought about all he had just heard. "Okay, so the empress and prince will be targets for obvious reasons and our first concern to protect. The village magistrate in Kallinstyne and his daughter will also be targets. They are direct descendants of when the Kingdom of Kallinstyne ruled everything east of the Santos River."

Borgroff continued when Luthias paused, "There are also the dwarven descendants of when a king or queen ruled before the dwarven republic was created. But who else has a connection to a royal family? The ancient elven capital of Tros'mura is nothing more than a ruined castle and fortress. I mean I guess there could be a distant heir anywhere but who could guess who to protect or who this demon means to kill?"

Justice Travon nodded. "I got the feeling from the demon that it doesn't think another demon is hunting these individuals. I got the feeling that the demon felt it was a mortal doing the hunting."

Nakira interjected, "Again, I scratch my head at the crazy thinking going on here. Why is this demon worried about another mortal killing mortals? I believe this demon has ulterior motives it believes this situation is hindering.”

Travon smiled at Nakira, “That is my thinking as well. Especially since it has no apparent master here within the realm of Terra.”

Nakira nodded her head. “A demon with no puppet strings wouldn’t want to draw attention to itself or its plans. That is why it chose to contact you the way it did.”

Travon nodded. “That and not a lot of mortals are going to believe the inclination of a demon being helpful.”

“Another question.” They all looked back at Nakira. “Why is this demon, mortal, whoever targeting you and Luthias? Where do your ties to the royal lines come in?”

Travon curtsied as best she could. “Third cousin twice removed and all that jargon from the empress and prince. I signed my rights to the throne over to her mother a long time ago. I had no intention of following in my father’s footsteps. But since I am still related down the line that makes me a threat.”

Luthias spoke up when they all looked at him, “As for me, I have no idea. No royal ties that I know of. My elven father, Demir, is a carpenter in Gatesboro, my human mother, Braelyn, is a priestess with the Church of the Divine Spirits.”

Travon looked directly into Luthias’s purple eyes. “You are the mysterious link in this particular Zjenica Robleus mystery.”

Luthias looked down to see a Zjenica Robleus book laid open and face down on a bench beside where Nakira was standing. “This demon could be the antagonist hidden in plain sight,” Luthias thought out loud as he spoke. “I’m guessing you want the three of us to be the protagonists in this storyline.”

Luthias chuckled as she smiled at the three of them.

Borgroff smiled, “The plot of this novel sounds like serious trouble for all involved. Especially for the three protagonists. An endless hunt for mortals with hidden royal blood. A demon antagonist hidden-in-plain-sight helping the protagonists save other mortals, instead of helping the presumed hidden antagonist kill other mortals.” Borgroff smiled, “Count the ornery dwarf into this hide-n-seek mystery novel.”

Travon laughed as she nodded her head at Borgroff, “Ms. Robleus is still drafting this novel. But I am giving you this news because you three are the best hope for the people of the Ellehcim Kingdom. You need to investigate this information, investigate this demon and its motives for helping and protecting the people we know to be of royal descent. Don't worry about finding out who has royal ties I have my staff already checking birth and death records in my chambers in Gatesboro. Luthias, only you can solve this. I know of your exploits as a Shadow Knight and as one of the knight hunters for the Council of Kings. You are the descendant of multiple generations of shadow warriors."

She winked at him. "My grandchildren will be telling their children of your daring tales and exploits. Borgroff's and Nakira's as well."

They all heard a bark from behind them and turned to see Nera walking up covered in dirt and mud. "Yes, and the tales of the majestic midnight blue wolf as well."

Luthias laughed as he watched Travon pet Nera. "A person in your powerful position should know not to believe everything she hears. Tales are usually just that, simple tales people exaggerate as daring exploits. Ask any bard." He leaned closer. "Or ask Zjenica Robleus if you don't believe me."

He watched as a smile crossed her lips. "I'll ask her when I see her next. Also, tales of Luthias Blackridge ripping an assassin and a mercenary apart using his shadow magic have been proven as true. Besides, people usually know better than to tell a person in my powerful position simple tales. Simple tales are for children, fools, bards, and idiots to believe and spread. People know it doesn't end well for them when I find out they told me a simple tale."

She sat down on a bench at the edge of the lake as Nera ran off jumping into the water.

Luthias watched Nakira pick the novel up off the bench as she sat down beside Travon. He chuckled knowing that was one of her favorite authors as well. He smiled as she read the title aloud, "The Dragon Fairy's Lost Love. I haven't read this one yet."

Travon leaned over and whispered, "Take the book with you and read it during your downtime between battling the forces of evil. It is my gift to you for agreeing to take on such a burden and keeping these two in line. You will not be able to put it down. This is my fifth time reading it." She winked. "I will just have Zjenica bring me another copy the next time she visits. She does some of her best writing here. In fact. I'll have her send a copy of all her books to Luthias's parent's house in Gatesboro for you."

Luthias stood in silence looking up at the majestic mountains then looked out and watched the dragons continue their aerial dance over the clear blue lake. He felt a hand grab and squeeze his hand. He looked over and saw Travon smile, "As you search for answers remember not all is as it seems. Also, that sword of yours is somehow key to discovering who this group, Jegere av Fijandsvarg is and what they have to do with this."

She breathed in a deep breath, "I'm sorry, I'm tired and must take my leave. I have another book and an old cranky elf waiting for me up at the house. You need to find Jadai. She should be in her room on the top floor of the spiral tower. Let the shadows guide you to the answers we seek, Shadow Warrior."

Chapter Ten

The three of them followed her to the main house and bid her farewell where the paths split. They continued over to the spiral tower looking for Jadai. Nakira and Borgroff chose Luthias to walk up the spiral tower and find her.

Luthias approached the top floor of the spiral tower and noticed a single door at the top of the stairs. As he approached the door, he saw it was open slightly giving him a small peek inside. Just as he was about to knock, he watched Jadai walk by the opened door, completely nude.

"Eyes off the prize Blackridge, there will be lots of time for that later. I need you to grab this gear and take it down to the stagecoach. I already have you all packed and loaded onto the stagecoach. I will meet you down there after I'm dressed."

He pushed the door open and looked around trying to keep himself from staring at her as she bent over digging through an ornate chest on the far side of the room. He saw three bags sitting ready just to the right of the doorway.

"These three bags are all that is needed to go right now?" When she didn't answer he turned to see her bent over at the waist nodding her head as she continued to dig through the chest. He looked at the brightly colored dragon fairy tattoo on the back of her thigh that extended down to the middle of her calf. The same one he saw in Traemorra. He quickly turned back to the bags.

"Question though, if you are her mage protector, why does she always send you off on errands? Why is she sending you with us?" Once again, she didn't answer so he turned to see her standing and facing him. Before she could answer his question, something Travon told Borgroff popped into Luthias' head.

"Because you're the ever-elusive angel wraith she mentioned. She can call out to you mentally from anywhere and your wraith cloak can take you there instantly. That's how you were at all three attempts on my life and now I see that is how I survived all three attempts."

"Your survival of the three attempts had nothing to do with me, that was all you. But yes, I am an angel wraith. I can hide in plain sight as many creatures. A dove, a cat, or vanish completely. I hate to ask this of you, but I need the other two to be unaware of my true nature for now."

She developed a mischievous smirk, "If you won't tell them I'm an angel wraith, I won't tell Nakira you stood here and stared at me while I was nude. Besides, as far as they will know, I'm going on from Traemorra. But I will be following and protecting you in spirit form, unseen and only heard within your thoughts. She knows you are the key to this mystery, and you are the only one who can solve this. She knows I need to be helping to protect you instead of her right now. If she calls me, I will whisper into your thoughts where I'm going and when I come back. I promise."

He nodded his head. "I will take these and meet you at the stagecoach." He didn't wait for a response as he picked up the bags and headed back down the winding staircase.

As he exited, Borgroff and Nakira were staring while Nera was lying down waiting patiently. Borgroff looked at the bags in his hands and asked, "What are these for? Wait, is she going with us?" Luthias shrugged his shoulders.

After a long time, Jadai came walking out of the tower with her black hair put up into a tail. They noticed she had replaced the dress she had been wearing all day with light brown leather armor that fit her body perfectly. "Eyes up guys, there is another lady present."

Luthias looked over at the driver and then to Borgroff, both of whom had also turned towards him. Nakira slapped Luthias on the arm as the guys all laughed at the fact, she had caught them staring. "Is everything loaded and ready?"

Luthias was still laughing as he answered, "Yes, several hours ago. So, we just sat here and swapped life stories with one another."

Luthias saw a sarcastic grin form on her lips as she tossed her last bag at him.

She looked at the stagecoach driver. "Driver, we need to go to Traemorra and drop them off before continuing on our journey." The driver took the bag from Luthias then bowed to Jadai and headed up to his seat. Luthias reached his hand out to help her up onto the coach. He was surprised when she placed her hand in his and allowed him to help her up inside. He then helped Nakira up onto the stagecoach and kissed her. Luthias smiled when he reached his hand out towards Borgroff.

"Not a chance lover boy and no kiss either." Luthias laughed and heard the girls laughing inside the coach.

Borgroff spoke again after the stagecoach started moving, "We know they are targeting royal families and we are just a short ride away from Kallinstyne. Shouldn't we do something about the magistrate and his daughter before we get too far away to protect them?"

Jadai looked up at Luthias. "Justice Travon expressed concern over the immediate danger to the empress and the prince. But if Luthias wishes we can head to Kallinstyne first."

Luthias shook his head. "No, I think we need to operate on most important first. That means our first step is to get the empress and the prince protected. They are the most exposed right now. Then we can work on the others."

Borgroff thought a minute before speaking again, "Then why are we heading to Traemorra instead of straight to the royal palace? Wouldn't it make more sense to head there and not clear across the kingdom?"

Nakira spoke up before Luthias or Jadai could speak. "If we could get an audience with the empress and the prince then yes it would. Also, if we could convince them this threat is more dependable than the other threats they receive daily then yes. But you must have a good reason to go before the empress or for the empress to call you to the royal palace."

Jadai looked up from a journal she had been writing in and added her thoughts to Nakira's. "I doubt us walking in and telling them a demon warned us a mortal is out to kill you is going to be considered a viable threat. Even coming from the distinguished shadow warrior and the Council's most famous knight hunter."

Borgroff chuckled. "That sounds crazy enough to get us thrown into the dungeons. I see your point. What is our plan of action then?"

"I'm going to have Knight Captain Brasscoat send troops from Fort Romnuuski to help with her protection." They all looked at Luthias as he continued. "As you all said, if we show up with that story, we are going to sound crazy and end up in a dungeon unable to help anyone as this kingdom then the rest of this continent crumbles into chaos. But if Dominion guards show up at the request of Chief Justice Travon and the Council of Kings, then she will take it as a serious threat.

"I will say, part of my job out here is to come up with a plan to move the empress and the prince somewhere hidden."

"Look into Tros'mura just across the border in Zukovia. People call it a ruined castle, but only one wing of it has collapsed. The main portion of the castle still stands. Luthias, I, and some others traveled there and defeated the assassin who killed the three counselors a few years ago."

Jadai smiled at Nakira for her quick thinking, "It was in response to those assassinations and the attempt on Travon's life that brought me to her protection detail."

"After we arrive at Traemorra I will find and talk to Knight Captain Brasscoat. Borgroff and Nakira, you two head to the Red Dog. Get Amunique and her group on this investigation as well. We need to get ahead of this."

Luthias turned back to stare out at the passing scenery, but it all faded as his mind wandered back to thoughts of his youth. He knew he wasn't born at the age of five but everything before that age seemed like murky fragments of old nearly forgotten dreams. He remembered nights of terror, voices speaking to him from out of the darkness, shadowy creatures sneaking about at night. He remembered his parents and grandparents trying to convince him the voices were the wind blowing through window seals. The shadowy creatures were just trees or moonlight casting shadows of trees and animals. He remembered wanting to believe them, but he couldn't. He can remember hearing the dark, demonic voice echoing all around him. Other times he remembered looking into a reflection in the faintest of lights. Reflections, revealing him as the shadowy creature lurking just beyond the edge of the shadows.

He remembered how much he hated and feared the darkness as a young kid. He remembered his paternal grandfather being the only person to help him overcome this shadow fear by starting his shadow warrior training. He taught him the secret art of being an Elven Shadow Warrior. He taught him not to fear the darkness but to use it to his advantage. Not to fear the voice but to use it as his own. Not to fear the shadows and their creatures but to learn to become them. That is what he's done.

He owed everything to the man but never got to tell him that or even thank him because he vanished from Luthias's world just before his tenth birthday.

The stagecoach coming to a stop brought him out of his thoughts. They had reached Traemorra. Luthias climbed down from the stagecoach and helped Nakira down. He then watched Borgroff and Nera exit. He looked back into the stagecoach seeing Jadai had already disappeared. But he acted like he was speaking to her anyway.

"I'm going to find Knight Captain Brasscoat and get the troops on the way to Santos Isle. We will see you when you return, or we hear from Chief Justice Travon again." He closed the door and signaled the driver to go on.

Nakira looked at Luthias as the stagecoach headed off. "Are you okay? You seemed to slip away for the rest of the stagecoach ride."

Luthias smiled at her, but Nakira could still see the sadness in his eyes as he replied, "Sorry, I slipped into some old dark memories."

"Tros'mura? Sorry if bringing up that subject brought those memories back up." Nakira reached out and grabbed his hand.

Luthias looked into her emerald eyes and smiled weakly, "Much older, much darker memories than Tros'mura." He kissed her. "I'll be okay."

She nodded. "We will meet you at the Red Dog after you talk to Knight Captain Brasscoat. Nera, stay by his side." She squeezed his hand when Luthias looked at his wolf then nodded.

Luthias watched her walk away and chuckled watching the same young gate guard from his front door smile, not taking his eyes off Nakira. No doubt remembering her little show that night.

"Welcome back Lady Karvina. And you as well Gate Captain Borgroff." They both just nodded as they passed through the gate. "Lord Blackridge, I'm sorry to hear about your house, sir."

"I've already got men rebuilding it for him," Brasscoat said before Luthias could answer. He looked up to see Brasscoat walking towards him from the edge of the surrounding woods.

"It is good that you're back. I will show you the progress they're making tomorrow when we can see. It's just clearing out the old debris right now but progress."

"Knight Captain Brasscoat, thank you for the help with the house. But I'm afraid this is more than just a visit. I am here on official

Council of Kings business."

Brasscoat nodded and led Luthias back to the edge of the woods where he knew they could talk freely. "Shadow Knight Blackridge, it is then."

Luthias smiled. "Chief Justice Travon brought me to her estate. We are investigating the possibility of attacks against people with royal blood. I need a battalion out of Fort Romnuuski to go help with the protection details for the empress and the young prince until we can find a safe place for them. Chief Justice Travon received a credible warning that they and others may be in danger. Also, while I am here, I know the magistrate here in Traemorra has distant royal bloodlines as well, so we need to double his security."

"The city magistrate and his family should be arriving in Gatesboro sometime late tonight or early tomorrow. He decided to go up there to discuss some business with the council. His family went with him to enjoy a little time away."

Luthias nodded. "Good, send a soldier out tonight to inform him and his family to stay put until they hear from Chief Justice Travon or me. I'm gonna go meet up with Borgroff and Nakira so we can talk to Amunique at the Red Dog."

"Luthias, keep Borgroff and Nakira as long as you need them," Knight Captain Brasscoat said then hurried off to find one of his messengers as Luthias headed towards the Red Dog Saloon.

Chapter Eleven

As the Traemorra magistrate's stagecoach approached the rocky gorge known as Twin Cliffs, the driver spotted a group of six men wearing black armor sitting atop their horses blocking the path through the gorge.

"Whoa there!" The driver pulled the team of horses to a halt as a callous, red-bearded dwarf with a deep scar cutting through his left eye smiled at the driver. The driver looked them over and spat on the ground.

"I'm sure I do not have to guess at your intentions here but know that you have stopped the private stagecoach belonging to the City Magistrate of Traemorra. You should also know there are eyes and arrows pointed at all six of you right now. If I give the signal, every one of you dies. Do yourselves a favor and live another day by kindly moving aside."

The callous, red-bearded dwarf continued to smile at the coach driver. "Death by six arrows it is. You can give that signal anytime. We are prepared for whatever happens."

He continued to smile as the coach driver raised his arm and then dropped it. All at once, six arrows flew in from the cliffs surrounding them. Five of the arrows hit their mark as the coach driver fell over dead causing the sixth to skip off the stagecoach landing at the hooves of the dwarf's horse.

"Idjit, I told you we were prepared for whatever happens next. That was a hint. Your men were dead before you could even see these cliffs. We are the Legion of Red Death."

He looked back towards his mercenaries who were sitting atop their horses smiling and laughing. "What are you idjits smiling and laughing at? Get the guest of honor and his family out of the coach. We don't make the guest of honor wait for his entertainment."

He watched the other mercenaries scramble down from their horses and drag the magistrate and his family out of the coach. The red-bearded dwarf climbed down and smiled a wicked smile. He walked over to the females of the group. "Ladies, today is your lucky day." He continued to smile as he got close to the younger of the two females.

He noticed the young brunette with suspicious, yet stern eyes didn't recoil back in fear as he expected she would. Instead, the young female smiled wide then bent down and patted him on the head. "Why is that little man? Is your mommy showing up to arrange a play date?"

One of the mercenaries behind him couldn't help but laugh at the young lady's bravery in the face of certain unpleasant pain and death at the hands of her captures.

The dwarf took the large red stained war hammer off his back and struck the mercenary down, smashing his head like a melon. He looked at the rest of the mercenaries who shut up immediately. He smiled and laughed as he gave a dirty look to the young, long-haired brunette female who was now hiding behind the younger of the two gentlemen. The dwarf laughed when the young man tried to appear brave as well. He put the war hammer back into the holster on his back.

He bowed as a king would when greeting foreign dignitaries. As he stood he spoke to the group. "My name is Crimson Shaw. I am the leader of the Legion of Red Death. This hammer is known as Red Death." He gestured towards the smashed head of the mercenary. "I think you can figure how it got its name."

He walked over to stand in front of an older distinguished gentleman dressed in gold and silver-lined chain mail armor. "My lord," Crimson bowed low once again. "You look rather dashing in your ceremonial armor."

Once again, Crimson looked over at the gruesome scene of the smashed head and twitching body of his mercenary before turning back and smiling.

"You don't think it's going to protect you though, do you? I mean this ceremonial chain mail alone will be turned into a pile of scrap metal by this hammer." He leaned in and whispered in his ear. "With you still inside it. Then who here will protect your beautiful daughter from me and my legion, Your son-in-law? He already looks like he is about to shit his britches. Your daughter is more apt to have to protect him."

The magistrate stuck his chest out trying to appear brave in the face of certain death. "I don't know who you are, nor do I care. All that matters is my family's lives. You can have and do what you want with me but please let them go free. My money, armor, jewelry, whatever you want is yours. Take my family's money and jewelry as well." He put his hands out in front of him. "Tie me up, beat me." He looked at dead twitching mercenary. "Turn me and my armor into a pile of bloody scrap metal. I am the one you are after, not them."

"My lord, how brave taking one for the family. I will be taking all of that any way. Go ahead and strip out of the armor." He turned to the magistrate's wife and admired the older blonde-haired female's beauty. He laughed as she too was trying to look unafraid, but he could see she was visibly shaking from the bloody show earlier.

"Does he let you tie him up in bed as well or does he only do that with his pet whores in the scarlet district?" He smiled as he looked over her body then turned back to look at the magistrate stripping out of his armor pieces.

"Ah, no matter, I am not the one who decides what happens to you and your family my lord. Just like you, I have a boss with an agenda." Once again, he turned back to the older female. "But I have good news for you, my dear. After years of dealing with your husband and his pet whores, he now gets to watch you and your daughter become someone else's pet whore."

He turned to look at the other mercenaries behind him smiling, "Both of you girls get to enjoy the company of me and my men." He leaned in and whispered to the older female, "But unlike him and his whores, he will watch you two enjoy our attention."

He looked back at the men behind him. "Tie these two men up and gag them so they can watch their ladies enjoy our pleasures without interruption. But remember we can't waste too much time. We have another job to do after we're done here."

Crimson smiled at the young brunette. "It looks like my mommy isn't going to show up so I will arrange the play date myself. Are you ready to play, date?"

***

When Luthias arrived at the Red Dog, the bartender directed him to Amunique's office. He looked over and saw Nera on the prowl through the bar keeping her eyes and ears open for trouble. When he walked in and shut the door, he saw Borgroff sitting in a chair with two tankards of ale. "One of those two tankards for me?" Borgroff finished off the first tankard and started on the second one. "Guessing not then." He shook his head and then looked over at Amunique. "What all have they told you so far?"

"Nothing yet, they said to wait on you."

"Justice Travon got a strange visit from a strange guest. A demon in wraith form warned her about someone hunting down people with royal blood. This demon also warned her about the first attempt on my life and the attempt on hers. But she didn't know enough to be able to tell me. She didn't know of a motive, a weapon, or even who. Travon was only able to help through a vision she had of certain dates, my face, and the image of fire."

Amunique nodded. "We would have just figured whoever she sent to warn you had lost their mind. What I want to know is who on her staff called forth a demon?"

Nakira looked at Amunique. "No one. She says this demon was untethered. No mage master. Justice Travon was the only person to see this demon and she only saw it in wraith form surrounded by red mist."

"She is not prone to telling tall tales and she is a druid expert in demonology. If she says she met with an untethered demon, then that is at the very least what she believed to be true." Amunique hung her head in deep thought after she finished.

"What is it, Amunique?" Luthias brought her attention back up to him. "That look on your face is more than deep thought. It usually tells me this information confirms something for you."

She looked up at Luthias and smiled. "You've been around me too long." She looked down and collected her thoughts before continuing.

"When I was young, our clan guards were all killed by a powerful demon. A black and red lace-winged succuba demon. Naked mortal body and head covered in red demonic snakeskin with black dragon scales. Black spiral horns grew from her scalp of fiery red hair and her eyes were black as raven's wings. My grandmother was the clan oracle, she could sense this demon was a slave to a mage master at the time, but she couldn't discern who its master was. They were shrouded within darkness and deception."

"If this demon killed your guards what stopped it from killing the rest of your clan?" Borgroff asked as he sat both of his empty tankards down on the desk and sat forward in his chair. "I don't see a demon leaving a job half done."

Nakira nodded. "I agree but we also don't see a demon warning people that someone is killing other mortals, yet, here we are."

Amunique shrugged her shoulders. "We never knew. My grandmother sensed the loss of its connection to its master, but it didn't return to the demon realm. The demon just became an untethered demon loose in the world and disappeared. Not completing its task of killing the clan."

After listening, Luthias spoke, "My knowledge of demons comes from my shadow warrior training. All the tomes say that when you kill the master, you send the demon back to the demon realm. A demon can't be in this realm without a master. They also say that when someone slays a demon, you are sending them back to the demon realm weakening their master's hold on them, but not breaking it entirely. So how does a demon lose its connection to its master and remain here untethered?"

Luthias looked around the room, but no one had an answer for him. "That is the biggest question we need an answer to. Another question we need to answer is who all has royal bloodlines. I have Brasscoat sending a battalion of men to help with the empress and prince's protection. He also said the Traemorra magistrate and his family were on the way to Gatesboro. I told him to send a soldier to have them stay in Gatesboro until they hear from Travon or myself."

Luthias noticed a smile on Amunique's face as she spoke. "The young female you kept seeing."

Luthias was waiting for her to make the connection. "Yes, she works for Justice Travon. She had been following me to help keep me safe until Travon could gain more information. Travon also thinks the sword I received from the nobleman should help us find a group known as Jegere av Fijandsvarg, the people we believe are behind the wolf's head tattoo and letters."

"Hunters of the Wolfiend," Amunique translated the words Luthias spoke. "That will help me out as well. But we need to get these runes deciphered. Leave the sword with the antique dealer and see if he can get us some more answers."

Nakira stepped forward. "Need I remind you all of the note

Luthias received in Ridgewood predicting his death if Luthias leaves the sword with him."

Luthias looked at Nakira. "Nakira's right, anyone but me in possession of this sword risks this group killing them. But I can have him make charcoal drawings of them and work on them while I keep the sword with me."

Amunique nodded. "Okay, we need to be aware of the base criminal element involved but we need to decipher who the main people behind all of this are."

"We also need to discern this untethered demon's interest in all this. There must be an angle for it but what?" They all looked at Borgroff as he continued. "So, find and hide people with royal ties, find and eliminate the base criminal element involved, decrypt runes on an ancient sword connected to Koraegin, the demon lord of Knarran, and discern if he has any interest in all this." He smiled and chuckled. "No big deal, we will have this solved by lunch tomorrow."

Luthias stood up as if someone had kicked him. "Borgroff, that's it. The demon's connection is Koraegin. It must be. Amunique somehow this sword, Koraegin, this cult, this untethered demon, and the wolfiend are all interconnected. For right now forget about investigating tattoos and the cult. Instead, investigate the legend of this wolfiend. Let's see if that gets us any closer. Nakira, tomorrow you and Borgroff check in with your tattoo guy while I take the sword over and have the dealer make drawings of the runes and wolf's head. I will also have him investigate the wolfiend legend as well and coordinate with Amunique."

Nakira stood up, walked over to Luthias, and hugged him. "Travon knew what she was doing when she hired you." She looked over at Borgroff and smiled. Are you ready for some sleep so we can solve this before lunch tomorrow?"

Borgroff laughed as he stood up and followed them out. "If only."

Amunique stayed in her office and shut the door after they left. "Is everything going according to schedule?" The mysterious wraith appeared within the black mist nodding her head. "Good, go see to it."

Chapter Twelve

The wraith demon floated invisibly within the shadows of the corner of the room watching the prince undress and climb into bed. She could feel the presence of the palace guards standing guard outside the door. She waited patiently watching him toss and turn until finally he settled down and fell asleep.

Silently, she hovered down out of the darkened corner and floated above him. She reached her invisible hand out and gently brushed the hair from his face waiting for her cue to act. "What the hell?" The guard's voice outside his door was her cue. She watched the prince's eyes open wide when he heard the guard's voice outside his door. He tried to sit up but something had him pinned down to the bed.

All he could do was stare wide-eyed as a dark red mist appeared above him. He watched the red mist take the form of a beautiful dark-haired female smiling down at him. He looked up at her as she straddled his midsection. At first, a look of confusion crossed his face, but that look turned to fear when she pulled a dagger from a sheath strapped to the leg of her red armor.

She stared at him for a moment, continuing to smile. She was reveling in the fear she'd created in his eyes. She leaned down and whispered, "I do apologize my liege, but certain deaths are necessary for the Fijandsvarg's return." She kissed the prince on the lips as she drove the dagger hilt deep into his chest. "Live in the darkness young lord, chaos will soon follow." She left the dagger sticking out of his chest and watched the life in his eyes fade until only death's mask remained.

She returned to her mist form then faded invisible as she exited the room. She floated above the dead guards who should have protected the young prince. "Failure is not an option when your job is protecting others."

She made her way down the deathly quiet hallway toward the empress's chambers. Soon her death wraiths would make their way through the castle killing everyone and disrupting the deathly quiet with the sound of blood-chilling chaos. She stopped just outside the empress's door where two death wraiths hovered above the bodies of two more dead palace guards.

"Her handmaiden warned her about the incompetence of the palace guards. Seems, the empress should have listened. Release the other death wraiths, let the chaos begin. But make sure you do not disturb me."

She floated passed as the hidden figures within the black veils of mist bowed. Once again, she hovered silently watching the empress as she slept in her elegant bed. She smiled as she floated to the side of the bed and then transformed into her full mortal form.

Gently, she lay down and felt the empress draw in close to her. She caressed the empress's hair as chaos broke out in the hallway. She laughed as she climbed on top and straddled the empress. She looked down into the empress's eyes and once again reveled in the fear she'd created. "Like mother, like son. He had the same look in his eyes." She slid a second dagger out of another sheath from the other leg and stared deep into the empress's fear-filled amber eyes.

"The fake royal bloodlines of today do not descend from true royalty. You must die so the rightful Emperor can reclaim his throne."

She leaned down and kissed the empress as she shoved the dagger hilt deep into her chest. She rose and watched life fade from her eyes and death's mask was all that stared back. "Live in the darkness your grace, the chaos has already begun. The Fijandsvarg shall return."

She climbed off the bed and walked out of the room where a death wraith floated over a dead elven female staff member. "Make sure everyone from the castle and the village is dead. Hang the empress and prince's bodies from a tree at the entrance to the royal grounds. Make sure no one touches or removes the daggers from the bodies. Let all those who pass by the Royal Grounds know what happened to their precious fake royalty. Leave the rest of the bodies where they fall." The wraith floated off quickly as the demon watched the chaos around her and listened to blood-curdling screams. "Beautiful chaos."

***

The sun blinded Luthias's left eye waking him from a deep sleep. "Not again!" Luthias raised his hand and slammed the shutter closed but kept his hand on it to hold it in place. He felt Nakira jump, waking up in bed next to him. "Sorry." He looked over at her and smiled. "I need to ask Amunique if she has any rat traps available. I'll line the floor and figure out who is delivering these damn letters."

She rolled over and lay on top of him smiling. "You'd just forget and trip every one of them when you woke up the next morning."

He looked up to see her beautiful face as he lowered his arm and wrapped her in a hug. He looked over at the table beside the bed. Lying on the table underneath the sword was another wax-sealed letter. She laughed as she rolled off him. He reached over and slid the letter out from under the sword. He opened it up and read it aloud.

"And the beautiful chaos begins. Not all is as it seems though. Those words never contained a truer meaning than right now. Remember to make the seconds count, because as you are witnessing it only takes a second for a person's entire world to go from making sense to complete chaos. Luthias, the darkness is coming. We are watching you shadow warrior."

Frustrated, Luthias folded the letter, got up, and put it in his pack. As he dressed, he looked over at Nakira getting up and around. "I'm headed out to see the antique dealer with the sword. You and Borgroff talk to your tattoo friend then we will all meet up here and see what we need to do next."

He walked over and kissed her. "I love you." He watched her tilt her head and stare at him. "What?"

She leaned in and kissed him again. "I love you too. But this is the first time you have said that to me during the whole time we have been together." She swatted him on the ass. "Now get going before this gets all mushy and we end up back in bed."

Luthias left the Red Dog and hurried to the museum. When he walked into the small museum, he saw a young female of human descent standing next to a display.

He smirked, "Is that a hat shaped like a dragon on your head?" Luthias chuckled seeing her jump at the sound of his voice, "I'm sorry, I didn't mean to startle you."

She smiled, "It's okay. Yes sir. I wear it when I read to the young kids. But I do apologize, sir, we are not having tours today." She smiled as Luthias watched her eyes light up. "If you would like to come back tomorrow morning though, it would be my pleasure to give you a private one-on-one tour."

"Easy dear, niece. This one is far beyond your reach." Luthias looked up to see the antique dealer standing in a doorway directly behind her. "Why don't you run to the saloon up the street and get you and I some breakfast?" Luthias watched as she looked back with a look of aggravation on her face. "Run along my dear and do hurry, we have a lot of research to get into today."

After she left, he led Luthias into the room then closed and bolted the door behind him. "I apologize, my sister passed away a year ago from an illness. Now at the ripe old age of fifty-three, I became a father for the first time to a hormone-driven, ill-natured young woman of fifteen. I've been trying to teach my niece to see the true value in everything around her."

Luthias just remained quiet as he sat down directly in front of an old akora wood desk. He looked around at the other furniture in the room and knew they were all akora wood and all older than several hundred years.

The old antiques dealer noticed Luthias eyeing the furniture. "This is all akora wood furniture made by a master craftsman from the elven tribes that used to roam the lands ruled by the royal family living in Tros'mura before it fell in battle. It's over seven hundred years old. This wood is the hardest wood to work with. It is rumored that only a master craftsman of these ancient elves could perform such work as you see within this room. They had to use magic to hone the tools to even make a scratch into the wood."

Luthias took the sword out of its sheath and laid it on the desk. "All interesting, but do you know as much about the wax seal as you do about this woodwork? I also need you to take some charcoal drawings of the wolf's head and the runes carved into the length of the blade. I need to know how this seal ties in with this sword so I can figure out who is sending these letters. I also need you to check into a legend known as the wolfiend. It and the demon lord Koraegin are involved with this, I just need to know how."

"Ye…yes of course sir, my apologies." He sat forward and cleared his throat seeing the serious look on Luthias's face. He quickly made the charcoal etchings he needed. "I will investigate the runes, their meanings, and this wolfiend legend."

"Good, keep up the excellent work. If you find anything out and can't find me, let Amunique over in the Red Dog Saloon know. I want you two working together. You can have your niece relay information back and forth." Luthias picked up the sword, placed it in its scabbard hanging from his belt, and exited heading back towards the Red Dog. Luthias walked into the Red Dog and noticed everyone staring at him,

Amunique greeted him, "Perfect timing. Clive just walked in and told us we have a big problem."

Luthias handed Amunique the letter. "That would explain this last letter then. Let me guess, the Magistrate of Traemorra and his family never made it to Gatesboro."

Before the knight captain could ask Luthias how he knew that, Amunique tossed the letter to the knight captain. "Nakira and I had another visit last night. I received this bit of cryptic writing last night while I slept."

Clive read the letter and then looked up at Luthias. "And the beautiful chaos begins. We are watching shadow warrior. What the hell does that mean?" He handed the letter back to Amunique and shook his head.

"Never mind, right now that doesn't matter. You three need to get to Twin Cliffs and investigate the scene. The guard I sent last night with your message showed back up this morning with the news. He asked Dominion guards to secure the scene until council inquisitors showed up. I figure that is you, now." He hung his head. "Luthias, according to my guard the scene is gruesome. Both men castrated, their heads smashed, both women raped and murdered. Violently"

Borgroff stood up, drawing Clive's attention away from Luthias. "Do we have any clue as to who did it?"

"We have one dead mercenary dressed in all-black armor with the crest of a red war hammer. But according to my guard, someone smashed the mercenary's head to a pulp just like the magistrate and his son-in-law. Everyone there was dead including the magistrate's driver and guards. None of them had a weapon that could cause this massive damage to a person's head."

"But a war hammer like the one in the crest could." They looked at Borgroff as he held one of his hammers in his hand. "A couple of the men my father served with in the dwarven legion carried large war hammers. He saw firsthand the kind of damage they could do."

"We better get out there. Nera, you ready girl?" Luthias asked his wolf. Nera barked as she trotted over to sit by the front door.

"Luthias," Amunique brought his attention back to her. "I am adding Borgroff and Nakira to my payroll as well. All my contacts will know you three have limitless expenses through my account. Did you remember to ask the antique dealer about the legend of the wolfiend, this Fijandsvarg?"

Luthias nodded. "I told him to coordinate with you throughout this investigation. I want you two working together. His niece will be helping."

Clive walked up to Luthias. "Traemorra will also provide whatever you need if we have it. But you four need to hurry."

Chapter Thirteen

Luthias, Borgroff, Nakira, and Nera approached the edge of the cliff and saw smoke rising from the burnt carriage in the gorge below them. This perspective gave Luthias the vantage point to see things that he and the troops on the ground may not see up close. He scanned the area around the carriage and then scanned outward. He sighed, "I was hoping to spot something from up here that we could miss on the ground."

Borgroff huffed, "All I see is senseless carnage."

Luthias looked over and nodded then urged his horse down to the scene. He saw one of the guards walking towards them. "Lord Blackridge, Lady Karvina, Lord Borgroff." He knelt to pet the wolf. "Lady Nera, Chief Justice Travon sent word you were the new Inquisition knights." Luthias just nodded his head as they climbed down from their horses. "The Traemorra city magistrate along with his wife, son-in-law, and daughter were heading towards Gatesboro last night. A group of bandits or mercenaries ambushed them. They raped and murdered the females." The young soldier hung his head after looking at the carnage before him. "I have seen my fair share of attacks sir, but never anything this brutal."

"Nakira, Nera, you two walk the perimeter. If you see anything call one of the guards over to you. Borgroff and I will work the main scene." Luthias looked over at the bodies of the dead.

"I have seen some brutal killings as well, but this brutality is more reminiscent of a demon attack than bandits or mercenaries. How sure are you that this attack didn't involve demons? I know a few mage assassins who conjure low-level demons to do some of their dirty work."

The young soldier looked over to the younger female lying naked and mutilated in the midday sunlight. "Sorry sir, the brutality of it all is overwhelming." The young guard turned and ran to a nearby tree and threw up. He walked back over after cleaning himself up.

"Once again, sorry sir. Six of the magistrate's guards hid up along the ridges overlooking this pass. One of those guards survived his wounds long enough to tell the first guard who showed, he saw six men dressed in all-black armor. He said the armor had a crest of the red hammer on the chest piece and their shields. He said their leader was a red-headed dwarf with a long red beard and a massive red war hammer. We also have a dead mercenary. We believe he made the dwarf with the hammer angry enough to squash his head like a melon. The same thing he did to the magistrate and his son-in-law. His armor matches what the guard described. The magistrate's gold and silver armor was removed before he was attacked. But it wasn't taken with the rest of their valuables and gold. For some reason, it was left behind."

Borgroff turned to Luthias. "Perhaps it was too bulky to carry during their quick escape from the scene. Either way, I have contacts within the Dwarven Republic and can find out information about him."

Luthias nodded his head. "Good, we can describe him to Nakira when she and Nera are done with the perimeter. We all need to be wary of this individual. He will be dangerous." He watched Borgroff nod as he stared at the carnage in front of them.

The soldier turned his head to look briefly at the magistrate's tortured, mutilated son-in-law, who the mercenaries castrated and smashed his head with the war hammer. "I had met the magistrate's son-in-law and daughter on several occasions. He was a lead investigator in Traemorra. The magistrate's daughter learned her husband's investigative skills quickly. She was also headstrong and as smart as the magistrate. She would have made an excellent investigative knight and could have even joined the knights of the council."

Luthias looked at some troops who were awaiting orders then at the young soldier in charge. "Get these people covered and ready for transport to Gatesboro. Make sure you treat these bodies as if every one of them was royalty. You are not to release them to anyone unless Chief Justice Travon or I give you verbal permission face to face."

Luthias watched as the young soldier saluted him then walked off and started barking orders. Luthias and Borgroff walked the area but didn't see anything that stood out.

As Luthias walked the area, a female voice appeared inside his head, *"This dwarf is going to be big trouble, Luthias. He is vicious with no remorse for his actions. You need to make sure Borgroff and Nakira know to not engage him unless they have lots of support troops."* Luthias mentally agreed with Jadai as he and Borgroff climbed up onto their horses.

Nakira and Nera came up alongside Luthias and Borgroff. "Nothing of note in the area. The mercenaries surprised the hidden guards and stabbed them. But there were more than the six mercenaries that were at the main scene. There were six more bandits, mercenaries, demon spawns, whatever you wish to call them, hidden in the same spots as the magistrate's guards. For some reason, after they fired the arrows killing the stagecoach driver, they took off and headed west."

"Headed off for another attack, but who?" Borgroff asked turning to face Luthias. "Luthias, we need to get to Santos Isle now."

"I agree. I will have one of the guards here inform Knight Captain Brasscoat we are riding to Santos and Kallinstyne. But I need you both to pay attention to what I am about to tell you. The leader of this mercenary group is a red-bearded dwarf who carries a massive red war hammer. From the damage of the crime scene and even to his own man, we can see he is vicious, cruel, and has no remorse for his actions. In his mind everyone is beneath him. If you two run into him, make sure you have plenty of support troops. Do not play hero and try to take him one on one." He looked at Nakira as she tilted her head and half-smiled, "That goes for me as well, I know."

Nakira turned to look at the guards overseeing the removal of the bodies. "This scene makes a lot more sense now. I'm guessing we can expect a lot more violence like this. Do we think he is behind this cult?"

Luthias shook his head. "No, he is just another hired leader of a goon squad. My guess is this Jegere av Fijandsvarg hires low-level goons until they need professional help. That is when they bring in groups like this Legion of the Red Death or Cut-throat and his goons."

"But Cut-Throat and his goons unwittingly took themselves out of play when they let revenge control their fate."

Luthias nodded when a rider rode up fast causing everyone to draw a weapon.

"Whoa! Sorry, I'm with the Fort Romnuuski battalion. I have been riding for a while to find you." Luthias let his crossbow drop back under his jacket as the others put their weapons away.

"What about?" He watched as the soldier bowed. "Soldier, dispense with formality, just tell me what you need to tell me."

He watched the soldier take a few breaths to regain his composure. "Sir, I'm not sure who I'm supposed to repeat this message in front of." The soldier looked at Borgroff and Nakira.

"They are Inquisition knights like me soldier."

He bowed again as he spoke. "The empress and prince are dead. Fort Romnuuski's general sent us to help protect the royal family. But when we rode up to the bridge crossing over to Santos Isle, we spotted the empress and prince hanging from a tree. Both had a dagger sticking out of their chests." The soldier looked to be about to tear up. "Sir, everyone on Santos Isle and in the royal palace is dead. The rest of my battalion is holding the scene for you."

"Thank you for your haste, help these guardsmen get the magistrate of Traemorra and his family to Gatesboro. You are to relay this information only, and I repeat only to Chief Justice Travon in private. Council of Kings Knight's orders." The soldier bowed and then rode off but stopped and rode back.

"I apologize, sir, I was also told to deliver this letter to you." He then turned and rode down to the scene.

"Well, the demon was right on with its knowledge. The empress, the prince, Traemorra's magistrate, and his family are all dead. Whoever is doing this is making sure there are no heirs left to fill the royal holes," Borgroff said looking at Luthias.

"Yeah, we need to get to Kallinstyne, but we also need to investigate Santos."

Nakira nodded. "Nera and I will head straight to Santos, while you and Borgroff ride to Kallinstyne." Nakira noticed Luthias look at her with concern but before he could speak, she continued, "Luthias, I know these scenes are going to be grislier than what normal soldiers are used to, but I'm going to have to face it eventually."

"I know and I apologize, that's not what I was thinking. I trust you both fully to oversee any crime scene as I would. I'm just thinking that you and Nera would be better suited to refit and bolster Kallinstyne's defense. You're a renowned scout and rogue agent. Nera, well, she is a wolf so enough said about her. We will all ride to

Crosspoint Fortress. I will have the commandant there send a battalion with you and Nera to Kallinstyne. From there, Borgroff and I will ride to Santos to conduct our investigation. After our investigation, we can meet you two in Kallinstyne. I need to see the carnage of Santos Isle with my own eyes."

Luthias looked over at Borgroff. "I apologize my friend. I don't mean to speak for you. If you'd rather ride to Kallinstyne, I can send you with Nera instead of Nakira."

"No, you are right about them both helping the defense more than we would for now. Besides, I too want to see Santos as well, I need to see this through. That means conducting this inquisition with you so let's go. We have been too late twice now I don't wish to be too late a third time."

"Especially, since the third time might just be Kallinstyne." Luthias looked at the royal crown inside the wax of the sealed letter. "It's a sealed council letter. I'll bet it's just the notice of our official titles as Inquisition Knights." Luthias broke the seal and opened the letter.

"To whom it may concern, Lord Luthias Blackridge, Lady Nakira Karvina, Lord Volf Borgroff, and Lady Nera, the wolf is henceforth known as inquisition knights for the Council of Kings. No one of any military rank, noble or royal status is to impede their investigation including the empress, the prince, or the chief justice of the Council of Kings. Any attempt to do so is treason. The Inquisition knights or other unseen parties will hand out the penalty of death. Immediately. Divine Spirits be with you."

They all sat in silence for a few seconds. Luthias finally broke the silence. "What are your thoughts, questions, and remarks on your new titles?"

"When the letter mentioned not to be impeded by anyone, what exactly does it mean?" Borgroff asked.

Luthias looked at him and Nakira. "No one and I mean no one, not a city magistrate, not a guard officer, no one can interfere with our investigation, questioning, or plan for protection. No one enters a scene unless we allow it. No one removes anything unless we verbally approve it directly to them. Until we end our investigation, we are the three most powerful people in Ellehcim." He chuckled when Nera barked, "And yes, you are the most powerful wolf."

"Will they try to influence us? Also, what happens if we use this power to our advantage?" Nakira asked making Luthias smile.

"Everyone you meet will try to influence you or direct you in a specific direction. The only direction we look at is where the information and evidence leads us. As for the second question, the other unseen parties also pertain to us. When we all woke up this morning, there was an assassin we didn't see watching our actions. That assassin will remove us from power permanently." He looked at them with a serious look. "And know until we officially end this investigation, we have at least two assassins watching us every second of the day. Let's get to Crosspoint Fortress." Luthias urged his horse forward.

Chapter Fourteen

Luthias's mind was on Nakira and Nera, he knew they could handle themselves with normal foes, but this dwarf and his mercenary army were no normal foes. He was glad he remembered Jadai was silently following him and convinced her to go with Nakira and Nera instead. Luckily, Jadai saw the intelligence in the decision and didn't fight him on it.

Once he and Borgroff reached the bridge to Santos Isle, he pulled his horse to a stop as he looked at the ropes still hanging from the trees. He then looked down at the two covered bodies lying on the ground. "Least they pulled them down."

Borgroff nodded as Luthias climbed down from his horse, walked over, and lifted the first cover. "It's the prince. The dagger they killed him with is still stuck inside him." Luthias pulled the dagger out and took it over to Borgroff. "Wrap this in a cloth and put it in your pack."

Borgroff inspected the blade closely. "Luthias, I know this dagger. It and its twin consist of obsidian-laced steel. My father, the dwarven forge master, made them as a gift for the young prince. But the dwarven messenger that was to deliver them never showed up here with the daggers. Dominion guards found him a year later just southeast of Traemorra in the Stoneback Mountains. Hellion beasts were feeding upon his corpse. There were signs someone tortured him before they left him to become hellion jerky."

Luthias walked over and lifted the cover off the empress. He reached down and pulled a bone-handled dagger out of her chest.

"Not the twin. We will bring both blades with us. We will let Chief Justice Travon and Amunique inspect them." Luthias looked at the men standing guard over the bodies. "Soldiers, make sure these bodies make it back to Gatesboro and you only release them to Chief Justice Travon in the council building. No one else."

Borgroff wrapped both blades in a cloth and then placed them in his pack. He spoke as he spurred his horse forward.

"And remember, this is your empress and prince, treat them with royal respect or meet the same fate. Let's get this brutal scene over with."

Luthias expected the same grisly scene from Twin Cliff only on a larger scale. But the scene in the village of Santos Isle was more reminiscent of a simple attack. "Borgroff, what is the first thing you notice?"

"The brutality of the Twin Cliff's scene is missing, even with the empress and the prince. I expected the prince to look like the magistrate but instead someone simply stabbed them with daggers and then hung them from a tree. I see no signs of brutality to any of the dead. They didn't castrate or behead none of the men, they didn't strip the women of their clothes or their dignity. None of the heads smashed with the war hammer."

They both climbed down and surveyed the village. "Luthias, these bodies show no cause of death. They have no sword or axe wounds, no bruising or damage from hammer blows. No holes from arrows. They are just… simply dead."

Borgroff looked over at Luthias when he didn't answer. He watched him as he looked closely at a strange black liquid before answering.

Luthias looked up at Borgroff. "Death wraiths. I believe our demon visited the royal family last night. The brutality is different because this dwarf and his crew were never here."

"The dwarf with anger issues goes overboard dishing out demon-like brutality while this demon and her death wraiths just get the job done and move on." Borgroff walked over to him. "So, who is in charge? Demon or dwarf?"

"Normally, the mortal who called the demon in from the demon realm is in control. But we know this demon has no mortal master. We also know it's hard to control someone with uncontrollable anger issues."

"And when you have no remorse for your actions, you're not going to be scared into doing as you're told. We dwarves are more immune to magical powers than other races. Although you can do damage to us with enough power, it would take a lot of power to force someone with that much anger under your control."

"Exactly, the only thing swaying him is the bags of coin being funneled to him from this cult." They mounted up and rode towards the royal palace.

They rode up to the large metal gates blocking their access to the royal grounds. "Halt, the royal palace is closed to all per Council of Kings Inquisition."

Luthias brought out the royal crown sealed letter and presented it to the gate guard. "Lord Blackridge and Lord Borgroff, council inquisition knights. We are here to conduct our investigation."

As the gate guard stared at the letter a large orc with commandant metals walked up. "Guard, do you know what happens to people who stand in the way of council inquisition knights?" Surprised by his superior's silent approach, the guard jerked to attention and saluted. "Give me that letter, soldier."

The large orc looked over the letter then bowed and handed it back to Luthias. "My apologies my lords. I will make sure I punish him appropriately."

"Nonsense, he was just being overly cautious at his job," Borgroff quickly responded. "He will accompany us, and you will play gate guard until we send a replacement."

The gate guard looked at the orc towering over him looking down on him with scorn. Luthias chuckled, "Don't worry about him soldier. Because if he says anything or does anything he will receive the punishment for interfering with an inquisition."

The gate guard still stared up at the large orc towering over him as the orc answered, "Immediate death." The orc looked at Luthias and then Borgroff as he bowed and forced a smile, "Your will be done, my lords. I will join you after you send a replacement to me."

"A dwarf could get used to this type of power." Borgroff's grin was ear to ear as he looked over at Luthias and the gate guard.

Luthias looked back at Borgroff. "I bet this dwarf we are tracking thought the same thing once, and now look at what he's accomplished. The only difference between you and him is there weren't two assassins staring directly at him as he reveled in the power."

Borgroff quickly looked around at his surroundings and shouted out, "I'm just kidding. No abuse of power going on here." He heard Luthias laugh.

Luthias looked at the soldier. "What do you know about what all happened here?" He looked over at the soldier when he didn't answer. He laughed again watching the soldier also frantically looking around. "I need you both to get your attention back to the task of this investigation or those two assassins will be the least of your worries." Luthias pulled the right side of his jacket back from his side to reveal a small crossbow hanging at his side. "Accessible in a minute, you're dead in two."

Borgroff nodded. "Sorry boss."

"My apologies my lord. I've just never..." The young guard looked at the crossbow again. "Sorry, only what they told me, my lord. They placed me on gate guard duty as soon as we arrived. A few of the guards who were patrolling the grounds swap out information as they pass each other. They give me details when they pass by me as well. According to them, everyone inside the palace is dead."

"Least it won't be the same gruesome scene as Twin Cliffs," Borgroff said as he looked around. "But we have two scenes with the same end goal, the death of royal bloodlines." Borgroff looked directly at Luthias. "Again, who is in control?"

"My guess is neither one is in control. They are simply doing the dirty work so this cult can keep their hands clean and remain unseen. Remember the multiple layers they went through to try and assassinate me. Also, if you have two unique style killings committed by two different criminals." Luthias let the thought hang there for a second to see if Borgroff would catch on.

The gate guard commented first, "You lead investigators in two different directions." They both looked over at him and nodded.

Luthias turned back to see royal guards sprawled out dead in front of him as they approached the Palace grounds. "Again, the same as in the village, dead but no visual violence."

Borgroff pointed in front of them. "I see another of those black blobs you inspected earlier. Why aren't we seeing more of them? Are they hard to kill?"

Luthias climbed down from his horse to take a closer look at the dead royal guards as he talked. "No, your hammers, his sword, my cross bolts will kill them. Killing them is simple. Seeing them to kill them is the problem. Remember the red mist demon the Chief Justice mentioned." Luthias watched Borgroff nod his head.

"That is how they first appear to you. If they wish, they can fully reveal the entity hidden within the mist, be it some form of demon, or an orc, elf, human, beast, or even dwarf. They come in many different forms. Usually influenced by what they were in life or dealt with in life. But before they reveal the mist, they are completely invisible. They normally only reveal the mist for two reasons, their boss demands their attention, or they are about to kill."

Borgroff stared at the black blob. "So if one appears you have a second at most to kill it before it kills you."

Luthias rubbed some of the liquid between his fingers. "More often than not, your buddy kills it in retaliation for killing you."

"So, most black blobs will have a victim beside it." Borgroff watched as Luthias nodded. "Let's go search the palace."

Luthias stood up and walked back to his horse. "Go relieve the commandant of his gate guard duty and have him meet us in the palace." The gate guard bowed his head and then rode back towards the gate as Luthias and Borgroff rode on to the palace.

Luthias and Borgroff were inspecting the dead when the large orc walked in. "My lords, how can I help you?"

Luthias watched Borgroff grin again as he heard the orc's words, but Luthias spoke up first. "What do you know about what happened?

"My lord, we don't know much. We first saw the empress and prince hanging from the," he shut up.

Luthias looked up when the orc stopped talking. "It is okay, commandant. Pulling the empress and the prince down was the correct thing to do out of respect. Please continue."

"We laid them down and covered them up with the daggers in place." He looked at Borgroff when he stopped. "I told them to leave the daggers for you to inspect. If they weren't there that is not on me."

Borgroff laughed, "They were. I have them in my pack as evidence. Please continue and don't worry about any punishment for anything done. It won't happen unless it was just completely stupid."

The orc bowed his head as he continued, "I left three guards at the entrance to guard the bodies. Then the rest of us rode up to the village. In Santos Isle, we saw the villagers as well as a few of the palace guards dead. I left a few soldiers there then hurried to the royal grounds. I placed the main group of the battalion on rotating gate and perimeter duty then sent the rest to lock down the palace and wait for further orders."

Borgroff looked up at the orc. "Your gate guard, is he the newest recruit to your battalion?" He watched a confused look appear on the orc's face as he nodded. "I figured so. Your other guards haven't been rotating him to perimeter duty.

"Damn, that Knight Hassleman," the orc said in anger. "I told him no more of his shit. I apologize I will handle him."

Borgroff laughed, "I take it this Hassleman was in charge of your perimeter guard duty."

The orc nodded. "Yes, he was my third in charge, up until a few seconds ago."

"Back to the task at hand, gentleman." Luthias stood up after he inspected a dead guard. "Have you searched every nook and cranny of every floor?"

"Yes, my lord. my second in command and my elite unit searched every inch of this island. I then followed behind and did the same on my own to verify their reports."

"Good work, commandant. Relieve your third of his command and send him to me. I have a report that I need returned to Knight Captain Brasscoat in Traemorra and then to Chief Justice Travon in Gatesboro." Luthias smiled at the large orc, "I figure bumping him down to the messenger of your battalion for a spell should force a little reality to his world."

The orc's grin looked purely evil. They watched the commandant walk off to do as told. "I don't figure there is much reason for us to continue our search here. If there was, we would have heard it from him. I will write up a report of what we know and send it to Clive and Travon. Then you and I can head on down to Kallinstyne after we stop in Pantreus for a refill of provisions."

Borgroff's eyes lit up. "Pantreus has a nice alehouse called, The Hunter's Ale. They have a special in-house brew by the same name that is one of the best I've ever drank."

"I've been in there but never long enough to drink. We deserve one after all that we've seen."

"More like a dozen but I will settle for one so we can get to Kallinstyne. I just hope everyone is still okay and we are not late a third time.

Luthias's mind went to Nakira and Nera as he spoke, "Me too buddy, me too."

***

The village elder of Pantreus sat at his desk when a young soldier walked in. Without looking up, the village elder addressed the soldier, "Did you finally get those men under control in the alehouse?"

"I don't figure it will last long, but for now, yes. Elder, one of the bartenders overheard them talking about their boss showing up."

"That is a situation we will address when he shows up. Right now, there are five of them and another only makes six. If we were a fishing village, I might be more concerned. But we are a village of hunters spanning multiple generations. Everybody here was born practically carrying a dagger straight out of the womb. Between you, your guards, and the hunters, we should be able to get them back under control, ran out of the village." The elder smiled, "Or buried in the cemetery. Just to be safe though, put a few of the hunters up high in some of the trees with crossbows or bows and rotate them out regularly." The soldier saluted and left quickly to do as the magistrate instructed. "Bothersome young people, always worrying over nothing."

***

To the southwest of Pantreus, Nakira, Nera, and the battalion from Crosspoint approached the main gates of Kallinstyne. "Halt, state your business within Kallinstyne." Nakira watched the gate guard look down at Nera and back away a couple of steps. "Your wolf will have to be tied up outside the gates," Nera growled at the guard.

"She is not my wolf. But I don't think she liked that idea," Nakira said smiling. "You are welcome to tie her up if you'd like though."

"I know she didn't like it and neither would Lord Luthias Blackridge of the Elven Shadow Warriors and Knight Hunter of the Council of Kings. Soldier, you better learn to recognize this wolf with or without Lord Blackridge at her side."

Nakira looked past the gate guard to see a light gray orc with black hair tied up in a tail atop her shaved and tattooed head. The tattoo art probably told of tribal battles and famous warriors who inspire her. She watched the guard turn and bow low. "You can bow later, right now open the gate for Nera and what I am assuming to be

93

an inquisition knight working with Lord Luthias. I am Knight Captain Xaika Ogresh, welcome to Kallinstyne."

Nakira laughed as the young guard looked embarrassed and Nera started wagging her tail as she stared at the orc. "Thank you, my lady," Nakira said as she bowed her head. "I am Nakira Karvina."

"Nakira Karvina, scout and rogue agent of Traemorra thrust into the world of the shadow warriors circle and inquisition knights by her beloved boyfriend."

"I guess you could call me a rogue agent of the council. I'm also guessing with the eager way Nera is wagging her tail and your knowledge, you know Luthias and Nera."

"The rumors are true then. We have Inquisition knights within the kingdom again. That hasn't happened for hundreds of years, at least." Nakira tilted her head a bit as Xaika laughed. "The magistrate of Kallinstyne is a massive history buff. Some of the books and scrolls within his library date back to the founding of the Kallinstyne Kingdom some two thousand years ago. Back then everything west of the Santos River was still part of the Kallinstyne Kingdom. I know Luthias from the many times he has come here to help or to seek some of the vast knowledge of the library. He has trained with me on many occasions as well as drag me along on some of his crusades. He is a formidable foe for anyone." She looked around and developed a look of concern when she didn't see Luthias. "I'm guessing Lord Blackridge is busy elsewhere?"

"Yes, we left his company in Crosspoint Fortress where I picked up my escort. He and Borgroff were heading…" Nakira stopped abruptly realizing she didn't know what all she could reveal.

The orc wondered if she was going to reveal too much or not. "It's okay, we can go see the magistrate. He will know more about what you can or can't reveal than we will." Xaika knelt to pet Nera. "I'm glad to have you back by my side my lady." She mounted up on her horse and led them up towards the castle. "Hopefully, the boys are behaving and hurrying up to get here."

Nakira saw a look of concern on Xaika's face and knew she knew more than she was letting on. Then it occurred to Nakira. She whispered the words from the bottom of the court letter, "Unseen parties," as she looked around at her surroundings.

Chapter Fifteen

It took Luthias and Borgroff a few hours to ride to Pantreus. They rode towards a guard on patrol along the outer roads. They nodded their heads as he smiled and spoke. "Welcome back to Pantreus, Shadow Warrior. The magistrate will be glad to see you, but we finally got the unruly men ran out of town."

They stopped their horses wanting more information. "What unruly men, and how were they dressed?" Borgroff asked.

"We had five men dressed in normal clothes. They were disrupting the village, causing trouble at the saloon, just being basic bandit or mercenary type assholes."

"When you say bandit or mercenary assholes, what exactly do you mean?" Borgroff asked once again.

Luthias looked at the guard as he added to Borgroff's question. "And be specific with your answer," He felt proud at how quickly Borgroff picked up the Inquisition knight role.

"Their clothing and actions revealed them to be just ornery travelers out for a fun time. That is also what they claimed to be. But their weapons told a different story. If you're from a small village, town, or just a traveler, your weapon will usually be old, nicked, and well-worn. A hand-me-down weapon from your parents or grandparents. A weapon used over and over by former guards. You are not going to be carrying a newer quality weapon like a Dominion soldier or big city guard would. But a bandit or mercenary might be though. The weapons these men were carrying were not hand-me-down weapons. One of the swords resembled the swords we now carry. We just got our new swords from the Crosspoint Fortress guards at the end of winter. With the way these men behaved, I doubt they were guards on furlough. But, I guess it is possible."

"Were any of these five men a dwarf with a red beard carrying a large red war hammer?" Luthias asked fearing the answer.

"No sir. There were a couple of orcs, an elf, and two humans. I'll let you both get into town. The elder will know more."

Luthias and Borgroff rode on into Pantreus and wanted to find the village elder before restocking. "We need to warn the elder about this dwarf just in case these five were scouting out this village for some reason."

"I agree but then we head to The Hunter's Ale for at least one drink," Borgroff said grinning.

Luthias looked at Borgroff and smiled, "How about two?" He watched the dwarf's smile widen.

After they tied up their horses, they walked into the small village to notice it was busier than they both thought it would be. An older woman with a flour-covered apron approached them carrying a plate of various slices of bread. "Would you gentleman like to sample some bread today?"

Both nodded and took a slice of bread.

"Can't beat freshly baked bread, thank you, mam," Luthias said, tossing her some coins. "If I may ask, what has Pantreus bustling with activity?"

"We've been mostly cooped up over the last couple of days due to some scoundrels causing trouble and harassing folks. Thankfully, our village elder finally jumped the guards for not doing their work and the guards finally ran them out of town."

Luthias and Borgroff bowed their heads and walked off to find the elder. As they walked around, Luthias noticed the elder walking toward them. "Lord Blackridge, if you're here about the troublesome travelers my men and I already ran them off. But I do appreciate you showing up either way."

"It's no problem, but honestly, we were just passing through to restock at the general store and refresh at The Hunter's Ale. While we are here though, there is an individual to be wary of. If you see a red-bearded dwarf carrying a massive red war hammer. Try not to aggravate him and send a soldier down to find me at Kallinstyne immediately."

"Sounds like more trouble than we need around here but if we see him, we will notify you immediately. Tell the bartender I said your drinks are on the house." They watched him turn and walk off in a hurry.

Borgroff laughed as he watched the lively old man trot off. "I hope I have that much get-up-and-go when I'm his age."

Luthias smiled. "He's always been that energetic for as long as I've known him. Let's get our supplies then get some ale. We need to get to Kallinstyne."

After they stocked up and grabbed a third ale, they set off to Kallinstyne to check on conditions there.

In what seemed like no time at all, they rode up to Kallinstyne's main gate. "Halt, state your business in Kallinstyne." The gate guard's voice rang out.

"Inquisition knight business." Luthias showed the Council of Kings letter to the guard. "I am here to speak with your Knight Captain, Xaika Ogresh."

"Of course, my lord," the gate guard yelled up to the watch towers. "Open the gates, inquisition knights entering. Send a runner to inform Knight Captain Xaika she has more visitors."

As the gates opened to allow them passage, he noticed a young female quickly riding off toward the main grounds of the castle. After arriving at the castle stables, they handed the reins of their horses off to a young stable hand. Luthias tossed the stable hand a couple of extra gold pieces. "Take extra care of the horses and there is a couple more where that came from." The stable hand smiled big as he bowed then walked off with the horses.

"Shadow warrior and knight hunter business must be good if you're tossing around gold pieces like candy. You could toss a couple of those my way," Xaika said smiling walking up to Luthias.

Luthias nodded. "It's been better, could be much worse." Luthias looked at Xaika and her companions. "We must speak with you, alone. This is inquisition business." Luthias watched her dismiss her companions. "I apologize but we don't want to start a widespread panic." Luthias hated to bring this kind of news to his longtime friend. "Did Nera and a dark-skinned human show up?"

Xaika smiled, walked forward, and hugged him, "I haven't seen you since just after Syn and Etherika Rein took off into Katerra and the first thing I get is business. These must be bad people to have you so tense. But yes, your girlfriend and Nera showed up. Nakira is out training with some of my scouts and I have the Crosspoint battalion spread out training with my crew."

Luthias smiled as he interrupted her, "And let me guess, Nera is resting at the feet of the castle butcher getting fat and spoiled again."

Xaika laughed as she nodded. "Our favorite war-hound." She

turned. "You must be Borgroff. Luthias tells me a lot about you when he isn't talking about Nakira and Nera anyway."

Borgroff looked at Luthias. "So I'm the third member of your friends to be discussed, huh?"

Xaika let out a hearty laugh as she patted him on the shoulder. "I wouldn't take it that way. Take it as you are the first friend he discusses after his girlfriend and spoiled pet." She leaned over. "Besides, since you don't know who I am and neither did Nakira, apparently I'm not even worth talking about."

Luthias shook his head as she laughed then continued speaking. "Let's head up to the castle. I will send a page for the blacksmith and court wizard." They approached a guard walking by them in the castle square. Xaika stopped him. "Guard, I need you to head out into the northern woods and have the inquisition knight return for a meeting with the magistrate."

They watched him bow his head and then run off toward the stables to get his horse. They walked on up to the castle and saw the magistrate in the northern gardens. Xaika started to interrupt him, but Luthias touched her shoulder and shook his head. They watched as he placed a white lily in the vase on top of the grave and then said a silent prayer. "Magistrate, I have returned with company."

The magistrate stood up, saw Luthias, and smiled. "Shadow Knight Blackridge! It is good to see you again, though you look a little worse for wear. Being an Inquisition knight takes its toll on you. My apologies to you and Lady Karvina for the loss of your house."

"Thank you, but we need to concentrate on what endangers Kallinstyne right now. More importantly, what endangers you and your daughter."

The magistrate saw two of the court pages talking as he approached the front castle entrance. He spoke to a young brown-haired female first, "Can you run and find my court wizard for me?" He then looked at a young blonde girl. "And I need you to track your father down for me as well. He should be in his blacksmith shop. Girls, have them meet us in the war room. Hurry, we don't have much time because tonight is the Spring Festival of Renewal. You wouldn't want us to start it late, would you?" Both girls shook their heads and then ran off.

Before they entered the war chambers the magistrate informed the guards who they were to let in. Once inside they took a seat at the large rectangular wooden table adorned with the map of Kallinstyne lands. Luthias stayed quiet a second but saw the magistrate gesturing for him to speak first.

"Magistrate, the Chief Justice received a warning, someone is out to assassinate people with royal ties, past or present."

Before he could continue, the blacksmith, the court wizard, Nera, and Nakira walked in. Nakira ran over and hugged him tight. "I'm so glad to see you." She realized they weren't alone and turned to the Magistrate and curtsied. "I apologize your grace."

"My dear, I would expect nothing more from you than that type of behavior. You all are out here fighting to save our lives, take every advantage you can to hug the ones you love. As the grave marker outside attests to, you may not get the chance to hug them tomorrow."

She blushed and bowed her head slightly.

"As I was saying, the Chief Justice received a warning that someone is out to assassinate people who have present or past ties to the throne. Someone has already killed the city magistrate of Traemorra, his family, and his private guards. I'm also sad to report someone has killed the empress and the prince along with everyone in the royal palace and Santos Isle. There was an attempt on the Chief Justice's life and strangely enough attempts on my life as well. I'm not sure how I fit into all this but the attempts on my life are what got this investigation started. Since our investigation began with the attempts on my life, we are using the information we have learned from those attempts as a starting point."

"Attempts?" Xaika asked. "As in more than one attempt?"

Luthias nodded. "Three so far. I'm sure more are coming since Chief Justice Travon named me one of the Inquisition knights." He drew the sword hanging from his waist and wax-sealed letters out of his pack and laid them on the table. "What we have learned so far is that a nobleman in Ridgewood was hired via a wax sealed letter to hire a mercenary who was supposed to lure the knight captain and guards out of Traemorra so a third person could burn down my house with me inside. But Cut-Throat and his goons somehow found out I was involved and messed up the plans by luring me out as well. Borgroff and I followed several leads tracking Cut-throat's whereabouts. Finally one led us to Hells Canyon. A now dead mercenary led me to the psychic in Riverwood, who in turn led me to the nobleman in Ridgewood who was carrying this sword."

"A lot of layers separating the person doing the first hiring from the crime," the magistrate said, picking the sword up. "Fijandsvarg's blade." Luthias knew if anyone else knew about it, the magistrate here in Kallinstyne would. "It's real then."

"Yes, the symbol in the wax seals of the letters match the wolf's head on the handle as well as tattoos on two dead individuals. We also learned of a group called, Jegere av Fijandsvarg, or hunter of the wolfiend. I know nothing about them other than they are knowledgeable, secretive, leave notes in the middle of the night, can get in and out of a room without me hearing them, and worship this sword."

The magistrate studied the runes on the sword. "Not the sword, the fiend itself. Well, at first it was the sword then it became the fiend." Everyone looked at the magistrate as he looked closer at the runes. When he realized no one was speaking he looked up to see everyone staring at him.

"Sorry, legend says Koraegin forged the sword originally to kill the one known as Fijandsvarg or wolfiend. The sword would collect the fiend's soul sending it to Koraegin. The legend continues by saying a passing druid gifted the townspeople the magical sword to cure their demon troubles. They formed the group to hunt down and kill the wolfiend plaguing their city. But somehow someone on the inside of the cult changed their thinking. Before they disappeared from society, they worshiped the wolfiend and had hopes of getting the sword into Fijandsvarg's hands so he could use it."

"Wait," Borgroff said interrupting. "I'm assuming the name wolfiend speaks for itself and means what it says. We are talking about a demonized werewolf of some sorts, correct? Why would a werewolf need a sword when they have fangs and claws."

"That is where the group went awry, the wolfiend had no use for it and didn't want the attention of the group," the Magistrate said still studying and writing down the runes he saw. "You see, the legend of the wolfiend states it was the spawn of a human/demon sexual encounter. According to the legend, a demon raped and mauled the Fijandsvarg's mother. The husband is said to have invoked the demon to kill his wife so he would inherit all her wealth and crown. Rumor was she was about to throw him into the dungeons for adultery with some of her maidens. But unfortunately for him, she lived long enough to have the baby who in turn inherited all the mother's wealth and crown leaving him broke and rotting in the dungeons."

"An untethered demon," Luthias said drawing everyone's attention. "I had forgotten about the untethered demon."

Xaika looked at him narrowing her eyes. "How in the hell do you forget to mention there is a demon loose in the world without a mortal master?"

Luthias shook his head. "Sorry, this untethered demon was the one who warned Chief Justice Travon. The chief justice said all she saw was a wraith wrapped in a red mist. But with what the magistrate just described this Fijandsvarg might be this untethered demon. We also think this demon committed the killings in Santos Isle and the Royal palace."

The magistrate nodded. "Yes, because if you kill the demon's master, you send the demon back to the demon realm. But since the demon was born and is half-mortal it could have the eternal life of a demon and remain here because of its mortal half."

"Okay, so I have a question." They all looked at Nakira. "If this cult worships this demonic wolfiend. Then why is it warning us that someone is killing people of royal blood? Wouldn't they be working together instead of against each other?"

Luthias answered, "It's like the magistrate said, the wolfiend doesn't want their attention. It has lived among the mortal realm for…" Luthias looked at the magistrate and realized he hadn't stated a period.

The magistrate looked up. "The source I have is from a two-thousand-year-old scroll. I keep it locked away where no one knows."

Luthias continued, "So, this untethered demon has lived in the mortal realm for at least two thousand years unbeknownst to any demons or mortals except this Jegere av Fijandsvarg cult. I bet this wolfiend just wants to continue living invisible because any attention brought to it would not only bring the mortal races against it but the demon realm as well."

"Which explains its motive for warning Travon in the first place. The demon knew what this was leading to," Borgroff said looking around. "But what do people of royal bloodlines have to do with it?"

The magistrate answered, "Simple, the Fijandsvarg was rumored to be of royal bloodlines, but no one knows which royal bloodlines or even if the child was male or female. I have found legends and tales pointing to male and some pointing female. The scroll I have only included certain details about the legend, keeping personal notes out."

"I'm guessing these new men of the wolfiend decided to go back to the original plan of killing the demon instead of worshiping it." Everyone looked at Borgroff as he petted Nera. "So now that we have this all out in the open, did someone say something about a festival, and does this festival involve ale?"

They all laughed before Luthias talked, "Xaika, Nakira, Borgroff, and I will work on a plan of defense." He pointed to the wizard. "Starting tonight after the festival, have your mages on duty on the castle walls with the archers on rotating shifts. Every other archer is replaced with one of your mages." He then pointed to the blacksmith. "Tomorrow conscript any men you need to repair armor, shields, and weapons."

Borgroff stood up and looked at the blacksmith. "Find me tomorrow and I will help as well. My father is the forge master for the Dwarven Republic. But I refuse to discuss work while getting my ale on so find me before I start or tomorrow at the forge."

The Magistrate smiled, "Then let's see if this festival is ready yet!"

***

The red-bearded dwarf sat atop his horse on the bank of the Santos River surrounded by thirty mercenaries. He looked around knowing all eyes were on him. They had all witnessed first-hand or heard second-hand accounts of him smashing the skulls of their fellow mercenaries who either failed in their work or failed to listen, so their full attention was on him.

"Pantreus is a few hundred paces west of us. My scouts brought back information that although this is a hunting village, we will have control once we smash a few skulls to prove we are serious. Round up everyone with a weapon and bring them all to the village square. Kill those that resist. The main individual we are here for is the village elder. He is a descendant of the royal family in the old

Drastinus kingdom down in the Soman Nation. Once you have him, bring him to me. Red Death will do the rest. The villagers are yours to play with as usual, but no one escapes, and no one lives. You fail, you die by red death as well."

The mysterious red wraith sat on a branch disguised as a red raven. She listened to the callous dwarf lay out his plans in detail. She knew Pantreus would be his next target after he killed the Traemorra magistrate. It gave her time to kill the empress and prince herself allowing their deaths to help her needs, instead of the needs of this callous dwarf and his employer. She knew his boss did not accept failure and the dwarf not killing the main royal family himself will be a major failure.

The dwarf's plan would also allow her to steal the deaths of the Kallinstyne's royal family from him as well. She just needed a few of the young guards to unleash her specialized pets in Kallinstyne to do her bidding. After the mercenaries leave Pantreus she could also release a few here to help her cause as well.

"Thank you for your assistance, dwarf. I just need a few of your mercenaries and a few guards for some special pets." The raven whispered the words of a spell into the gentle breeze. She watched four of the mercenaries out of view of the dwarf turn and wander off towards the tree she was perched in.

Chapter Sixteen

Back in Kallinstyne, Xaika stopped with Luthias, Borgroff, and Nakira as they watched the others head off to do as Luthias instructed. "Luthias, is there any specific information you want me to tell my men?"

"You know your men better than I, so you know what they need to be doing and where they need to be. Use the Crosspoint troops in the same manner. But I do want their attention on men wearing all-black armor with the crest of a red hammer on it or their shields. If they see anyone other than a red-bearded dwarf in this armor, they are to kill them and let us know immediately. They have a history of raping, castrating, and beheading. Their attacks are more like demon attacks than mortal attacks."

Xaika nodded. "And if they see this red-bearded dwarf?"

"Get back to find us immediately. They are not to confront this dwarf unless they absolutely must."

Borgroff shook his head. "I still find it odd that mortals are leaving scenes looking like a demon attack, but the demon attack looked more like a normal battle sight, only without weapon wounds. There were just a few victims with claw marks, most looked like they just fell over dead."

"Death wraiths." They all looked at Xaika. "Meaning the ones that look like they fell over dead, did fall over dead after the wraith snatched their soul."

Luthias nodded his head. "Borgroff and I assume the attack in Santos didn't include these mercenaries. I doubt the type of rage and brutality they display would be missing anywhere they go."

Xaika had a look of worry on her face as spoke, "Death wraiths are going to be difficult to watch for. Their victims are usually dead two seconds after they appear."

"And the victim didn't even know anything but death and darkness. The Pantreus elder did say they had five travelers causing trouble. But he said they got them under control and out of town on their own. He and a guard we talked to stated these men were wearing normal clothes instead of armor. Have your men keep your eyes open for these people as well."

Nakira stepped forward speaking, "They might be advanced scouts for the mercenaries. We use this method in Traemorra sometimes when simply watching from afar doesn't give us enough information." Luthias and Xaika nodded at Nakira.

Borgroff looked around. "Looks like there is still decorating to do, so I'm going to head over to the blacksmith's shop and familiarize myself with his setup."

Xaika bowed towards Luthias. "I will go get my guards set up at their posts and meet you all at the festival."

"Well, my lady. . ." Luthias started talking to Nera but watched her trot off with Xaika. He turned to look at Nakira. "Are you leaving me too my lady?"

She looked at him and winked. "Sorry, I'm going to go meet back up with the magistrate's daughter and her handmaiden to get ready for the festival. She is loaning me a dress for tonight." He smiled as she winked and walked off.

Luthias thought about Jadai and was surprised when she spoke without him mentally speaking first. "I'm just going to ask, does that thought mean you are inviting me to make an unannounced appearance in Kallinstyne just in time for the festival?"

Luthias smiled as he walked towards the stables to ride down to the main gate. "Yes, besides earning the right to a visible appearance after invisibly stalking us for so long. I fear we will need all the help we can get here within the next few days."

"I fear the same. I heard back from Borgroff's contact in Stoneback so that gives me a reason for why and where I have been. Once you get to the gate, I will head off down the road and show up."

Luthias arrived at the main gate and was looking over the guest list when a guard walked up. "Lord Blackridge sir, someone is out at the gate for you." Luthias walked out to see Jadai on horseback looking in his direction and waving.

"She is my contact for the Council of Kings and Chief Justice Travon, she is expected." He looked back at the guard. "Make sure everyone here knows about the guests to detain and let us know immediately if they do show up." The guard bowed as Luthias climbed up on his horse and headed to Kallinstyne with Jadai. "Where did you find a horse out of thin air?"

"It's a spirit animal. They look, act, and feel like the real thing. Yes, the dog is a spirit animal as well."

Luthias nodded his head. "What did Borgroff's contact have for us?"

"This dwarf goes by the name, Crimson Shaw. His father was a hero within the older dwarven legionnaire ranks. His father had a few instances of violence, but the evidence proved that violence was necessary and done in defense of the Republic. The legionnaire ranks Crimson served with frowned on him due to his extreme tendency for violence. His mother was the matriarch of the district they lived in. Although she wasn't physically violent, she was extremely mentally violent. She didn't look kindly on failure by anyone. She would use her underlings to make her points clear. Crimson included."

"Great," Luthias said rolling his eyes, "a vicious manipulating mother teaching and raising her son while the father is a legionnaire doling out violence as a means of protecting the Republic. She feeds Crimson the information she needs him to know about his father to follow her footsteps instead of the hero father."

"Well, it gets worse. Because her plan worked. According to records, she had one of her minions give him a nasty scar across one of his eyes for failing to do a job she asked him to do. In turn, he smashed the minion's skull and then smashed his own mother's skull with his war hammer. He took over the district for a while. Then one day for reasons no one knows, the legion of Red Death as he renamed them, left Stoneback never looking back. The father died a couple of years later fighting some mountain scorpions. Did you know those scorpions grow to be eight feet long and have an eight-foot tail?"

"Yes. I had to fight a few of them before. But it sounds like this guy had no chance of growing up normal."

"You sound like you feel sorry for him," Jadai said looking at Luthias.

"I don't feel sorry enough to forgive him for the violence, but yes, I do. He is like this because his mother corrupted his moral values by raising him like this. His father was a dwarven hero but is not around him enough to sway his attitude. She teaches Crimson what she wants him to know so he will be another tool for her to use as she wishes."

"I see what you mean, this is the only path he knows because it was the only path he was taught. But we are still killing him on sight, right?" she asked smiling.

Luthias smiled and chuckled as they rode up to the stable. "Oh, hell yes."

Luthias and Jadai quietly walked up as Kallinstyne's magistrate placed another white lily upon his wife's grave. Luthias stood quiet, lost in thoughts of how he could have been doing the same for Nakira had it not worked out differently.

"I can't believe it's already been five years since she lost her fight."

The magistrate's voice brought Luthias's mind out of his own dark thoughts. Luthias wiped a tear from the corner of his eye before the village magistrate stood up and faced him then continued talking.

"I know you barely met her before her death, but how mad do you think she would be right now? We haven't hosted her Festival of Renewal since her death."

"I'm sure Xaika would need to become your personal knight protector to keep her from killing you."

The village magistrate laughed as he reached his hand out to his newest guest.

"This is Jadai, my contact for Chief Justice Travon and the Council of Kings." The magistrate kissed her hand as he bowed his head. "She brought us some information on the leader of this mercenary group, the Legion of Red Death."

She curtsied. "Long definition short, he is violent due to manipulative mommy issues who he killed to take over the dwarven district she was the matriarch of."

"He has a violent temperament, a huge weapon, and no respect for women, got it."

"I got with the gate guards and let them know to notify us immediately if anyone not on your guest list tries to gain access to Kallinstyne."

"Good. If you all will excuse me, I need to dress for this evening." The magistrate walked off.

"If you don't mind, I'm going to take a look around and see what defenses we have to work with," Jadai said looking around.

Luthias nodded as she walked off. He then headed off into the garden area. As he walked through the gardens, he came upon Xaika surrounded by a group of children sitting and listening to a story.

"Here is the hero of our story now. Shadow Master Blackridge and his grandfather, Daemon the Dragon Slayer had tracked the young dragon to an area northeast of Gatesboro. The young dragon trapped a young girl against a group of trees. She was around sixteen years old, the same age as Shadow Master Blackridge at the time. She was terrified, but Shadow Master Blackridge snuck around the dragon just an arm's reach away from the damsel in distress. Then as Daemon, the Dragon Slayer brought his mighty sword down hard onto the dragon, Shadow Master Blackridge rushed in and swept the young damsel in distress off her feet and saved the day."

Luthias shook his head as he saw the children staring up at him. "Does Knight Captain Ogresh tell you all made-up fairy tales like this about me often?" The kids all laughed and nodded their heads as Xaika released them to run off. Luthias laughed, "You know not a word of that is true."

"Yeah, but Daemon the Dragon Slayer and Shadow Master Blackridge, are their favorite characters. I started off just using your grandfather. I threw you in when I started to miss you."

Luthias chuckled and shook his head as they followed the kids back to the castle square. "I'm guessing since you have time to make up lies about me that you took care of duty rosters?"

Xaika laughed and nodded as Borgroff walked up.

"Wait, I missed out on making up lies about the great hero that is Lord Luthias Blackridge of the famed Elven Shadow Warriors and Knight Hunter of the Council of Kings? Oh and now knight inquisitor, how many more titles do you have?"

Xaika smiled, "You can add Shadow Master to that list. At least according to the kids from my stories anyway." Borgroff laughed.

Luthias snapped his fingers and pointed at him. "Borgroff, you're a genius."

"We've been friends for how long and you just now figured out I'm a genius. Now, what did I do to earn that remark?"

"I bet this cult is targeting me because of my rank within the Elven Shadow Warriors. I know royalty isn't involved in my bloodlines, so the ancient shadow warrior organization must fit in with all this somehow."

"I see what you mean. We know from your grandfather's true stories." She winked at Luthias who just shook his head. "The shadow warriors have been in service secretly for thousands of years. The two factions would have crossed paths at one time or another due to this untethered demon of yours."

"Exactly, from what I have learned from my grandfather's demon and beast hunt stories they would not protect this wolfiend. So, when this cult was hunting the wolf fiend they may have worked together within the shadows."

Borgroff filled in the silence when he saw where Luthias was taking the conversation. "But when they switched to protecting the demonized werewolf, the shadow warriors broke whatever treaty they had and hunted them down. We know from the stories and legends of the shadow warriors they are among the best warriors, rogues, and mages in history."

"We were taught traditions handed down from warrior to warrior, taking what we were taught, improving upon it, and teaching new warriors."

"Like you did with Syn and Etherika and are now with Nakira, even though she's human," Borgroff said, looking at him. "Doesn't that go against the elven portion of the name Elven Shadow Warriors?"

Luthias laughed, "No, there are records of humans, orcs, and even dwarves in our ranks. The elven portion of the name was just a holdover from their beginnings within the ancient nomadic tribes. At one time the leaders, all elves at the time, voted to remove it and just go with Shadow Warriors, but the warriors of all races shot it down stating it gave alms to its roots."

He looked up and around them at the finished decorations. He then spotted a villager carrying around a bottle of The Hunter's Ale special stock. "Borgroff, time to get your ale on. I see they are serving The Hunter's Ale from Pantreus." Borgroff spotted the bottle and hurried off towards the bar without a word. As he laughed at Borgroff he spoke to Xaika, "This is news we need to bring to the magistrate's attention tomorrow to see what he might know. But for now, it's time for all of us to follow Borgroff and get our ale on."

Xaika nodded and walked off.

The staff had finished setting things up and were mingling with the early guests. Off to Luthias's left was the bar with tables for people to sit, eat, rest, and talk. Off to his right were garden benches, trees, shrubs, and flowers, and in the middle of both was the dance area. Overhead there were decorations of pastel colors streaming back and forth mixed in with lanterns to light up the area. Luthias looked off towards the mountain peaks in the distance. The sky faded from a dark blue above him into a lighter blue mixed with various shades of red, yellow, and orange as the sun seemed to rest on the horizon.

Someone placed their hand upon Luthias's shoulder, he turned to see Nakira wearing a lilac-colored low-cut off the shoulder dress. He spun around and bowed as she curtsied low before him. "I... I..." He stuttered out as he pulled her in against him and kissed her.

"Am speechless?" She continued for him when she pulled from the kiss. She laughed as he simply nodded. "I saw Jadai stopped being your creepy stalker wraith and showed up visually." Luthias pulled back and looked at her. "Honey, I'm a rogue scout. That's not to mention that the best shadow warrior alive is teaching me his craft. But don't worry she and I talked, and I know why you two decided it was the best course of action." She leaned in and hugged him as she whispered in his ear, "But she better not be going from creepy stalker to creepy peeping tom at night."

"Wouldn't she be more of a peeping Tom-ette or peeping Tamra?" She popped him on the head. He laughed, "Believe me she knows not to. But let me say, you look ravishing in this dress. I hope our room is private and away from people tonight."

"But how would either of you know if I am watching the action and listening to the moans?"

Luthias tried not to smile and laugh as Jadai popped into his head and spoke. He decided not to repeat her words or acknowledge she spoke at all.

He stared into Nakira's emerald eyes as she commented, "Like you and I are going to be inside a room tonight instead of out on patrol with Nera."

They both got quiet when they noticed the magistrate walking up to them. "I can't believe the work the staff has done on setting up the festival. My beloved had always overseen every detail and insisted on it being perfect. She would always say this festival signified new beginnings blooming forth with flowers, roses, and trees. She honestly believed that if we had a great festival the entire year would be set off on the right foot. It looks to me like the staff continued her pursuit of perfection. Are you two ready to kick this year off on the right foot?" Luthias and Nakira smiled and nodded.

The festival got underway with all the villagers and visiting nobles laughing, dancing, drinking, and having fun. The magistrate and his daughter were mingling and making their rounds. Luthias noticed Borgroff dancing and Nera, being her ever-watchful self, patrolling the boundary of the garden area. Always on alert. As he looked around, someone tapped him on the back. Luthias turned around to see a young blonde female standing there all dressed up. "My lady, you look beautiful." She curtsied and thanked him. "Is there something I can do for your majesty?" Luthias asked as he bowed low and dropped to one knee making her laugh.

"Yes sir, I have been waiting for the boys my age to dance with me, but they all just sit around like bumps on a log. Can you make one of them dance with me?"

Luthias laughed, "I guess I could have my wolf bite them in the seat of their britches. I'm sure that would get them up and about."

The young blonde was laughing when the magistrate's daughter walked up and put her arm on the young girl's shoulder. "I don't think Lord Blackridge would feel good about forcing a boy to dance." She smiled at him, "I also don't think Nera would like to bite young men on the seats of their britches either." She leaned down to the young girl and whispered, "Unless they deserve it. But I bet Lord Blackridge would love to make the boys jealous by dancing with you himself."

She winked and smiled, encouraging him to dance with her.

Luthias stood and once again bowed. "It would be my pleasure to show these young boys the fun they are missing by not dancing with a beautiful lady. Their loss is my gain." He reached out his hand and took hers as he led her to the dance floor. As the band played a waltz, he noticed how well she danced. "You dance beautifully, your grace. Have you been taking lessons?"

She smiled her sweet smile at him as she nodded her head, "Yes sir, the magistrate's daughter and her handmaiden knew I came of age to dance this year. They have been teaching me in her room. They suggested that if no one asked me to dance I should ask you or Sir Borgroff."

"Well, my lady you are a quick study and a smart student then." The music ended as the magistrate approached them. Luthias bowed as the young girl curtsied.

"My lady, I see you learn quickly. Would you give me the honor of this next dance?" she chuckled as the magistrate bowed before her.

She curtsied as she replied, "It would be my pleasure, your highness." But as they walked into the dance area, she stopped and looked up at him puzzled. "Your Highness, I thought, uh… we were going to dance? Why is everyone leaving?"

He looked at her and laughed. "You and I are going to dance. This is the dance I would normally dance with my beloved wife. Since she is watching over us from within the spirit realm, my daughter and I decided I would pick one of the guests to dance with." He bowed his head slightly at her and winked. "You are my pick this year. I watched your progress with my daughter and your dance with Lord Blackridge. I knew you were my dance partner for this year."

He looked up and pointed at the band. Everyone watched in awe of the young girl dancing with the village magistrate. In years before he and the lady had always mingled and allowed the villagers to attend the festivals but neither of them had ever danced with anyone that wasn't of noble rank. As the music ended the crowd applauded. The village magistrate bowed while the young girl curtsied and giggled.

The rest of the night was great. The blonde girl had every young man in the village wanting to dance with her. Luthias danced with Nakira, the magistrate's daughter, Xaika, Jadai, and the young girl when she could pull away from the boys. As the evening neared its end, Xaika walked up and leaned back against the bar beside him.

"Well, my friend, I have not had that much fun in a few years. The magistrate has offered you and your guests a room within the castle for the night. If you all choose to use it." She leaned over to him as Nakira walked towards them and spoke so she could hear. "With how good she looks in that dress, I say you'd be a fool to pass up that offer."

Nakira blushed as she approached and changed the subject. "The castle is a magnificent sight. One of the few still standing from an old bygone era."

Luthias looked towards the castle. "The magistrate and his

daughter are direct descendants of the old rulers who once ruled these lands. The Council of Kings granted them funds for a full repair as well as lordship over the surrounding lands. Which is everything south of and including Shadows Pass. It was the only remaining castle in repairable condition, well, except for Castle Tros'mura just across the border in Zukovia. Any repairs to it is still on hold pending debate of whether to or not. That's been going on for years."

Xaika looked around at the empty gardens as Nera came up and laid down at Luthias's feet. "Looks like most everyone's left except the staff, the castle steward, and the lady's handmaiden cleaning up." They all started to pitch in with the cleaning when she noticed the village magistrate and his daughter standing at the grave site. She walked up to the staff and pointed. "What do you say we leave the cleaning until tomorrow morning and give them time alone?" They all nodded their heads and then walked off toward the castle entrance.

Luthias knelt and petted Nera as the magistrate and his daughter walked up. "No disrespect to my beloved but I think that was our best festival ever." He looked to his daughter. "Your mom would be proud of us I think."

Luthias stood up as she nodded and spoke, "I'm headed to bed though. Goodnight, Lord Blackridge. Goodnight, Lady Nakira." She leaned in and whispered in Nakira's ear, but everybody still heard. "Keep the dress. You look stunningly beautiful in it. It is my gift for risking your life to protect us and the villagers." Nakira curtsied as she blushed and smiled.

The Magistrate watched his daughter leave and then began to speak. "You two have a room on the bottom floor. The only bedroom on that level. I know you are here for defense and will want to stay up all night, but at least get rest in shifts." He looked over at Borgroff passed out on the bar and pointed at him. "Just like him, you all need your rest. I will have some guards come to help him into a room."

"He'll be okay, let him stay right there. He always slept on a stone slab in Stoneback instead of a normal bed, which drove his mom crazy. He'll appreciate the hard bar top. Hell, he will be in better shape than the rest of us."

Luthias looked at Xaika as the magistrate walked off into the castle. "Get your guards settled in then let them know to wake you and me up if anything at all happens. The magistrate is correct. We all need rest so we can be at our best. This enemy will wipe us out if we are weary. With the carnage they've left behind, we would just become more carnage in their wake." Nakira and Luthias watched as Xaika bowed and then walked off towards the stables. Nera stood up and walked over to the bar. She then lay on the ground below Borgroff as Luthias spoke to her, "Keep him safe." Nera laid her head down on her paw and let out a low bark.

Chapter Seventeen

Crimson smiled an evil grin as he looked at the horror showing on the Pantreus elder's face. "Elder, have you ever seen a criminal's head on the chopping block awaiting execution?" The elder tried to shake his head, but a mercenary pressed his boot down on the side of his head keeping it still. The mercenary smiled as he smashed it against the tree stump.

"Well sir, the criminal looks an awful lot like you do right now. Without the mercenary boot smashing your face of course. When the headman's axe comes down, it cuts through skin, muscle, and bone. Hell, it cuts the head clean off." Crimson removed the large blood-stained war hammer off his back and looked at it still grinning ear to ear. "Luckily for you, I don't carry a headman's axe so your head will still be attached when Red Death's work is done."

Crimson squatted down until he was face to face with the elder. "Well, some of it will be attached, the flattened part. The rest will be over there," Crimson stood and pointed off into the grass as he continued. "Some over there, most of your head will end on me though. Oh well, even fun has its cost."

Crimson raised the hammer as he looked at the mercenary with his boot still smashing his head down onto the stump. He quickly moved his foot as the hammer came smashing down. Crimson looked down at his armor. "See elder. Most of your brains ended up on me."

Crimson looked around at the grisly scene of the Pantreus village square. "Everyone dead?" The mercenaries nodded, smiling. "Good, let's get to the river and clean up before we travel to the camp. We will rest up tomorrow before we hit our next target. Buddy up and keep your eyes open for more of them damn wraiths. If your buddy dies because of a wraith, you die because of Red Death. Head to the damn river, idjits."

***

The next day, a knock at the door woke Luthias up from a deep sleep. "Yeah...what? Oh, hold on." He reached over and noticed Nakira wasn't in bed with him. Thoughts of the carnage he'd seen and the image of his house in flames flooded his mind. He quickly dressed and opened the door to see Xaika and Borgroff standing at the door both with serious looks on their faces. "What happened? Nakira, is she okay?"

"Sorry, yes, she is fine. She and the scouts were out training when one of them saw a soldier sneaking around the lands east of the village. Nakira sent the scout to find us while the rest tracked the soldier. We would have woken you up earlier, but Nakira said you were restless last night, and we should let you sleep." Luthias hurried out of the castle with Xaika and Borgroff.

"Earlier?" He looked up and noticed the sun was already just shy of its mid-point in the sky. Nera barked, walked up, and nudged him.

Borgroff laughed at Nera. "Yeah, it's just past eleven in the morning. Xaika told me what you said last night about us needing rest. We agreed with Nakira and left you alone until we needed to wake you." Borgroff looked at Luthias as they mounted up onto their horses. "I also appreciate you letting me sleep where I was. Best sleep I've had since leaving the stone slab in my bedroom in Stoneback."

The scout led them to the area where he saw the soldier. Luthias climbed down and searched around. He smiled as he dropped low while pointing to the north. They all climbed down and followed him as he crept forward to a fallen tree. Beyond a few other fallen trees, they saw a ragged, old guard post hidden among vines, thickets, and brush. It looked like it hadn't been used in a century or so. "I'm guessing this is where you tracked the soldier too?"

"I didn't track the soldier, sir. Lady Nakira sent me back to find you and Knight Captain Ogresh."

Luthias looked at the scout. "Sorry soldier, I was talking to Nakira above you." The scout looked up at a branch above his head. He fell backward when Nakira appeared from nowhere. Luthias laughed as he helped him up, "You'll get to where you can spot them. Don't look for the individual hidden within the environment, instead look for the distortion their cloak causes to the environment. A slight ripple in a pond's surface reflection, or heat rippling and distorting the scenery as you peer through the flames."

Nakira sighed as she dropped to the ground quietly then whispered, "I hate how you spot me so quickly. It always takes me longer." She nodded her head towards the building as she continued. "We tracked him here and witnessed three others enter from other directions as well. They aren't wearing black armor and they looked more like kids than hardened mercenaries."

Xaika looked from the building to Nakira. "As Luthias always reminds me, looks can be deceiving." Nakira nodded as Xaika continued, "What's our plan?"

"Nakira, you have the scouts in good spots. You all remain hidden and keep watch. Arrows trained on the door."

Borgroff looked around bewildered and whispered, "I don't know how you all see anyone in that damned cloak state."

Luthias laughed as he shook his head, "Xaika, Borgroff, Nera, and I will head in. If anyone other than one of us walks out first, wound them."

Nakira nodded and whispered, "Kappe opp." She then disappeared.

Luthias drew Fijandsvarg out of its sheath, Borgroff drew his battle hammers while Xaika drew her sword. They looked at each other, nodded then walked quietly towards the building. Luthias expected to find some mercenary scouts when they entered. But was surprised when he saw a group of frightened young men wearing armor bearing the hunter's crest of Pantreus. But as Xaika just reminded Nakira, first appearances were often deceiving.

He expected Xaika and Borgroff would wait for him to talk but smiled when Xaika took the lead. "I am Knight Captain Xaika Ogresh with the Kallinstyne guard. The two gentlemen beside me are Inquisition knights with the Council of Kings."

She noticed the young soldiers never looked at them. Instead, they stared at the large midnight blue wolf standing guard blocking the doorway. "The majestic wolf you all are staring at fearfully is Nera, wolf guardian of the Council of Kings. Good luck if you're thinking of trying to get past her and out the doorway. We, three, will even step aside and allow you the chance if you wish." They all sat staring then shook their heads. "You boys have trespassed onto Kallinstyne lands. We have the road well posted that the magistrate of

Kallinstyne forbids entrance into the lands to any but guards and groundskeepers. Therefore, we consider your presence a criminal act against the people of Kallinstyne. Unless you can give me a worthy explanation for your presence here, we will arrest you all and place you in the dungeon to await trial by the Council of Kings. Also, before you get it in your heads that you have us outnumbered, we have scouts cloaked and hidden throughout the area outside this building. They have orders to kill anyone who exits this building unless one of us leaves first."

The young soldiers looked from the wolf to the three knights standing before them. A young soldier with a claw mark scar across his right jaw spoke up first. "My lady, on behalf of our village, we apologize. Our intent was not to trespass. Mercenaries attacked our village, our people..." He looked like he was about to tear up before pulling himself together and continuing. "They raped and murdered our females, both young and old. They forced our men into their service and savagely killed those that didn't comply."

Luthias spoke to the young man with sadness. "Where are you from soldier?" Although he already knew the answer, he wanted to see how the young man would reply.

"We hail from Pantreus, sir. Our village..." he stopped mid-sentence and dropped his head to the ground as the tears fell from his eyes.

Luthias looked at each of the young soldiers. "I've been through there several times." He returned his attention to the young man with the scar. "Do you know who attacked? What did their crest look like? What direction did they come from?"

"At first, we had five strangers in town and although things got a little unruly, the guards and our village elder were able to keep things under control. Then an angry dwarf with red hair and beard led a large group of mercenaries into town from the north-eastern border along the river's edge. They wore all black armor with a crest of a red war hammer that resembled the one the dwarf carried on his back."

Luthias watched him look down as thoughts appeared to flood his mind. When the young man looked up, he spoke with a tone of hatred. "They carried no banners of pride, only those of hatred, murder, and rape in their hearts. There were no cries of heroism, only the cries of those they savagely raped, butchered, and murdered. During the chaos, we slipped away and were on our way to see the magistrate of Drastinus. We hoped he would help us fight and kill these vermin.

Xaika looked at Luthias as she interrupted the young soldier. "Why go past Kallinstyne to get to Drastinus?"

"Our village magistrate is…" He hung his head as tears ran down his cheek. "He was a distant relative of the magistrate of Drastinus and descendant of the royal lineage. We figured the magistrate would be more apt to be as angry as we are. None of us have ever been there but the elder once told us Drastinus is located just across the Soman border, south of Kallinstyne and the mountains. We took the main road, but we were too tired to continue so we started looking for a place to rest. We followed the wall through the woods until we reached this abandoned guardhouse. Once we got here, we caught some rabbits and squirrels for food."

"That must have been when the scout saw one of you. If your magistrate was related to the magistrate of Drastinus, that would make you soldiers under his rule now. The scouts outside will lead you down to the barracks by the main gate where we will give you a place to rest for the night and food. In the morning, soldiers will escort you to the edge of Drastinus' lands. Next time make sure you keep to the roads."

The young soldiers rose and followed Nera and Borgroff out of the building. Luthias stopped the young man with the claw marks. "Where did you get this scar?"

"I got it fighting a large jaguar that was troubling Pantreus. It had been killing our chickens and small animals. I came across it while I was out checking on the animals and it attacked me. One of the guards killed it and saved my hide." Luthias nodded and sent the soldier out with Xaika.

Luthias counted the men as he followed them outside, then whispered. "Eight young soldiers. I hope that's not all that's left." He looked at the scouts. "Show them to the barracks at the main gate for rest. Provide them with food and drink, then ride back along the south road to the castle. Make sure to report back to Xaika when you get back to the castle grounds." They nodded and led the strangers toward the barracks at the main gate.

"Borgroff and Nakira will ride with me to Pantreus and check on the village. Xaika, I want you to find Jadai and have her help you get the defenses set up. Once finished, Jadai does not leave the side of the magistrate's daughter until I tell her differently."

"Luthias, if you don't mind, I'd rather stay here. If Crimson and his legion are in the area, I'd rather be here to help the scouts get ready."

Luthias nodded. "Good thinking. If Borgroff and I do spot the mercenaries, we will return and help prepare for them." He bent down to Nera. "You stay as well and watch their backs. Keep them safe." Nera barked then ran to stand tall beside Nakira.

The ride to Pantreus was quick and quiet with both Luthias and Borgroff keeping watch for Crimson and his legion. Luthias spoke quietly as they rode into Pantreus. "Keep your eyes open."

"You think this could be a trap meant to capture us?" Borgroff asked, looking around.

"Anything is possible but with the carnage they leave behind, I doubt they would intend to capture us alive."

"Yeah, more like make an example of us." Borgroff rode around the corner just ahead of Luthias then abruptly stopped and brought one of his hammers up. "Luthias, I see bodies."

Luthias climbed down from his horse, drew Fijandsvarg, and then walked forward as Borgroff climbed down from his horse. "Yeah, we need to search for survivors but keep your eyes open for any of the mercenary soldiers. You cover the south side of the village I will search the north."

Luthias's anger rose as he looked over the carnage in and around the first few houses. He walked carefully over a man the mercenaries stabbed and beheaded. He then had to step around a female stripped of her clothes, stripped of her dignity, and her life. Lying beside her was a tray of bread scattered across the ground. Sadly, he recognized her as the baker they bought bread from on their first visit. "No remorse. No respect for life," Luthias commented to himself.

He walked past more dead villagers and a guard the mercenaries strung up from a tree by his hands and then castrated. Judging by the pool of blood on the ground and the splatter on the tree trunk, the guard was still alive. He used Fijandsvarg to cut the rope letting the body drop. He searched through more houses, the trading post, and the village magistrate's home but found no survivors and no signs of an enemy. Besides being angry, the carnage done to the good people of Pantreus sickened him. He saw women both old and young stripped of their clothes, mutilated, raped, and murdered. Men were also stripped of their clothes and castrated; some were also beheaded. Other villagers hung from the rafters of buildings or limbs of trees, blood pooling on the ground underneath them.

"Luthias, what kind of mortal being can commit such heinous acts to another? The south side is mostly empty except for a few townspeople and a couple of dead guards. Looks like most were herded into the village square."

Luthias was standing inside a house when he heard Borgroff's voice behind him.

He didn't turn around, he just stared at the mutilated couple lying on the floor in front of him. "These two were killed while eating." Luthias shook his head. "I've only seen this kind of violence done by demons. The Traemorra city magistrate and his family and now the village of Pantreus. These brutalities were committed by mortals. Mortals like you and me."

Luthias swung his hand out in frustration, causing an oil lamp to fly off the hook that held it, hit a wall, and burst into a small flame. They both heard a loud shriek and watched a black sticky liquid appear on the floor within the fire. "Death wraith?"

Borgroff stepped back looking around. "But why didn't it attack us?"

"I don't know. I haven't seen any proof of them being involved in this attack, yet." Luthias stared mesmerized by the black liquid burning within the flame as he continued to speak. "I know there are evil men. I've killed more than my fair share."

Luthias watched the flame from the oil lamp flicker out as it finished burning the black liquid of the dead death wraith. Luthias shook his head as he snapped out of his trance and looked at Borgroff. "But that's always been one or two individuals killing one here and another there. Crimson may be a sadistic leader, but he isn't the only sadistic mercenary in this group."

"I was thinking the same thing. They might not start sadistic but spend enough time in one's company…"

"And you start thinking and acting like them." Luthias finished Borgroff's line of thought. "You become a product of your environment. There might have only been a handful when they killed the Traemorra city magistrate and his family but more than that did this much carnage."

Luthias exited the room and brought Borgroff's attention to the village square. "Borgroff, what do you see?"

"Death, mutilation." Borgroff stilled himself against the rising mixture of emotions caused by the carnage. "Evil."

"Yes, evil for sure. But look beyond the emotions of the scene, look underneath the death, mutilation, and evil carnage. When you do, you will see a pattern. You see most of the guards brought to the village square before the mercenaries killed them. All these guards, not to mention the other men and women hunters here in town would have overwhelmed a handful of mercenaries. Pantreus is a village of hunters. Knowledge and training are handed down from generation to generation. The people here know how to handle their weapons to defend themselves and their loved ones."

"Like what you said about the knowledge handed down with the shadow warriors."

Luthias nodded. "There had to be a larger group of mercenaries joining the men from the Twin Cliffs group. The first group of travelers, as the elder called them, returned to the village, and started the violence to draw out the village guards and villagers that would defend their families. Then Crimson and the mercenary soldiers showed up and started slaughtering them."

"Yeah, I concentrated on the carnage and ignored the pattern. But again, I ask, what kind of man takes people that have surrendered and do this type of carnage to them? No remorse for his actions."

"That is one of the questions we need to answer." Luthias and Borgroff walked back to the saloon where he had earlier found two of the mercenaries dead. He rolled one of the mercenary soldiers over and saw the armor bore the crest of the red hammer. Luthias also noticed the dead mercenary had a dagger stabbed into the side of the codpiece of his armor. Luthias looked to the left of the dead mercenary and noticed a young red-headed female whose clothes had been torn and partially stripped. He noticed the clothes were animal skin armor and she had more of the same type of daggers strapped to a belt bearing the name Tlesha.

"She never gave up. That's a girl with a warrior's spirit," Borgroff said, staring at the scene.

"They have the red hammer crest. Looks like this feisty young lady killed her attacker but this one finished her off." Luthias rolled the other mercenary over. "Borgroff, the death wraith we killed earlier killed this mercenary."

"Wait, if they are killing each other does that mean they aren't working for the same person, demon, group, whatever?"

Luthias shook his head. "I don't know. We're missing something here. Be wary and stay close."

He stood up and looked around the village square once again. He could feel the rage building inside him. He walked away from the saloon and headed north of the village. As they reached the edge of the village, they walked into the church and graveyard. Luthias walked forward and stared at a red raven sitting atop an old headstone of a young teenaged female.

"I guess this graveyard is about to get a lot more residents." Luthias looked around then thrust the sword just behind Borgroff's back. Borgroff heard the shriek of the death wraith as it collapsed behind him. "Come on! We need to get back to Kallinstyne, quickly. I'll get a messenger to ride to For Gambit to send a platoon to bury the villagers here."

Chapter Eighteen

Luthias and Borgroff rode towards Kallinstyne quickly, both were thinking of the impacts of losing everyone in Kallinstyne. They felt relief when they heard the voice of one the guards patrolling atop the guard towers. "Open the gate, inquisition knights approaching."

Borgroff turned to face Luthias with a huge grin. "It's like a melody on the breeze."

"Yes, things are normal for now. But we both know we have two different enemies coming at us any minute from who knows what direction. Come on, let's get to the castle square quickly."

Luthias had just walked out of the stables when Nakira walked up and hugged him. "Thank the deities you two are back and safe."

Luthias hugged her tight as he spoke, "I'd love to do this all day, but we have trouble brewing. Let's get everyone into the war room."

They entered the war room just before the magistrate walked in with the blacksmith and court wizard. "What did you two find in Pantreus?"

"Is the carnage the same as at Twin Cliffs?" Nakira asked as she looked at Luthias.

Borgroff nodded his head. "Those eight young men are all that's left of Pantreus."

Luthias hung his head in thought before talking. "Judging from the carnage we just witnessed in Pantreus, I'd say yes. But the scars on the young man's face we spoke with make me fear it is less than that."

Xaika looked at Luthias. "I figured you asking about his scar was more than just curiosity. I take it you don't think a large cat did that."

"Large cats and wolves like Nera usually dig in with all four claws when they attack, it is how they hold their prey while they bite down to kill it. He only had three claw marks on his face. It is possible for only three to land but from the scar placement on his face I'd expect to see four claw marks if it was a large cat." Luthias opened his tunic to show a similar scar on his left shoulder as he developed a serious look on his face. "Hellions only have three claws. Their first and last talons grab the prey then they extend the middle claw into their victims. They can then fly their prey back to their nest and feast in private. Hellions are extremely territorial even around other hellions."

Xaika caught on to Luthias's point. "Meaning, if it is from a hellion then he has been to the lava flats between here and Drastinus."

The magistrate nodded. "Meaning he didn't get lost and wind up in the old overgrown guardhouse by accident. He had been down this path before and possibly even knew this guardhouse would be a good place to hide until Crimson and the others showed up."

Nakira looked at the magistrate. "He is part of the advanced scouts for Crimson."

Luthias nodded. "We noticed Crimson and his legion rounded up the guards as well as the people with weapons into the town square. If that is the case, then how did these eight young soldiers escape notice as they rounded up all the grizzled veterans and hunters? None of these eight young men are older than eighteen to twenty years. None are what we would call a seasoned soldier. We have investigated two completely different types of scenes. We saw the carnage left behind at Twin Cliffs by Crimson and these mercenaries. Then we saw Santos attacked by demons. Neither sight was at all like the other. It looked like everyone in Santos died of natural cause or fright. There was no weapon damage of any kind on anyone except for the dagger wounds on the empress and prince. Twin Cliffs, however, looked like demons showed up and destroyed everything and everyone. Neither scene incorporated violence or lack of from the other scene."

"I'm sensing an until Pantreus," Xaika said as Luthias nodded.

Borgroff looked around at everyone. "Exactly, until Pantreus, but if the clues Luthias and I saw are correct then our two enemies are not playing well together."

"We discovered two dead mercenaries. One had a dagger sticking out the side of his codpiece. Stabbed there by a feisty young female who didn't give up her dignity." Luthias watched all three girls smile and nod approvingly. "The other mercenary showed no sign of death just like the victims in Santos. Before we discovered the mercenaries' bodies though, I was standing in someone's house. The mercenaries killed this couple while they sat and enjoyed a meal. I stood there for a few seconds and lost my temper. I swung out in anger, knocking an oil lamp down off a hook from the ceiling. The lamp hit a wall and burst into flames not even a foot from me. When it did, a death wraith screeched as it went up in flames."

"Then you stood there alive a few seconds too long." As Jadai spoke, Luthias sensed Nakira's angry reaction, so he reached out and took her hand. "What I mean is, death wraiths show up one second, and the next second you are dead unaware of what killed you. Only your soulless body remains."

Luthias nodded. "Exactly, then when we investigated the area around the graveyard, I killed another one floating behind Borgroff. Wraiths show up for one of two reasons, to kill you or because someone commanded them to. Neither one of us are into commanding death wraiths so why aren't we dead? This demon has an agenda separate from this murderous cult."

Jadai held her chin with her hand thinking as she talked. "We know the demon who warned Travon spoke of mortals trying to kill people of royal descent. Crimson and his goon squad. We know from the attempts on Luthias, that this cult is our prime suspect. They are trying to find and kill this wolfiend who legend says is half demon, half-mortal of royal blood. We assume Crimson and his legion of goons are working for the Jegere av Fijandsvarg or murderous cult since they are brutally killing royal families. After the demon attack in Santos Isle and the royal palace, we also assumed the demon might be working for them as well, but if they are, why are they killing each other? If not, who are they working for then?"

Borgroff shook his head. "Don't know yet. That is another mystery we must solve along the way. But like Nakira and the magistrate mentioned, these young soldiers just might be the advanced scout team for the mercenaries."

Luthias nodded. "Crimson is cruel and violent, but he didn't get to his position through cruelty and violence alone. He is also smart and conniving. He knows word of the first group of scouts might get around and we would all be looking for strange unruly travelers."

Nakira smiled as she finished Luthias's thought. "When your enemy learns your plan, it's time to change the plan."

Luthias nodded. "Exactly, while we are watching for troublesome travelers, he sends in a unit of sad displaced soldiers."

"Then let's replace his sad, displaced soldiers with a unit of our own." They all looked at the magistrate as he continued. "I'm assuming this old guard gate would be the point of entry they wish to exploit. I want guards posted heavily tonight and through the next few days. If any of our guards see anyone sporting this black armor, they are to kill on sight and then find Lord Blackridge immediately."

Xaika saluted. "Would you also like me to send a couple of men to Drastinus and see if their magistrate knows about any of this?"

The magistrate nodded. "Yes, I want two guards to head out tonight."

Luthias looked at Nakira sensing her hesitating from speaking. "Nakira, do you have an idea as well?"

She smiled at Luthias and then looked at the magistrate. "Your grace, I don't mean to overstep, but may I trade spots with one of the two guards?"

"Young lady, this here," she watched the magistrate spread his arms out pointing to the war room around them. She hung her head and held her breath as she waited for him to chastise her. "This here is a war room. In a war room, I am simply one of you, strategizing ideas. We are all equals with equal say." He leaned over as he watched her let out her breath and smiled timidly. "Besides, you are one of four Inquisition knights. Inquisition knights don't answer to anyone but the assassin no one's noticed." As the magistrate said the word assassin, she noticed he looked directly at Luthias, an assassin of the Shadow Warriors. "What is your thinking?" he asked bringing her attention back to the group.

"Something doesn't feel right. I can't explain it, but I think sending guards out might be a setup to lure them out to their deaths."

The magistrate smiled, "Thin the enemy's overwhelming number however you can. But if a master rogue detected their trap and turned the trap against them…" He looked at Luthias. "I like it and can see why you keep her around." He leaned over to her again and pointed at Luthias and Borgroff. "You are the brains behind the brawn."

"We can discuss strategy after the meeting before you leave." Luthias smiled proud of her.

The magistrate asked, "Where are our sad displaced soldiers?"

"They are at the main gate barracks," Xaika replied. "I have extra guards posted there. I will have every guard on duty tonight."

The magistrate looked at the others as he spoke. "Master Blacksmith, make sure to finish repairing the guard's armor and weapons. Conscript any men you need. Mage, keep your people on duty with the archers atop the castle walls until Lord Blackridge says otherwise." Both men bowed and then left.

"Luthias, come find me after the meeting. I am going to go help at the forge." Luthias watched Borgroff head out as well.

Luthias addressed the others left in the war room. "I'll be watching over the young soldiers at the main gate barracks and awaiting Nakira's return. Then if by chance they were from Pantreus and telling the truth, we will see these soldiers off to Drastinus in the morning."

"Luthias, if these young men are truly who they say then protect them. But not at the cost of your own life in case they are Crimson's scouts and are attempting to deceive us. If these mercenaries are anything like you say, they will have you outnumbered eight to one. Seasoned or not, that's tough odds even for you. Any men you need to protect the people of Kallinstyne, you have. This includes my silver crown guards."

He looked at Xaika, Nakira, and Jadai before looking back at Luthias and continuing, "I trust the guardsmen and Xaika here in Kallinstyne with my life and that of my daughter's obviously. But I want to thank you all for helping to protect us. I know Lady Jadai Velair here would lay down her life for any of us, otherwise, Chief Justice Travon wouldn't have hired her. Lady Nakira Karvina has made our scouts a hundred percent more effective than they were before she showed. Lord Volf Borgroff has raised the morale of the soldiers and even showed our Master Blacksmith a few new tricks at the forge." He walked over and patted Luthias on the shoulder. "Thank you. No matter what tomorrow brings I am proud to be among your friends. Luthias, follow your instincts, they have served you well over the years. Give me whoever you feel is necessary from the remaining guards, but please make sure you protect my daughter."

Luthias bowed. "Your Highness, I am going to hold a meeting in the throne room with the guards and staff members left inside the castle walls here shortly. I will have the castle steward reduce the staff down to a bare minimum and send the rest home to be with their families tonight. Jadai will be heading back to your daughter's side. I'm going to send Nakira off with a plan for the trap before Xaika and I see to the outside defenses."

After the magistrate released the rest from the war room, Luthias walked into the garden area with Nakira for privacy. "Be watchful of your surroundings and remember the teachings of the shadow warrior."

She pulled him close and stared into his purple eyes. "Don't worry I have the best teacher." She smiled and kissed him. "I will take one of the scouts with me.

"Do you have a plan? These aren't the training games you and I do." He reached up and touched the spot where his blunt tip arrow hit her and broke the skin. "Their arrows won't have blunt tips."

She reached her hand up and placed it over his. "I know, and I promise to be the worst demon spawn they ever dealt with." She winked at him and kissed him again. "I will be careful and wary of my surroundings, I promise. Hood up and cloak spell on."

He shook his head at her attempt to ease his worry. "Let me know as soon as you get back." He watched her until he couldn't see her anymore then whispered into the wind. "Shadows guide you." Luthias looked to his left and saw Nera standing in the woods staring at him. "Go protect her but keep to the shadows. Not even she is to know you're there until it is time." Nera barked then disappeared into the woods.

Chapter Nineteen

Borgroff helped the blacksmith finish the repairs before he joined Luthias and Xaika to address the villagers, guards, and Nakira's scouts. After they made sure all the preparations were done, they walked into the throne room.

When they entered, they saw a small crowd conversing at the common tables. Luthias expected to see the magistrate sitting on his throne but was surprised to see him sitting at the common tables conversing with the blacksmith and a few others. The young blonde page from the dance was standing to the magistrate's left, leaning against him. She was the first to spot them. "Lord Blackridge! Lord Borgroff! Lady Ogresh!"

The magistrate looked up and gestured his hand toward the throne. "The throne is yours. We are here to listen to your plan so you three need to be where we all can see you. My daughter, her handmaiden, and Jadai will hold a meeting with you all in the privacy of my daughter's quarters."

With that said, Luthias reluctantly took to the platform while he watched Borgroff and Xaika take to it like they belonged there.

"This is Volf Borgroff, I am Luthias Blackridge. We, along with Nakira Karvina and Jadai Velair are here representing the Council of Kings. Knight Captain Xaika Ogresh will oversee the castle's protection detail. The scouts Nakira's been training are hidden within the castle and castle grounds already. You will not see or hear them unless needed and no one, not even I, knows the locations of each within the castle. Jadai will stay with the magistrate's daughter inside her room along with two female silver crown knights. Xaika will be using her outer chamber as her main guard post. She will divide the guards and the castle into perimeters to patrol. Guards, make sure you vary your patrol routes and lengths. Do not become predictable in your perimeter patrols. The guards inside the magistrate's outer chamber are not to leave for any reason. The same goes for the silver crown guards that will be inside the bed chamber with him. For reasons of protection, the staff will sleep in an upstairs room adjacent to the bedroom of the magistrate's daughter. I know you all don't usually sleep in such elegant surroundings but I'm sure you will be able to manage for a night or two." The staff nodded as everyone chuckled nervously. "The blacksmith, who is an excellent swordsman and helps train the guards of Kallinstyne, will be in with you all to help with your protection. No matter what you hear outside the room you are guarding, no one is to open for anyone unless Jadai or Xaika acknowledge themselves at the door? No matter what you hear outside the castle walls no one is to open the outer castle doors until I do so myself. I don't mean to scare anyone with all this extra attention to protection, but I need to know that everyone will be safe. Your Highness, is there anything you wish to add or change?"

The magistrate walked up and stood between Luthias and Xaika. "Lord Blackridge and I have good reason to offer up this kind of protection detail. I am sad to say it may continue in whole or in part over the next few days. When the threat has passed, we will slowly return things to normal. Lord Blackridge, Lord Borgroff, Lady Nakira, and Lady Jadai will be helping me oversee the castle, its grounds, and all Kallinstyne lands until I deem it safe again. Their word is my word." With that, he bowed to Luthias which caused everyone else in the room to stand and follow suit. "Good night. May the divine protect your path."

The room emptied quickly leaving only Luthias, Xaika, Borgroff, and the castle guard awaiting their orders. "Your knight captain will see to your duty rosters for the night. I'm going to go check in with the others. Xaika, I will check with you one last time before I leave."

The guards and the Silver Crown saluted Luthias as he turned to leave. "Your will be done, shadow warrior." Those words echoed off the walls of the empty throne room as he headed off.

As Borgroff and Luthias walked into the outer chambers, Jadai, the two female guards, the magistrate's daughter, and her handmaiden were talking. The handmaiden looked passed the guards to see them enter the room. "Well here are our dashing heroes now."

Luthias smiled halfheartedly as he bowed. "Your grace. Jadai and these two silver crown knights will be in your room with you, while Knight Captain Ogresh will be outside your door with another guard. Borgroff and I will be down at the main gate barracks until morning.

Under no circumstances do you open this door for anyone but Xaika, Borgroff, Nakira, or me."

She curtsied. "Thank you all. I feel safer knowing you are here."

"You're welcome, Your Highness." Jadai curtsied and then noticed Xaika walking in behind Luthias and Borgroff.

"Luthias, wait." Luthias noticed a bit of worry in Jadai's eyes as she walked up and hugged him and Borgroff. "Both of you be careful, please."

Luthias nodded as Borgroff smiled and replied, "You as well. Be smart." Xaika followed them out but before she shut the door behind them she heard Jadai whisper, "Shadows guide you."

Xaika decided not to ask about it considering how low she whispered it. "I reiterate what she said, be careful out there. We have an entire battalion, unseen scouts, and specialized knights within the castle. You two will be alone." She hugged Borgroff then Luthias. "Please be vigilant and come back safely. I will protect them with my life." She watched them bow and then walk away not sure if any of them would see the dawn of the next day. "Tomorrows are never promised, only received as blessings." She quoted the words her mother would always tell her before bed each night.

***

Luthias and Borgroff left the castle and headed to the stables. As they rode through the village, they made sure the villagers and guards locked everything as Luthias requested. "Should we head over and check on the soldiers in that old guard post?"

"No, if they have anyone watching, it will tip them off that we know of their plans. I have some of the scouts positioned out there watching anyway. We just need to get down to the barracks and keep an eye on these soldiers." As they continued towards the main gate, Luthias noticed the same eerie chill he felt each time he saw Jadai in Traemorra and Ridgewood. Luthias kept quiet about the feeling but paid extra attention to his surroundings.

They tied their horses up and then instructed the guards to head back and patrol the castle grounds. "Borgroff, disappear into the woods but keep your eyes open."

Borgroff looked at Luthias. "I need to ask a question and I need a straight answer." Luthias nodded. "We think the guard post is the main point of entrance for the legion since that's where we found their scouts. Why aren't we watching over these young men there with the other soldiers?" Borgroff walked up to him and gave him a hard look. "We aren't here watching for the legion, are we?"

"They're not our top priority, no. As dangerous as they are, we know when they are about to strike us with a weapon. Their attack is an attack we can see coming and defend against. We both know if these wraiths wanted to, they could decimate everyone in Kallinstyne as they did on Santos Isle. Not a soul would know anything was happening until death stared at them face to face. Something tells me Crimson and his mercenary legion of Red Death is being used by the demon as a distraction. We know they are going to attack at some point as well but…"

"But your gut has us here, so this is where we are needed. Your gut is usually correct." He smiled as he looked down, "All my gut ever wants is ale and food." Borgroff shook Luthias's hand and pulled him into a hug. "Let's kick all their asses then."

He watched Borgroff head out into the darkness of the surrounding woods. He then whispered the words to his cloak spell, "Kappe opp," disappeared, and quietly walked into the barracks to watch over the young men. He sat down in a corner of the barracks fully cloaked to wait till morning… or until the worst came to happen. He hopes he's wrong about everything, and these young men will make it to Drastinus Kingdom without any more problems. As he thought about it his eyes immediately settled on the young man with the scar. He said a silent prayer praying everyone would see the daylight of morning. As he finished the prayer his mind immediately showed him visions of Nakira. He hoped Nakira would make it through her journey safely. Luthias hoped he didn't make them an easy target by sending only two. He almost lost her once and ended up in a vengeful spiral he regrets. This time there would be no regrets, only the vengeful spiral.

***

Nakira and the scout followed the road south of Kallinstyne toward Drastinus. As they rounded a small bend in the road, Nakira nodded at the scout, spoke the words to her cloak spell, "Kappe opp," disappeared, and quickly rode off into the woods. She doubled back until she came upon the soldiers she suspected were following them. "I hate being right sometimes." Nakira rode through the woods shadowing the five men.

When they rode around the corner where she had doubled back, one of them spoke up. "Wait, why is there only one rider? Where did the other rider go?"

"She is right here!" Nakira shouted as she rode out of the woods. She directed her horse to ride in between the soldiers startling them and their horses. She swung her dagger and hit an arm knocking a soldier off his horse. Nakira heard a growl and a bark as she saw a blade coming at her.

She threw her dagger up and blocked the incoming blade at the last second. The block jarred her and the other soldier, but an arrow whizzed past her head and hit the soldier in the neck knocking him from his horse. Nakira spurred her horse towards another soldier as she heard Nera finish off the fallen soldier. The soldier was paying more attention to the large wolf killing his friend and didn't see Nakira's dagger until the last second as she thrust it into his chest.

She pulled the blade free and then rode off for another soldier. The next soldier raised his sword to block her blow but left his midsection open. Nakira swung the other dagger out landing a hard blow cutting into the soldier's stomach and ribs, knocking the soldier from his horse. She looked up to see a fourth guard go down from an arrow. The arrow didn't kill him, but she knew Nera would finish him. She rode after the fifth soldier, but an arrow whizzed past her again striking the soldier in the back of the neck and causing him to fall forward from his horse.

Nakira waited for the other scout to ride up. "That's all of them." She turned to look at the scout. "Good shooting with that longbow." She then looked down at Nera. "I see Luthias had you shadowing me." Nera barked as they climbed down from their horses to look at the men they had just killed.

Nakira walked up to the man she had sliced open as the scout knelt and commented, "I'd much rather face my longbow than face your daggers or Nera." Nakira smiled at the compliment. The scout examined the dead soldier closely. He noticed the soldier's tunic partially open where she had sliced through it. "Lady Karvina, this man has a strange rune burned into the center of his chest."

Nakira checked the other soldiers. "They all have the same rune burned into them. We need to get back to Kallinstyne, quickly!"

Chapter Twenty

Luthias watched the young men sleeping as he listened to the sounds floating in on the breeze. The familiar chill he felt hadn't faded, Luthias knew something was coming, perhaps even watching. He felt the hours creeping by minute-by-minute hearing only the normal sounds of the night. Frogs croaking, cicadas buzzing, and crickets chirping. He was beginning to believe he had over thought the danger of these young men. Just as he relaxed a sound from outside caught his attention.

He listened to try and hear the sound again but didn't. Still cloaked and invisible, he quietly made his way over to check on the young men. Noticing they were all still asleep he walked out of the barracks to have a look around. He was looking up at the full moon when he heard the same sound again.

Still cloaked, he crept in the direction the sound came from. He walked up to a large tree and peered around it. Slowly Luthias's head cleared the side of the tree and he saw a raven fly up and land in the tree. Luthias let out a sigh of relief. He looked around a bit then decided to return to the barracks to watch over the Pantreus guards until morning.

Before he reached the barracks door, Nakira and the scout quickly rode up. "Luthias, where are you? I need to show you something."

"Kappe ned." Luthias appeared out of thin air, standing between the two horses.

"Hell's Realm," the scout said nearly fell from his horse as Nakira jumped.

Luthias grinned, "What did you learn?"

"I'll explain while we ride." Nakira pointed at the scout. "You watch those soldiers. Keep your eyes and ears open." He saluted and went to watch over the sleeping soldiers.

Nakira began talking as she and Luthias rode away. "You were right, there were more soldiers. Five more soldiers dressed the same as those young men followed us. I told the other guard to keep riding on while I doubled back behind them. Luthias, we killed them but, these men have a strange rune burned into their chests."

When they reached the battle sight, Luthias examined the rune Nakira told him about. He stood and drew Fijandsvarg. "Damn! It's a soul rune. It's an ancient demon rune that lets the soul of a demon inhabit the body of a mortal. A mage will burn the rune onto the mortal using a form of magic known as demon branding."

He lifted Fijandsvarg and brought it down, cutting off the dead soldier's head. As the severed head rolled over a bright blue light showed from the mouth and something within shrieked loudly. They watched a blue ooze leak out of the wound.

"Help me cut their heads off. It's the only way to kill these demons before they get loose. Then we need to hurry back and check those men at the barracks."

As Nakira climbed down, one of the bodies started convulsing. She watched as the chest burst open spewing blue liquid everywhere. A large blue bi-ped demon with the horns of a bull sitting atop a jaguar's head roared and swung its large paws and claws wildly. Nakira ducked and rolled out of the way barely escaping. One of the paws caught Luthias and knocked him to the ground. He landed hard but rolled quickly to his feet.

"Cut the other heads off quickly while I deal with big blue." Luthias backed away, attempting to draw it away from the other bodies and Nakira. "Come on blue, let's play follow the leader!" The large demon stood and stared for a bit then charged him quickly. Luthias barely rolled to the side in time. "Agile for such a big boy aren't you blue." Luthias stood up luring it to charge him one more time. "Charge me again blue, come on!" Luthias yelled at the bull-horned large blue jaguar standing half-again taller than him. It looked around and then charged Luthias.

This time he stood his ground and waited until the last second. He shoved Fijandsvarg out then stepped to the side as the sword sliced through the beast.

Nakira cut the last head off then watched Luthias cut through the beast severing its left arm and cutting through the ribs of the beast. She watched the beast stagger a bit, but it didn't go down. Then out of the woods, Nera jumped onto it clawing the beast and biting down hard on its neck. She watched the beast go down hard with Nera landing on top of it, ripping part of its neck out with her teeth. Nera dropped as the beast quickly turned into a puddle of blue liquid.

"Good job girl. Let's get back! If these beasts get out, they will wreak havoc on Kallinstyne." Luthias and Nakira quickly rode back to Kallinstyne with Nera shadowing them in the woods.

They jumped off their horses and ran into the barracks. But the scene before them had already turned gruesome. The Kallinstyne scout and five of the young men lay in pools of blood. The scout's longbow lay gripped tight in his fingers and his throat was slashed by claws.

Borgroff ran out of the darkness startling Luthias and Nakira. He looked at the young men and noticed some had their chest cavities torn open. "Luthias, why does it look like these men have had their chests ripped open from the inside?" Borgroff noticed one of the chests covered in a yellow liquid. "Wait, did that strange yellow armored oversized squirrel with bat wings and saber teeth I just killed come from inside him?"

Luthias looked down to see one of Borgroff's hammers covered in the same yellow liquid and nodded. "Yes. There are four more of varying types roaming Kallinstyne."

Nakira checked for the marks on the rest and severed their heads. They ran outside as Luthias looked around quickly. His head darted back and forth as he tried to catch a glimpse of the demons, but none were around. He ran back inside to see Nakira severing the head of the young man with the claw marks.

"The last three bore the soul rune as well."

"Damn, just as I suspected. The demon wanted us to concentrate on Crimson so her pets could rip through the chests of these young soldiers and do her bidding. Eliminate two enemies at once. Nakira saw runes burnt into the chests of the men they killed on the road. One of the demons broke loose from a soldier's chest. It was a large blue jaguar with huge bull horns. The beast stood half again taller than me. These demons nurtured on the soul of those men devouring it until they burst forth."

Luthias looked at the holes torn open in the young men's chests. "Red, green, purple, yellow and another blue. Borgroff killed the yellow demon, but we must hurry and get to the castle. We have at least four more specialized demons, more death wraiths, and their master on the loose. Borgroff and Nera will head over to check on the old guard post while Nakira and I ride to the castle. Be quick Borgroff."

Borgroff nodded, ran over, and mounted up on his horse then rode off with Nera chasing after him.

Nakira and Luthias jumped on their horses and rode hard toward the village. As they rode into the village, they noticed doors smashed in, shutters ripped off, windows broken, and bodies lying in houses and on the streets. Luthias saw bodies of villagers mangled, killed by the mercenaries. But he also saw villagers and mercenaries killed by the wraiths as well. Just as they started to ride toward the castle, they both heard a loud scream and saw a bright red glow from one of the destroyed houses.

"Come on let's destroy this demon." They jumped down. Luthias drew Fijandsvarg while Nakira drew her recurve bow and notched an arrow. "Stay back, watch for openings." Luthias didn't wait for a reply as he ran towards the glow. "Hey red! Let's play!" They watched an elven female float out of the ruined house. She was bright red with demon horns and a long scorpion tail. "Oh shit!" Luthias rolled to the side, the tail's stinger narrowly missing him as it slammed into the ground where he was just standing. But he heard the twang of Nakira's bow and watched an arrow lodge into the demon's breast. The demon screamed and pulled the arrow loose tossing it aside. Luthias assumed an attack position daring the demon to strike again. "Come on scorpion bitch, try that again."

The demon screeched loudly and swung her tail but instead of straight down on him as he expected the tail swung sideways knocking him several feet. He rolled over shaking his head as he spoke to himself,

"Mom always told me to be careful what you ask for, you'll get it." He watched the demon head for Nakira. "Oh no you don't." He stood up and raced towards it as Nakira kept its attention on her. He raised Fijandsvarg high as he approached the back of the demon. He sliced through severing the head clean off. The body slumped to the ground, dissipating into a bright red liquid.

"I missed the action of a large demon again?" Luthias and Nakira turned to watch Nera and Borgroff quickly approach. "I better not be stuck just fighting oversized yellow armored bat squirrel demons."

"I will save you big blue number two when we see it, but we also have green and purple to go as well. What did you find?"

"They were all dead. Crimson and his crew killed them. Two of the Kallinstyne soldiers had their heads smashed, the other guards were gutted and sliced open."

Luthias shook his head. "Demons, wraiths, and mercenaries…"

"Oh my!" Nakira interrupted him. He looked over to see her pointing towards the castle. He saw a stream of purple flames rising high into the air.

"Damn!" They mounted up and rode fast towards the castle. He only hoped they could catch and kill the demons, wraiths, and mercenaries before they killed everyone in Kallinstyne.

As they arrived at the castle grounds, they saw the gates splintered open with one on the ground. They jumped off their horses and drew their weapons. They ran into the castle square searching for whatever had been shooting purple flames. Borgroff nudged Luthias and pointed at a group of burnt corpses lying in the courtyard. Sitting in the middle was a purple rabbit licking its fur. Borgroff looked up at Luthias. "Is that a rabbit?" The rabbit looked over at them and stood up. "That rabbit is as tall as I am." They watched the rabbit breathe in. They jumped out of the path as a streak of purple flames shot out of its mouth.

"I'll keep its attention while you two get behind it and kill it," Luthias said drawing the rabbit's attention. "Yeah, try that again. You missed."

Borgroff watched Nakira shoot an arrow that stuck into it but only seemed to annoy it. The rabbit started breathing in as Borgroff drew out both hammers and ran towards it. He noticed Luthias waving his arms just as he jumped and brought both hammers together smashing the rabbit's head. The resulting blast blew Borgroff hard into the fountain.

Luthias and Nakira ran up to check on him. Luthias chuckled at the sight. "I was trying to tell you we needed to kill him from a distance as he will most likely explode."

Borgroff looked up at Luthias and grinned, "And miss out on that kind of fun." Luthias and Nakira shook their heads as they helped him up and out of the fountain. "At least I landed in water to put out the flames."

Luthias looked at the sight around them. It was the same gory scene as the village. Castle guards, wraiths, and mercenaries were all dead covered in a purple liquid. They searched and checked every corner of the courtyard. The archers and mages that were supposed to be up on the walls were nowhere in sight, which Luthias figured would be the case. They would have been the first ones taken out. He imagined the main demon took care of them as she released her wraiths on the rest. "Nera, go do your thing girl." Nakira and Borgroff watched Nera head out into the woods as they followed Luthias to the castle, seeing more dead soldiers and even some scouts uncloaked and dead.

They noticed the grisly scene continued into the castle as well. Castle guards, mercenaries, and scouts dead. Some were taken by surprise and killed by wraiths. Others were killed by the mercenaries as they marched through on their way to their targets. Luthias whispered, "Keep your eyes open for the other two demons as well."

"Least the demons and wraiths are helping us kill Crimson's men." Luthias looked at Nakira. "What? The bright side of things!" Luthias heard Borgroff chuckle behind them.

The magistrate's room was the first room they hurried to. The scene inside was as he expected after seeing the rest up to this point. Castle guards were dead in the outer chamber with one of them showing evidence Crimson had been there. Inside the magistrate's chambers, the silver crown guards all lay dead.

Nakira pointed out two more dead wraiths staining the magistrate's royal bed sheets with their black sticky liquid. They also noticed the magistrate dead from a blow from Crimson Shaw's hammer. "I hope the divine grant your passage to the beyond." Nakira whispered as Luthias nodded.

As they searched through the rest of the castle, Borgroff stopped and pointed at a soldier who had a bright green liquid covering his chest. The liquid was slowly dissolving his black armor, flesh, muscles, and bones. "Don't get that stuff on you, for damn sure."

As they looked at the green glowing acidic liquid, they heard a commotion coming from down the hall. They rounded a corner and saw a group of mercenaries doing battle with Xaika and one of the female silver crown knights. Luthias sheathed Fijandsvarg as Borgroff ran off toward the fight. He raised his crossbow, letting a bolt fly. Nakira raised her recurve bow and searched for a shot. "Time your shots and watch our backs." Luthias dropped the crossbow back beneath his jacket and drew Fijandsvarg again. He heard the strings of the recurve bow and knew an arrow was coming.

He ran in a straight line as the arrow whizzed by him and struck a thin elf in the neck, who dropped his sword and fell to the floor dead. The Silver Crown knight quickly turned her attention to another elf coming at her.

Borgroff joined the fight and landed a blow on an unsuspecting orc who was paying attention to Xaika. Luthias raised his sword and swung forward but a large burly dwarf blocked his blow at the last second. Luthias jumped backward as the dwarf's axe swung through. The dwarf over swung and had to lower his shield arm to steady himself. This left his neck and shoulder open. Luthias stabbed the mercenary causing him to drop his axe.

Something caught his attention, so he turned, bringing the dead mercenary's body with him raising his shield arm. He ducked as the dead dwarf and his shield blocked the incoming green liquid. "Green demon!" Luthias yelled, trying to get the others' attention. But before anyone else could move, Nakira had shot an arrow through a green guinea pig demon the size of a small fox.

Nakira notched another arrow and refocused on the battle. As she watched two more mercenaries ran up from another hallway. She took one of them out as he swung his hammer at Xaika. The arrow hit the mercenary in the side sending him and his hammer to the ground. Borgroff brought both hammers up and smashed the other one's head between them.

As Luthias thrust the sword forward into a human, he watched in horror as a dwarf severed the head of the silver crown knight. Luthias pulled Fijandsvarg from the human's chest as the silver crown knight's head hit the floor with a sickening thud. Luthias watched Xaika stab another human, sending him to the floor. Borgroff landed a blow to both sides of the dwarf's head smashing his skull. Nakira ran to check on the magistrate's daughter, her handmaiden, and Jadai.

Xaika took several breaths. "Jadai led the magistrate's daughter out of the castle, her handmaiden didn't survive. A death wraith killed her before we knew it was there. You need to hurry though because three men were chasing them, Crimson and his red war hammer was one of them."

Borgroff could see Luthias's anger had turned to rage. "Luthias, you and Nakira go help them. Xaika and I will find you after we finish clearing the castle. But damn it, leave big blue to me."

They watched Luthias and Nakira run off toward the castle entrance. "Crimson is a dangerous foe for anyone, but Luthias's rage makes him just as dangerous."

He watched Xaika nod then look at him quizzically, "Big Blue?"

Borgroff smiled, "You'll see."

Chapter Twenty-One

Luthias and Nakira ran toward the front entrance and heard more commotion outside. Exiting the castle, they saw a platoon of dwarven soldiers battling against more mercenaries from Crimson's legion. As Luthias scanned over the battle scene in front of him, he saw a dwarven female battling with a particularly tough-looking elf. They watched her sling one of her blades out. Nakira raised her bow and aimed. The arrow flew right into the right side of the neck sending the mercenary to the ground. Luthias watched as the dwarf looked in their direction, bowed her head, and then pointed to the north.

Luthias nodded, pointed into the castle, then quickly ran off into the woods with Nakira speaking as she ran to catch up, "She had a chain connecting her daggers! Luthias, I need a set of those." Luthias ignored her banter as they ran into the woods.

***

Borgroff followed Xaika as she hurried to check on the room with the staff. Borgroff watched her reach for the door handle, then stop. She turned to him. "The young castle page stayed with her father."

Borgroff nodded then stepped up to the door. He dreaded opening this door as well, but he also knew it would be easier for him to face the carnage than Xaika. Borgroff opened the door slowly hoping that someone was alive. As he surveyed the scene, he noticed only the blacksmith made it out of bed before dying.

The young page lay in the bed cuddled up to the female castle steward. Her position didn't allow him to see her face, but her stillness told him all he needed to know. The only solace he could offer Xaika was that at least it wasn't the mercenaries who got to her and the rest of the staff.

Borgroff turned away from the sight and saw Xaika stab her

143

sword out beside his side just under Borgroff's arm. They both heard a deafening shriek as the sword cut through the death wraith sending it collapsing into a pool of black liquid.

She looked up to see Borgroff thrusting his hammer directly at her. She flinched and ducked down as she heard the shriek of another wraith die just behind her. She turned to see a pool of black liquid. They both saw an auburn-haired dwarven female holding a set of black stained daggers connected by a chain. "Borgroff? Hells Realm!"

Borgroff stood in disbelief as he stared at his childhood friend. Her hair was pulled back into a loose tail hanging long down her back. He stared at her oval-shaped face, petite nose, and dark red eyes. "Goyrok? What are you doing all the way over here?"

"Chasing down that bastard dwarf, you can't seem to kill." She smiled and winked at him.

Xaika stepped back to stand beside Borgroff. "Thank you, glad you showed up when you did." As she spoke, she noticed the dwarf throw a dagger toward Borgroff's right side.

Borgroff turned and watched the wraith dissolve into the black liquid. "Show off! This is Kaci Goyrok, she is a Knight Hunter with the Dwarven Republic Guard. Goyrok, this is Xaika Ogresh, Knight Captain of Kallinstyne."

"You're welcome, but your friends might have just run out to their deaths. He took off after the others, but Crimson and his Legion of Red Death were already out there hunting. Another group of the Red Death mercenaries headed that way afterward. I sent my battalion after them and decided to come to check if anyone was in here."

"We have some hunting of our own to do then," Xaika replied as Borgroff nodded.

***

Luthias sent Nakira off to try and lure the big blue demon back to his location, he wanted to use it to create chaos and help distract Crimson. Luthias stayed cloaked as he searched the woods behind the castle. He knew the dense forest in this area was why the princess and Jadai chose to run north instead of south. Jadai didn't know the area, but the magistrate's daughter knew they had a chance to disappear into the dark forest and hide from the mercenaries. He just hoped they didn't run into Big Blue or Crimson before Nakira or he did. Luthias slowed when he started hearing footsteps and whispers just ahead of him.

Luthias crouched low and pulled Fijandsvarg out of its sheath. He quietly crept towards the voices. He stopped just behind two elven mercenaries whispering and looking around. He stabbed one. As he pulled the sword free, the second mercenary fell to the ground with an arrow sticking out of his forehead. "Nice shot," Luthias whispered as he looked around and spotted Nakira before she disappeared again.

He knew these two were here searching for something or someone. He looked through some tree branches and spotted Nera crouched on a cliff face behind the tree. He heard a noise coming from his right. He turned and quickly lifted his crossbow. He fired a cross-bolt at a human who had just fired an arrow toward Nera. Luthias watched the mercenary fall to the ground with his cross bolt sticking out of his temple.

Then he turned and watched in horror as Nera fell from atop a large cliff bouncing to the ground below. "No!" Luthias bellowed out as he ran towards his wolf. But as he reached her, he noticed the arrow had hit her hind leg passing through. He knew she needed to be bandaged but also knew Nera would survive. "Stay here girl, I will be back after I kill this damn dwarf." Nera barked and tried to get up, but he pushed her down, and petted her a second. "Stay." He then got up and ran off.

***

Xaika led the others into the northern woods until they came across the bodies of two mercenary soldiers. One shot with an arrow, the other stabbed. She watched Goyrok silently use hand signals toward her men. The men took off in different directions. Xaika returned her attention to the area in front of them.

Borgroff kept his hammers up and ready for any enemy who dared to show their face as he whispered, "Any idea where they would have headed from here?"

Xaika kept searching the area as she answered, "Out here they can disappear anywhere allowing themselves to track and kill the mercenary soldiers one by one. Out here, Luthias and Nakira have the upper hand over the dwarf."

Goyrok huffed, "Getting the upper hand on Crimson is tough to do, he is as smart as he is evil. I've been trying to catch him for three years."

Borgroff looked at them both. "Out here the demon, her wraiths, and big blue have the true advantage."

"Hey over here," someone shouted from a few yards in front of them. They ran to find a soldier standing over Nera as she whimpered.

Xaika bent down to examine the wound as Borgroff spoke, "He must have taken chase after the mercenary who fired the shot at her."

"And to find Jadai and the magistrate's daughter." They both turned to see Nakira walk out of the darkness.

Another soldier called out to get their attention. They arrived, to notice another of the mercenaries. "A cross-bolt to the temple killed him." Nakira looked over to follow its path. "By the looks of it, we found the man who tried to kill Nera. His path faces her and the path of the cross-bolt that killed him leads to wear Luthias was standing."

"That means, Luthias watched this mercenary try to kill Nera then fired the cross-bolt that killed him." Borgroff looked back at the others.

Goyrok interrupted him, "I know this all seems important right now, but we need to find the rest before Crimson does."

Xaika nodded. "Kaci is right."

"You all go find and help Luthias I still have the blue demon to find." Nakira headed out as Borgroff caught up to her.

They had been searching for a bit when Borgroff whispered, "Just how big is big blue anyway?" As Borgroff asked, a mercenary flew out of a group of trees and landed a few paces in front of them. Borgroff watched Nakira run off to the side so she could flank the demon. Once she was out of sight, Borgroff walked forward with both hammers up and ready. "Okay, big blue let's play." He walked forward and noticed a large bull-horned jaguar charging some fleeing mercenaries. He noticed the demon's cat-like reflexes and speed when it caught them and sent them flying with a slap of his paw. Borgroff smiled, "Finally a real challenge and not a flying yellow pest or exploding purple bunny."

Nakira watched Borgroff smile and knew he was going to do something stupid. She watched him but kept her bow trained on the demon. "Just don't get in my way," she whispered as she watched him bang the two hammers together drawing the demon's attention.

She had a shot and took it.

She knew it would take a precise hit for her to take it down but any damage she could do would help him take it down quicker. She watched the arrow hit making the demon roar. She watched Big Blue turn and see Borgroff. Nakira followed Big Blue as it charged at him. "What's your plan dwarf?" She noticed he wasn't moving. He stood there smiling with his hammers ready.

Just as Big Blue lowered its head to hit him, she watched Borgroff roll forward and stretch his hammers out wide. He cut the legs out from under the demon sending it flying into a large akora tree. The tree was large enough for both horns to get stuck deep into it from the impact. Nakira watched Borgroff finish in a standing position and run back to the stuck beast. He brought both hammers out and slammed them into the demon's side.

She heard the demon bellow out and watched it raise its head quickly in pain. When it did, the demon broke both horns releasing itself from the tree's grasp. She watched Borgroff roll out of the way of its large, clawed hands. She concentrated and followed its flailing as its claws barely kept missing him. She shot the arrow and was surprised when the demon dissipated into a blue liquid. She looked over at Borgroff lying there with blue and purple liquid covering his body. "Borgroff!" She watched him stick his thumb up into the air and could tell he was laughing. "Stupid dwarf."

***

Luthias walked quickly and quietly through the woods. He had his crossbow ready under his jacket and Fijandsvarg in his hand. He knew the girls were in the woods somewhere. He wanted to holler out to get their attention, but he also knew that Crimson and more mercenaries were out here as well. He knew hollering would alert them to him and the girls. He would never forgive himself if he was the reason either of them died. He already had the guilt of an entire village on his hands. He stopped, crouched down, and listened to his surroundings for a bit. He hoped to hear something, anything that could lead him to the girls or Crimson and eliminate him before he got to them.

"Crimson Shaw, you evil bastard. I've heard lots of things about

147

you." Jadai's voice carried through the woods to Luthias's ear. He turned to his left and sheathed his sword. He quietly brought his crossbow up as he crept toward her voice. He just hoped he was creeping up behind him, and not behind her.

"I hope you've heard nothing but dreadful things!" Crimson said his voice reaching Luthias's ear. "I do have a reputation to keep up with."

Luthias smiled when he approached a small clearing and saw Crimson facing away from him. Luthias aimed at his head. But before he could fire, a wraith dug its claws into Luthias's right shoulder. Luthias dropped the crossbow and brought out Fijandsvarg. He quickly turned and sliced through the wraith sending it down into the dirt.

He spun back around watching Jadai square off against Crimson. He hurried towards them as Jadai stepped into the swing of Crimson Shaw's hammer. Luthias jumped and thrust the sword towards Crimson's back. Both weapons hit their marks. Luthias pulled the sword out, spun, and swung it at the dwarf's head, but Crimson ducked the slashing sword and rolled out of the way. Crimson bounced up fast swinging his hammer.

Luthias dropped and rolled to the side narrowly escaping the crushing blow of the deadly war hammer. He looked up to see Crimson's evil grin,

"You are prize number one. Out of everyone I've been paid to kill, you are the one they want dead the most. They claim you are a hard target to cage." His evil grin got bigger. "I told them that's your mistake. Don't cage what you can pulverize." He looked from Luthias to his prized hammer.

Luthias watched a dagger fly in and hit Crimson on the back of his shoulder. Luthias watched the female dwarf from the courtyard yank on the chain and pull the bloody dagger out of his shoulder along with a chunk of his flesh and a bit of muscle. He hollered and dropped the head of his war hammer onto the ground. Luthias quickly stabbed forward but Crimson brought the handle up and knocked the blow of the sword to the side.

"Goyrok, I figured we would eventually meet up again," Crimson said as he kept his attention on Luthias. "I'd love to play, but I have bigger worries right now." As he finished talking Luthias heard the faint sound of a bowstring. He watched Crimson duck and roll forward causing the arrow to miss him. Luthias caught it just in front of his chest. "Nice catch. I'd heard whispered rumors that you were good at that."

Luthias followed the arrow's path to see Nakira looking down her recurve bow with a look of hatred on her face. But her look quickly turned to shock when she realized what had happened. Luthias gave her a quick smile. "Nice job of ducking. Do you always avoid attacks instead of battling head-on?" Luthias caught the female dwarf's stare and looked down at his hand.

She quickly read the sign he flashed her and smiled, "You got it!" She whispered and readied her daggers once again. She watched Luthias lunge at Crimson. Crimson brought the large war hammer up favoring his right shoulder. She sent the dagger flying and hit him on the back of the left shoulder. She then threw the other dagger at Luthias. She watched him catch the dagger and then shove it deep into Crimson's chest.

Crimson dropped to the ground, but Luthias saw his hand weakly reaching for his war hammer. Luthias reached down and picked up the war hammer. "Death by war hammer!" He brought it down hard squashing his head like a melon. He dropped the handle as he looked over to see Jadai lying dead from the hammer's blow. As he hurried over to her, Nakira ran to his side. Luthias looked up at her. "Go find the magistrate's daughter."

"We already have." Luthias turned to see Xaika carrying her lifeless body with a bone-handled dagger sticking out of her chest. Luthias walked over and removed the dagger as Nakira kicked Crimson Shaw's corpse. Xaika smiled, "There is no doubt he deserved that kick a thousand times over, but my guess is it was one of the other mercs who killed her. I don't see Crimson using a dagger when he could have used his pride and joy hammer."

"It wasn't a mercenary." Luthias dropped his head.

"It was the demon," Borgroff said finishing for Luthias.

Nakira looked back to Luthias and Jadai. "Luthias, how is this possible? How is Jadai dead? She should have been able to vanish before the blow hit her."

Luthias saw the others looking confused. "I don't know. Let's get the dead buried then head back to Traemorra. We may have eliminated the mercenaries, but we still have a demon and her wraiths."

Xaika nodded. "I also think we should head to Chief Justice's place to check on her husband and staff. Then I suggest we head to Gatesboro to inform her of Jadai's fate before we make the trek to Traemorra."

Luthias looked up at Xaika nodding. He looked back down at Jadai once again. "I'm not sure about her spirit but this body will be buried up on Knight's Hill with the rest of the fallen heroes." He looked up to watch Xaika nod. Luthias walked over and handed the female dwarf her daggers. "These are a handy weapon." He looked over at Borgroff and smiled at the purple and blue-covered dwarf. "Now if only I knew a dwarf whose father was the Forgemaster of the Dwarven Republic. I could commission a set for Nakira." He looked at Borgroff and smiled. "I see you met up with Big Blue."

"Met big blue, kicked big blue's ass, and let your girlfriend have the kill while I bathed in big blue's goo." He laughed as he looked down at himself. "Goyrok here will inform my father to make the blades and chain for you when she takes this piece of shit and his weapon back to Stoneback." He looked over at her. "Hell, you might as well travel with us until we get back to Traemorra."

He watched her smile. "Only if you promise to clean up in the creek at least."

Luthias laughed at her, "First, we need to at least bury the magistrate, his daughter, and Jadai. We need to honor their souls. When we stop in Fort Gambit to get Nera bandaged up, we will send another platoon to also bury the rest of the dead here in Kallinstyne."

Chapter Twenty-Two

After burying the magistrate and his daughter by his wife and Jadai up on Knight's Hill, they headed out of Kallinstyne. While they buried the three of them, the dwarven battalion cleared out an area just to the east of the village to make enough room for the Fort Gambit battalion to bury them.

The trip out of Kallinstyne had been quiet with no one in the mood to chat after losing an entire village. Luthias looked back at Nera who laid on the handmade stretcher whining as his horse dragged it behind him. "Sorry girl, I know you don't believe you need it, but you are a hero and deserve to rest until we get you to Fort Gambit to get that leg bandaged and healed."

Xaika smiled halfheartedly as she rode beside the stretcher and looked down. "I tell you what girl. I will trade you spots and relax the rest of the way to Gatesboro while you pull me." Nera barked making her laugh. Even though her laugh was genuine her heart was still broken for the life and friends she was leaving behind.

"Luthias, a body." Borgroff pointed forward as he climbed down and ran over. Borgroff rolled the female over then fell backwards when he saw her throat ripped to shreds. "What the hell? Crimson and his legion came through here before hitting Kallinstyne."

Luthias climbed down and walked over. He examined the wound and saw claw marks on both shoulders. "This is more recent, and it wasn't the legion. Hellions did this." He ran back, jumped on his horse, and rode hard into Travon's estate.

He jumped off his horse and was halfway to the house by the time the rest caught up to him. He hollered back without looking. "Search everywhere. Kill everything not mortal or animal."

A little while later, Luthias walked towards the edge of the lake carrying an old elf when the others walked up as well. "No sign of Travon anywhere," Xaika said watching Luthias. "Hopefully, she is still in Gatesboro unharmed." Luthias didn't respond to Xaika as he laid the old elf's corpse down on the ground by the lake. Luthias stared at him for a second then looked out onto the lake to see all three dragons still alive floating on the water. The eerie chill came over him again as the three dragons suddenly took flight. He drew Fijandsvarg and startled the others causing them to quickly follow suit.

"What? Did you hear something?" Nakira asked looking around.

Luthias looked around and saw a hellion flying in quickly from the south. "Hellions!" Luthias watched the dragons take flight from the lake. He assumed they were scattering but was surprised when he watched each one attack the first three hellions. He watched them battle with their claws, spiked wings, and fire breath. The dragons made short work of their prey as they headed towards more.

Luthias put Fijandsvarg up and brought out his crossbow. He started firing cross bolts into the hellions. He saw Nakira's arrows and even Goyrok's chained daggers when they got close enough. After a few of the hellions died the dragons chased the rest off with their fire breaths.

Borgroff huffed, "I know I'm a dwarf and all, but I'm about battled out for the day."

Luthias looked at Borgroff. "I hear you." He looked down at the old elf once again. "Anyone else alive?"

"No, everyone else looks the same or worse, death by hellions. But Luthias, hellions don't leave the lava flats," Xaika said making Luthias look at her.

"Unless they are told to." Everyone looked at Kaci Goyrok. "Hellions are nothing more than beasts. Like other beasts, you can train them to do what you want."

"Who in the hell is stupid enough to train hellions? They are nothing more than this realm's version of dumb ass demons with the temperament and disposition of an evil dwarf and his red war hammer." Borgroff noticed everyone staring at him as he spoke. It was then he realized they were all staring at a dwarf carrying the infamous red war hammer on his back.

"Perhaps a demon who tried to warn Travon about the deaths of royal bloodlines," Nakira said drawing their attention. "I mean we just left Kallinstyne leaving everyone but Xaika dead, including the two people we were supposed to protect." She quickly looked at Xaika. "Sorry I didn't mean that to sound... like it did."

Xaika held up her hand and smiled weakly, "It's okay. I understand what you are saying. We lost the Traemorra magistrate and his family to the mercenaries. We lost the magistrate of Pantreus to the mercenaries. We lost…" Nakira placed her hand on Xaika's shoulder as she dropped her head and continued. "We lost my magistrate to the mercenaries. I guess we pissed it off for not living up to its expectations."

Luthias looked at them. "But this demon is doing the same thing. If anything she isn't mad at us for failing to protect them, she's mad because we didn't protect them long enough for her to kill them before the mercenaries could. She killed the empress and prince with daggers. She also killed the magistrate's daughter before Crimson could. She may have warned Travon about their deaths, but it wasn't to protect innocents. It was to protect them long enough so she could kill them for her own agenda."

"But like the empress and the prince, the magistrate's daughter died by a dagger to the heart. A dagger left in her heart until you pulled it out of her." Borgroff finished for Luthias following where he was going with the conversation.

"Okay, but a dagger to the heart, a war hammer smashing a skull, hellion's teeth to the throat, and a wraith behind you all end up with the same result, dead royal bloodlines." Luthias looked down at the old elf as he repeated the words Crimson told him, "You are prize number one. Out of everyone I've been paid to kill, you are the one they want dead the most." Luthias looked up to see everyone staring at him. "Crimson said this to me just before Goyrok took a chunk out of him. By 'they,' I am assuming he means his employers, this Jegere av Fijandsvarg cult."

"Also consider the fact this all started with an attempt on your life that Cut-throat and his goons messed up," Nakira said staring at Luthias. "Luthias, this demon, and this cult are trying to kill you. We need to get you back to Traemorra and the Red Dog now."

"I agree this crazy cult is trying to him for some reason, but I don't think this demon is." Borgroff held up his hands in defense of the evil look appearing in Nakira's eyes. "Hear me out at least before killing me. The death wraith in Pantreus didn't attack him when it had the chance. Instead, we only knew it was there when it went up into a ball of flames. Then he killed another one who was simply following us into the graveyard. It had the chance to kill me as well so why didn't it?"

"So far, the only wraith that attacked me is the one who attacked me before I could shoot Crimson to prevent him from killing Jadai. But lots of them had the opportunity to do so. I am in this demon's cross hair, but it doesn't want me dead." He looked at Nakira as he continued. "I won't go into hiding but I do agree we need to get back to see Amunique. Hopefully, she and the antiquities dealer will have information for us."

Xaika looked down at the old elf's corpse. "But we also need to inform Travon of the tragedy here."

Luthias looked at Xaika and nodded. "Yeah, we will head to Gatesboro then on to Traemorra after we get Nera to Fort Gambit to get healed. Let's get everyone here gathered and buried by the lake shore. Hopefully, these are the last people we bury for a long time." Luthias walked over to Nera and petted her. "Sorry for the rough ride earlier but we had to get down here quickly." He smiled when she barked and wagged her tail.

After burying the dead at Travon's estate. They made good time getting to Fort Gambit. Luthias made sure to tell the fort's commander about the bodies needing buried in Kallinstyne. He immediately dispatched several platoons. The veterinarian in Fort Gambit kept Nera in her office for observation and rest. She watched over her for a few hours before she allowed her to leave. But her condition was that Nera had to ride not run or walk, so she had the commander of the fort give them a wagon. Luthias and Nakira hooked their horses up to pull it while Borgroff, Xaika, and Kaci tied theirs trailing the wagon. They all rode to Gatesboro. Nakira wanted to sit next to Luthias, but Nera was sitting tall and proud between them. She just laughed and petted her.

The trip from Fort Gambit to Gatesboro felt like it took hours longer than it did. Exhaustion from the battles, lack of sleep, and depression from losing so many people in such a short span, all took its toll on everybody. It hit them all at once when they relaxed in the wagon. A quarter way through the trip, Luthias realized he and Nera were the only two awake. "Girl, after we're through, you, me, and Nakira are taking a long time away. We're hiding from the public." When they approached the city of Gatesboro, Luthias woke everyone up giving them time to wake up from their naps.

Luthias and the rest awaited Travon inside one of the private rooms reserved for sensitive council business. He knew she would assume the meeting was about the Inquisition and wonder why they were meeting this way. He requested the room so they could break the news to her in private. This gave her the space and freedom to show her emotions instead of having to be stoic in front of the councilors in chambers.

They watched her enter and take the seat they purposely left her. The seat at the head of the table. She raised her hands and gestured at the room as she looked at Luthias. But Luthias spoke before she could, "Chief Justice Travon," he bowed his head. "The room is needed for the news we have for you."

Travon looked at who was in the room and bowed to each. "Clandestine meetings are never good news." She saw Xaika. "You are the knight captain from Kallinstyne are you not?"

Xaika bowed and was going to go through the events in Kallinstyne but figured it needed to come from the others, she wasn't sure she could make it through without breaking down. "Yes, Lady Travon."

"Kaci Goyrok, Knight Hunter of the Dwarven Republic Guard. It is good to finally meet you. Like our own Knight Hunter, Lord Blackridge here, I have heard of your daring exploits. You are a welcome sight among the Inquisition knights. I will add you to the roster as such once we finish with our clandestine meeting."

"Thank you, my lady." Kaci bowed.

Luthias dropped his head and sat in silence for a second as everyone in the room turned to him. He looked up at her with sadness in his eyes. "Chief Justice Travon, I apologize but Jadai died in battle in Kallinstyne and your estate… my lady. I'm sorry no one survived."

Travon fell back hard against her seat. "What? No! They were after me! They should have been safe without me there. I'm the target of the assassinations, I left… so… they…" She dropped her head and started crying. Luthias watched Xaika walk over and hug her. Soon after Xaika joined her in tears. After a few minutes, Travon pulled out of the hug and looked at her through red puffy eyes. "I'm guessing from your reaction, Kallinstyne met the same fate." Xaika looked over at Luthias to speak for her because she was too emotional.

Luthias nodded. "Yes, mam. I'm sorry for the loss of your husband, your staff, and Jadai. But it wasn't an assassin. Hellions flew up from the lava flats and attacked your estate."

Chapter Twenty-Three

Travon looked at Luthias surprised. "But, hellions don't leave the lava flats. They certainly wouldn't fly that far away from their nests without provocation. What caused…" She stopped and dropped her head when the realization hit her. "The demon commands them now."

Luthias nodded solemnly. "Yes, the demon had the hellions attack your estate though we don't know why, especially since this demon is the one who warned you in the first place. But I will say we think she has been interfering in the plans of a cult known as the Jegere av Fijandsvarg."

Travon looked up and patted Xaika on the back as she stood up and walked back to her seat. "Hunters of the wolfiend? What in the hell do they have to do with any of this? I thought they disappeared a thousand years ago, killed by the Elven Shadow Warriors. Are they behind these assassinations?"

Luthias watched Xaika take her seat as he continued, "We believe so. They killed Traemorra's magistrate and his family, Pantreus's magistrate, and the village of Pantreus, as well as Kallinstyne's magistrate and most of the village of Kallinstyne."

"The empress, the prince, but why? Please don't tell me these idiots believe in the silly legend. Half-demon, half-elf…" She looked at Luthias and shook her head. "Half mortal whatever. They can't believe this wolfiend has been alive for all these thousands of years walking among us."

Borgroff watched Luthias tilt his head a bit as if something Travon said or did caught his attention. He would need to remember to ask him about it in private later.

Nakira spoke up as Luthias sat silent. "That is exactly what they believe. They are killing people with royal ties to eliminate it. But these hunters of the wolfiend aren't responsible for the death of the empress, her son, or the Kallinstyne magistrate's daughter."

"We knew this demon had an agenda. They always do. We still aren't sure what it is yet. This demon has been having its wraiths cause chaos killing people, but the demon chose to kill these three victims with daggers."

Luthias watched Borgroff bring out a cloth wrapped around three daggers. "We see nothing extraordinary about these daggers. No difference other than their material. We pulled a bone-handled dagger out of the magistrate's daughter in Kallinstyne, the black obsidian-laced dagger out of the prince, and the other bone-handled dagger out of the empress."

Travon's head snapped up quickly. "Who pulled the daggers out of the victims?"

Confused by the abruptness of her reaction, Luthias answered, "I did. Were we not supposed to for some reason?"

"No, sorry, yes." Travon struggled with a half-hearted smile and looked around. "Sorry, that's not what I meant to imply. You all are the Inquisition knights and answer to no one." She pointed to her newest appointee, Kaci Goyrok when she said the last part. "I just wanted to make sure some random guard wasn't trying to collect keepsakes from the dead, that's all." Luthias watched as Travon smiled uncomfortably. "The dagger that stabbed the prince and the empress would be the talk of the family as an heirloom for generations."

Borgroff decided to bring the attention back to the point of the meeting. "Did any of your staff find anyone else we need to try and protect? Also, did you all find any connection to Luthias in your royal gene pool? I mean this all started with three assassination attempts on his life." He looked over at Nakira. "Sorry, and the one attempt on Nakira's life which would have gotten everyone involved killed."

Nakira smiled at Borgroff as she recounted Luthias's victims so far. "The mercenary in Hells Canyon, the nobleman and the Bagswell brothers in Ridgewood, the assassin in Traemorra, countless mercenaries, Cut-Throat along with his goon squad, and now the infamous, Crimson Shaw who was killed by his own infamous hammer. He is still closing in on everyone involved. All we need is the hunters of the wolfiend and this demon." She reached over and grabbed Luthias's hand as she finished. "Who we believe to be this Fijandsvarg fiend. Untethered."

Luthias chuckled, "And here I thought I came back from Ridgewood to be steered from this course of vengeance." Travon was examining the daggers throughout their banter. "Do you see anything we missed, hidden runes, magic inscriptions, anything? Borgroff also stated the black and red obsidian dagger has a twin somewhere. They were a gift to the Imperial Prince from the Dwarven Republic."

Travon shook her head. "Nothing other than the value of the obsidian dagger and its missing twin being more valuable than the two boned-handled daggers. They are all regular daggers for as far as I can see, but then I'm not trained to see hidden runes. If anything, this demon placed a spell on the daggers before killing them. But the order of the kills and the daggers used in each kill may be what's important. We know the magistrate's daughter in Kallinstyne was last and the demon used one of the two bone-handled daggers. We also know the demon stabbed the empress with the other bone-handled dagger. Although we don't truly know the order in which she killed the empress and the prince, I would hazard a guess she killed the prince with the black and red obsidian dagger then the empress with the first bone-handled dagger." Travon wrapped the daggers back into the cloth and handed them to Luthias.

"Meaning the prince's death was most important to the demon's narrative and is connected to how she uses its twin," he replied as grabbed the bundled-up daggers.

Travon nodded. "For reasons I can't go into until I can confirm my thinking. Luthias, I need you to always keep these with you." She looked at the others. "If I didn't trust you, you wouldn't be a part of this inquisition. But whoever carries them is in more danger than the rest. I'm not comfortable putting any of you in more danger than I already have by naming you, inquisitors."

"But he is the one most likely to survive an attack for the blades," Borgroff said understanding her point. "You think this cult might come after the daggers, don't you?"

She smiled at Borgroff, "Yes, I'm not sure why yet. But I know the daggers fit in with this wolfiend legend somehow." She looked down to see the Fijandsvarg sword hanging from Luthias's side. "I see you have chosen to carry the sword out in the open. Another trap to lure attempts?"

Luthias nodded as he looked at Nakira. "Yes if it is out in the open and a member of the Jegere av Fijandsvarg sees it."

Nakira pulled her hand free of his and slapped his arm. "You've had three attempts already and are trying to attract more? The battles we just endured weren't enough for you yet. Even the dwarves with us are battle-weary. Also the dwarf you just killed with his own hammer said you were number one on his employers list."

Travon laughed at Nakira's response as Luthias spoke, "I have always had one or both of you with me. Now, we also have Kaci and Xaika. So, one of you will be there to save my life."

Luthias looked at Xaika who hung her head in thought for a second then looked back up at him. "If you wouldn't mind." She stood up and walked to stand by Travon's chair. "I believe I will stay and be Chief Justice Travon's knight protector. I believe with the loss of Jadai she could use the protection." She turned and looked at Travon. "If she will have me that is."

"It would be my honor to have the oldest daughter of the Orc Republic's High Priestess as my knight protector." She winked at Xaika. "I don't know if it speaks ill of me or Luthias that he needs three protectors while I only need one." She turned to look at Borgroff and the large red war hammer on his back and the two battle hammers on his side. "You sir, look like the epic image of a hero dwarf if I've ever seen one."

He looked down at himself then over his shoulder and realized he was carrying all three hammers. "Sorry, with everything we've talked about, I forgot I had it on my back. I guess I do look a little hammered."

Travon chuckled, "That war hammer has nothing but evil deeds in its history considering I hear he was also the blacksmith who forged it. An old elven man once told me shadow warriors believe not only in the restoration of the mortal soul but also in the restoration of a weapon's soul. If any weapon deserves to earn a good soul, it is one that has never experienced a good soul to begin with."

Luthias looked down. "I had forgotten those words. My grandfather once told me the same thing. He said he once had a sword when he was young. He had given it a bad reputation then someone stole it from him. He told me he wished he could have given it a good soul. I never really understood what he meant until now."

Kaci smiled, "When we leave here, I will take it back to Old Man Groff and have him reforge it for Borgroff." Travon nodded at her.

Borgroff smiled at the mention of his father's nickname. "If anyone can reforge Red Death and give it a good soul, dad can."

Travon stood up and walked over to Luthias as he stood up. "Thank you for all you have done so far. Your payment is waiting at the front desk. I hope you put an end to all this tragedy soon."

Luthias bowed. "I hope you don't mind we took the liberty of burying everyone at the estate just up from the lake's edge. We chose a spot near the bench you sat on and watched the dragon's fly." He saw her look up at the mention of the dragons. "All three were there and still alive. They helped us defeat the hellions when they returned to kill us."

He watched her smile and nod her head. "The old man would sit down there for hours watching them while I read my books. You picked the perfect spot for him to rest and wait on me, thank you."

They bowed as she walked out. The rest quickly got back into the wagon and headed towards Traemorra. It was dark once again by the time they arrived. Kaci left the group just past Twin Cliffs and promised to meet up with them the next day in Traemorra. Inside the Red Dog, Luthias didn't even stop to talk to Amunique, instead, he headed upstairs to his room after getting a kiss from Nakira. "What's up with Luthias? He never misses a drink and a chat before bed, especially when there are important matters to discuss."

Nakira looked upstairs towards the room as she spoke. "I'm not sure. He was quiet the whole ride here from Gatesboro. Asked if Borgroff and I minded updating you and he would talk to you and Clive in the morning."

Borgroff sat quietly wondering if it had to do with what caused Luthias to tilt his head while Travon was talking about the wolfiend. He knew he should bring it up, but he wanted to bring it up to Luthias first just in case it wasn't important or about the case. Nakira had enough to worry about, he didn't need to add to it without reason, so he just remained quiet.

Amunique could see the worry in her eyes when Nakira turned back to look at her. She could also see unspoken worries in Borgroff's features as well. "I can imagine you all are tired from whatever happened and from your ride back here." She looked over at Nera, limping a bit. "It also looks like Nera could use the rest." Amunique walked over and let Nera into her office. "You my dear can sleep in here with me tonight. You all need your rest as well.

Once you all get up, we can talk. I will make sure Clive is here as well. Borgroff, the first room in the back hallway is open and yours." She watched them all disperse, appearing tired and beaten, which told her the news in the morning was going to be unwelcome. She walked outside and whispered into the wind then watched a raven take off in flight. "I just hope we are not too late."

Chapter Twenty-Four

Luthias sat on the edge of the bed. He'd barely been able to sleep. When he woke back up for the hundredth time since laying down with Nakira, he'd looked over and saw another note on the side table. Now, he sat there dressed in his armor and gambeson jacket. In his hand, he held the last note he'd discovered.

He read over it after writing a personal note to Nakira. But two sections seemed to pop off the paper at him. He repeated the lines aloud. "The chaos brings with it a tainted darkness. A darkness that captures whoever dares enter, caging them for eternity. The path into the darkness leads to the only fate worse than death, eternal imprisonment." He looked up from the paper and saw Nakira sleeping peacefully. "I love you. You'll know what to do."

***

A female figure enveloped within the red mist floated down from the graveyard in Kallinstyne known as Knights Hill. She floated through the courtyard of Kallinstyne. She looked around at the thick red cloud settling over the area. "Magnificent work. I want everything from the west Katerra border to the Santos River in the east and from the Ziamicawl mountain lava flats south of here to the Sea of Souls coastline in the north bathed in the tainted darkness." She watched the wraith before her bow then felt the breeze as it disappeared.

She looked up when she heard the wings of a hellion fluttering above her descending into sight. "I want the Santos River dug out down to the Soman border. I need this red taint confined so it can strengthen enough to call the Fijandsvarg forth to the surface." She waved her hand and watched the hellion disappear back up into the dark red fog settling down over the area.

A brown terrier walked out of the dense cloud and came up to the figure in the mist. It stood on its hind legs waving its front paws begging her to pick it up. She bent down, picked it up then headed into Kallinstyne castle. "He is the only original royal bloodline. The rest were simply born of pretenders who bought and lied their way into their prominent titles. This kingdom was supposed to be the might of his rule. Our rule. What was once torn asunder will be reforged again. We will rule together what we once should have. Blackvale was to be ours. It will be ours once again." She looked down at the dog. "Go back to the void for now my sweet. I have lots to prepare."

She heard the dog whine a bit just before it disappeared into a black mist that dissipated from her hands.

***

Nakira smiled a sleepy smile and rolled over. She reached for Luthias but only found a cold pillow and empty sheets wrinkled up on the bed. She looked at the nightstand and saw another note with a wax seal lying beneath the sword Fijandsvarg's blade. But unlike the rest of the notes, it was already lying open.

She wanted to hope she could walk out with the letter and find Luthias down at the bar looking up at her smiling and teasing her for sleeping in. But deep down she knew he had left alone with Nera before anyone awoke. Nakira reluctantly picked up the note and read it. As she did tears filled her eyes and streamed down her cheeks. She quickly dressed and ran down to the bar.

Borgroff looked at the letter in her hand and saw the tears in her eyes. "What's wrong? Where's Luthias?"

"Judging by the tears in her eyes and the letter in her hands." Amunique answered, "He has run off to finish this after putting together the final pieces." Borgroff and Nakira looked at Amunique. "Let me see the note dear." Nakira walked over and handed the note to Amunique. She then sat down and leaned against Borgroff as he wrapped his arm over her shoulder and consoled her.

Amunique read the note aloud, *"As the seconds tick away, chaos spreads across the land. The chaos brings with it a tainted darkness. A darkness that captures whoever dares enter, caging them for eternity. The dragon fairy naively thinks darkness leads to chaos. But in her defense, darkness caged her soul two thousand years ago, when the dragon fairy lost her love. In the second true love was torn*

163

asunder that night, her world went shadow and stopped making sense. It was at that second that the chaos truly began.

Luthias, return to the ancient city where darkness and chaos were born. Return to Blackvale City and reforge what was once torn asunder. It is the only way to stop the chaos and bring her out of the dark cage encasing her heart. We will always be watching. Don't forget the daggers and your beloved companion.

Nakira, I know I promised to always keep you or Borgroff with me, but for what I must do next, I must do it alone with Nera. I love you and promise to try and return to you when I'm able. Please, whatever you hear do not follow my path into chaos and darkness. Do not let Borgroff follow me either, tie him up if necessary. The path into the darkness leads to the only fate worse than death, eternal imprisonment. I fear the chaos I would wreak if anything were to happen to either of you. Know that my heart is always yours and only you can restore my tainted soul from the chaos and darkness. Signed, Luthias Blackridge, E.S.W."

As Amunique finished reading the letter aloud, Xaika walked in with Travon, Kaci, and Clive. "He didn't say anything about Kaci and me not following him into the darkness. Tell us where Blackvale City is, and we will help him end this."

"As much as I would love to be on board with the plan to disobey him and follow him anyway," Borgroff said lowering his head. "I fear this is how it has to finish." Xaika looked at the dwarf and started to protest when Travon cut her off.

"You are correct my dwarven hero, but his quest is only half of what must be done." Travon bowed and looked at Amunique. "It is good to see you again."

Amunique bowed her head as well. "It is good to see you as well. It has been too long. You all come sit down beside Borgroff and Nakira. It is time we tell you what we now know to be true." She watched them sit down as Travon came and stood beside her. "Chief Justice Travon and I are half-sisters."

"Wait, you're an orc, she's elven," Clive said making Amunique and Travon smile.

Borgroff pounded the bar. "Half-sisters meaning they are sisters in the cult. They are the Jegere av Fijandsvarg."

Amunique chuckled at Borgroff shaking her head. "No, we share the maternal bond in our mother, but it is our fathers who are different. My mother and father are both orcs, her father was of elven descent. Our mother was an oracle like me. She saw a vision showing her the death of everything. This vision showed her an image of the wolfiend being reforged into one being. Then it showed him imprisoning the world in darkness and bringing about a demon apocalypse. She then saw another vision which could avoid the demon apocalypse.”

“Having a child with an elven druid.” Both looked over at Xaika and smiled.

“What does a fortune-telling old elven druid and a psychic orc have to do with this wolfiend and its demon apocalypse?” Clive asked as he sat confused shaking his head. “Never mind, I know he told us not to help but if we told him not to help us, we all know he would be walking into the fires of the demon realm right beside us. Why are we not trying to track him down?”

“To answer your first question, where oracles see visions of what might happen, elven druids see how the present and past shape different paths into the future.” They all looked back over at Xaika as she spoke. “Kallinstyne library had extensive knowledge and I was bored with plenty of time to read.”

“We need to see about bringing that library to the council chambers and preserving it. If the demonic taint isn’t ruining them already. Kallinstyne library has thousands of years of texts, letters, books, and arcane knowledge. Volumes of books dating back to the time when it was known by its original name, Blackvale City. It used to be the biggest city anywhere.” Everyone looked at Travon as she spoke.

“The city named in the letter! Come on Kaci, Xaika, Nakira.” Borgroff stood up and headed to the door.

“Sit down little man, you are not going anywhere, yet.” He turned and stared at Amunique in anger. “I want to do the same thing. I want to march off to Kallinstyne and save our friend. All of us in this room want to do that. But my sister, Vanya and I are telling you if we do it wrong, then the first vision our mother had will come true anyway. Death to all.”

Borgroff hung his head. “Not only do we lose Luthias, but we kill everyone else depending on us.”

“Yes,” Vanya spoke as they watched Borgroff walk back over and sit down. Amunique poured some ale for everyone as Vanya spoke.

"The two visions our mother had, showed her different versions of events surrounding the Fijandsvarg fiend. The first vision should not have happened after I was born. Our mother told us both visions just in case." She looked over at Amunique. "Then she told us we were not allowed to see each other ever again nor speak of our relationship unless the inevitable happened."

"The inevitable meaning portions of both visions started coming true." They looked at Nakira and nodded. "The vision before Travon's birth showed the demon and the daggers. The vision afterward showed the sword and the Jegere av Fijandsvarg which came to be known as the Elven Shadow Warriors. But here we are dealing with both groups and all of the blades from the visions."

Amunique nodded at Nakira. "How did you figure it out?"

"When you two were talking I was sitting here going over what all we learned in my mind. Going over the events, swords, daggers, letters, everything. Then this last letter popped up in my head tying everything together. Every other letter with the wolf's head seal came unsigned simply saying we are watching. Luthias signed it with ESW telling me about the Jegere av Fijandsvarg, shadow warrior connection. I also know who the demon is, it's Jadai. She planned her death in Kallinstyne." She looked at Borgroff. "That is why the wraith attacked Luthias allowing Crimson to kill her. It allowed her to stay behind as the demon and work on her plan without having to hide her identity from us."

Borgroff nodded. "You two did seem confused about her death."

Nakira nodded. "Jadai told us she was an angel wraith."

Borgroff pounded his fist on the bar. "The dragon fairy naively thinks darkness leads to chaos. But in her defense, darkness caged her soul two thousand years ago, when the dragon fairy lost her love."

Nakira smiled halfheartedly at Borgroff as he recited a portion of the note. "Yes, she also has a dragon fairy tattoo on the back of her thigh extending down her leg."

"So, wait. Are we saying Luthias Blackridge is the…?" Clive sat the tankard of ale down on the bar. "Luthias is the descendant of this wolfiend, how many of them have there been, and how many knew?"

"Only one Fijandsvarg has ever existed," They all turned to see the antique dealer standing inside the doorway. "But he has been known by many names over the two thousand plus years. Also, at any given time only two people at a time ever knew. Jadai was not the wolfiend. Luthias is."

"I hope you have news that will help us save Luthias." Borgroff turned back around and stared at the full tankard of ale he hadn't touched. "The deities know all we are doing is sitting around telling tales while he goes off to fight alone."

"He's not alone. He took his wolf. I also have agents who are following him. Though they don't know why. All they know is to keep him safe until such time he reaches the Santos River."

Clive stared at the thin, aged, scholarly-looking man as he closed the door and walked up to the bar. "I don't mean any offense but what kind of agents could an antique dealer have? What are your agents going to do? Recite ancient texts at the demon? Bore it with a story?"

The scholar laughed as he sat down beside Clive, "I take no offense as that means my disguise has worked, keeping me safe and unseen. Allow me to reintroduce myself to you all, I am Russington Restwell. I am a direct descendant of the founding member of the Jegere av Fijandsvarg. Well, the Elven Shadow Warriors after they infiltrated and changed the original group's mission anyway. I come from a lengthy line of individuals who have all quietly watched over the Fijandsvarg since the original council separated the demon half from the mortal half. The original mage council died performing the separation, they chose my ancestor to remain and watch over both souls. He was also given a special spell that was handed down from generation to generation. This spell allowed the original soul of Riven Blackvale to be reborn over and over again as a new identity." He looked over at Nakira. "Although, he does die it's not a literal death as we mortals know it. Upon death his soul waits between realms in what is known as the void. Once the spell is spoken and the magic performed, a chosen individual within whatever community we've moved to is blessed with a pregnancy. Riven's soul is pulled from the void into the chosen female and he is reborn."

Borgroff stared at him with a confused angry look on his face. "He is reborn? How the hell many times have you all messed with his head like this?"

"Many more times than anyone wanted to. The procedure uses a powerful magical spell that leaves the job of watching over him to the next descendant in line." He watched as they all looked up at him. "As the original council can tell you, all magical powers come with a cost. In my case, since I couldn't father children, my niece was to take over the next life cycle. But with the events currently ongoing, that option I'm afraid might no longer be available. May I see that note you hold?"

Amunique handed the letter over to him. "It's just like the others you sent. You are the one leaving these, correct?"

"No, I have never left notes for him. The only note I ever wrote that he possessed was the first one he took from the nobleman. I didn't, however, write the rest addressed directly to him. But I believe this note might be about his former lover, Zoriyah Ralinder of Blackvale City." He looked up to see their confusion. "Sorry, you all know her as Jadai. Zoriyah was, according to legend, the girlfriend of the original soul and knew about the wolfiend. A distant relative a thousand years ago was the first to report her appearance. We didn't know until Jadai appeared who she was exactly. We only knew that she was either a demon or a daemon and following the soul through his lives. She would assume a new host and change her appearance with each new rebirth of Riven to hide among the masses. But each generation since him has learned who she was just before we moved him. We need to get Fijandsvarg's blade to him before he uses the daggers. He did need to go to meet her, but he needed Fijandsvarg's blade as well. Someone laced the daggers with a shadow magic spell that captured the souls of whomever they killed. She will have him stab her with the daggers believing he's releasing the souls into her. He will think the souls are helping to release her from the demonic power she is under by making her a mortal spirit again, thereby sending her soul back to the spirit realm with the Divine Spirits. But she is absorbing the souls so that when she stabs him with the last dagger all the souls will travel into him, demon included. The three tainted souls from the daggers will help bind his soul so hers can take control over Fijandsvarg. We are not a hundred percent sure, but that's the theory handed down through the generations."

"Reforging what was once torn asunder." Nakira looked down as she continued, "Their love. She doesn't want to just be with the man she knew, she wants to become a part of him. Once joined, she can never be apart from him again. Her soul forever linked to Riven's."

Russington looked at Nakira and nodded. "That's the theory. He needs the sword so he can join his demon and mortal sides back together before this happens. It is the only way he can see the truth through the darkness and chaos."

Amunique spoke up, "Two halves of anything combined becomes one. The two halves of the demons will combine to become one full-blood demon. An untethered full-blood demon loose in this realm unbound to any mortal soul."

Russington shook his head. "Again this is all based on theory and two thousand years worth of speculation. But the full blood demon would be bound to Luthias's soul, if we hurry and make it to him in time. Without his wolf side, they would be bound to one of the mortal souls she possesses. Empress, young prince, or the magistrate's daughter. Jadai, the mortal soul she possessed in this life cycle died due to Red Death. The darkness within would have his mortal soul caged for eternity."

"That is why she stabbed the prince with the obsidian dagger. He is meant to be the soul in charge," Vanya said drawing their attention.

"Wait, I'm confused. If he and Nera stay as two separate beings, isn't that better? I mean she is the beast here not Luthias. He is the mortal half. She is the beast or demon half."

Russington looked down. "According to information handed down through the generations, the original council disguised the mortal half so that it was hidden in plain sight."

Borgroff drew one of his hammers off his hip, slammed the bar hard with it then pointed it at Russington. "We are sitting here chatting and telling tales while my best friend is walking into a demonic death trap that will turn him into a who knows what. I am at my wit's end. Speak without the idjit riddles or the next swing is upside your infernal head and we look for a new scholar." Goyrok reached over and put her hand on his shoulder. As he looked at her, she shook her head.

Russington bowed his head. "Sorry, good sir. I didn't mean to upset you or anyone else here. What I mean is, we believe Nera is the mortal soul, and Luthias is the demon. With each rebirth process the demon, Luthias, goes through, his mortal side dies and is reborn as well. Rebirthing a demon and keeping it in mortal form is difficult enough and as I said costs the mage their life. Re-birthing an actual mortal in this form would take many mages and cost every one of them their lives each time. As was the case with the first council. But rebirthing a mortal soul in animal form is easier, and we combine it with the demon's rebirth. No one pays attention to the animals of the wild, so the original council decided to hide the mortal side in the form of an animal of the wild. The people scared enough to hunt and kill him, the ones who formed the original Jegere av Fijandsvarg already classified him as a wolfiend. Thus, the original members chose to hide his mortal soul in the form of a natural wolf of the wild. Though it hasn't always returned as a wolf, other times it has been a jaguar, a raven, and even a few times as a dragon but always male. This is the only time I know of the mortal side showed up as a female.

Nakira dropped her head. "So, if he is not combined with his mortal side from Nera before she performs her ritual, he will lose his chance to become mortal."

"We do not know for sure but that is the working theory." He watched Borgroff's hand tighten up on the hammer in his hand. "None of this has ever happened. All we have are theories and speculations. I was in the process of moving Luthias when things went beyond Luthias's control."

"Okay, you, I, Kaci, and Nakira ride to Kallinstyne, Blackvale City, wherever, and do what is necessary to save Luthias. The rest will do," He paused and looked at Vanya and Amunique. "What else is needed to be done?"

Amunique smiled at him, "We need to rid the world of this darkness. In the original vision, the darkness is kept in place by the elements of fire and water until the demon was healed into one being. Then the demon used its power to spread the darkness and chaos imprisoning the world in eternal darkness."

Vanya spoke up when Amunique went silent, "But in the altered version with my birth, the darkness is driven back by Fijandsvarg's power. We need to help everyone west of the Santos River escape the area before the darkness overtakes, imprisons, or kills them. Then we need to make sure it has no escape. We need to destroy bridges and dig trenches extending water routes. I will call the dragons from the lake to help with their fire where needed."

"But little man, there is one flaw with your plan. The chaos brings with it a tainted darkness that captures whoever dares enter, caging them for eternity." Amunique looked at him then at Clive. "Yes, he would walk side by side with any of us into the fires of Knarran. Hell, he'd be leading the charge. But let's face it, even before we knew what and who he is now, we all knew he was no normal mortal. I mean he is an elf the size of an overgrown orc. Hell, I bet even the dark lord, Koraegin himself would tremble at Luthias' approach. Anyone who follows him into the darkness of the taint may die before they ever reach him."

"I have us covered in that respect." They all turned to look at Russington. "I can keep the four of us protected from the taint long enough to get the sword to him and explain what we know." He looked hard at Nakira, Kaci, and Borgroff. "But any longer and we all become hideous wraiths doing the bidding of a master for eternity. Not even a reforged Fijandsvarg can help us then. Hell, if he is evil then we would still be doing Luthias's bidding."

"And I fear the chaos I would wreak if anything was to happen to either of you." Amunique quoted the note making Borgroff nod somberly.

"I understand. Nakira, Grab the sword. Let's go save the hero of this Zjenica Robleus novel."

Vanya smiled and nodded. "We will travel with you to the Santos River then begin our preparations to make sure the demon apocalypse won't come to fruition." She sighed, "Or at least is contained."

Chapter Twenty-Five

Luthias and Nera approached the bridge leading to the royal palace. Nera hunkered down into an attack position growling as she peered across to the other side. He knelt and petted Nera. "Yeah, I feel it too. We need to torch this bridge to stop its advance." Luthias walked to the edge of the bridge as he looked towards Santos Isle. "I hope the soldiers got out of there and back to Romnuuski before the taint took over. Divine be with them if not." He closed his eyes and spoke softly, "Brannkaste." Black fire shot from his hands spreading across the bridge. He stood there staring into the blackened flames as the bridge burnt then fell into the dark waters of the Sea of Souls.

Nera's bark brought his mind back to the present. "Sorry girl. I know we need to get moving." They traveled to the bridge crossing over to the west side of the Santos River. "We need to burn this one too." He looked at Nera who barked and growled at him. "Yes, I know they are going to need it to help get people out of danger." He sighed, "Okay girl, but I hope they see what we have done with the bridge to Santos Isle and do the same here." He chuckled halfheartedly as she barked again wagging her tail. "You have a good soul girl. I am a better person having you as my companion."

He looked at the road leading to Ridgewood then at the river's edge. Nera must have had the same thought because she walked over to the edge of the river and then looked back at him. "Yeah, the river's edge is the safest route. We can follow it down to Pantreus. But from there we'll have to brave the taint into Kallinstyne to find the demon. The antagonist hidden in clear view. Keep your eyes and ears open. We don't know what she has planned." Nera growled then turned and trotted off along the river's edge wagging her tail. Luthias watched her. "Shadows hide us in our battles, divine preserve us if we fall." Luthias looked back towards Ridgewood hoping his friends would evacuate everyone before the tainted darkness reached them.

He knew Nakira and Borgroff will want to help him but entering the darkness is a death sentence. If he is what he thinks he is, then hearing about their deaths would set a vengeful untethered demon loose upon the world. It wasn't until Travon spoke that he understood what was happening. He looked back towards the east as he rode on to catch up with Nera. He knows they will try anyway because they know he would as well. He just hopes he can defeat the demon and find a way to rid the darkness before it can kill or corrupt them.

***

Borgroff and company rode up to the gates of Fort Romnuuski quickly. They watched the guards draw weapons at the hurried approach of seven riders. "Whoa, it's okay. This is one of the inquisition knights." Borgroff looked up to see the orc commandant from Santos Isle and the royal palace. "Whatever he needs of us we provide."

Vanya looked at Borgroff and smiled, "The epic dwarven hero." She turned back to the orc. "The dwarf needs a rider to head to Crosspoint Fortress. They need to send a battalion of soldiers to help evacuate Fort Gambit at the Council of King's request. I will need every other soldier from Crosspoint to meet the inquisition knights at the bridge crossing over towards Riverwood." She watched as a young elf quickly mounted a horse and rode off.

"I need the soldiers of Romnuuski to ride with Lady Amunique and Chief Justice Travon to help with the evacuation of people from Shadow Pass, Ridgewood, Terra Muse, Souls Port, and Orc Point. There is a tainted darkness coming up from the south. It contains demons and wraiths. We have ships arriving from Traemorra to carry everyone, but they must have time to evacuate them."

Borgroff rode up beside the orc and leaned over. "I personally need the men from the elite group you told me about in Santos." He whispered low to the orc so no one else could hear his words. He leaned back and the orc nodded his head definitively and gave him the evil smile he and Luthias saw in the royal palace. Borgroff smiled, "It's up to every man if they wish to come because this will most likely be a suicide ride. Let them know the truth about the danger. But if they don't help then they help protect the people evacuating." The orc bowed and hurried off.

173

The rest rode up beside Borgroff as Nakira asked, "Are you sure it was wise to tell them this will lead them to their deaths? We have Luthias and Nera at stake in the taint, but they don't. They have loved ones here."

"They will show up. These are hardened veterans," the gate guard from Santos said as he walked up to Borgroff. "We all will gladly lay our lives down for the inquisition knights. I know I am green but if you have me, I will gladly accompany you."

Borgroff climbed down from his horse as the commandant walked up. "I have a better idea. I have a feeling the commandant will be riding for me. I need someone I trust to lead the rest of the men from Romnuuski protecting the villagers and people helping with the evacuation." The young soldier looked at his superior officer.

"I am indeed riding and so are all the elite soldiers. They are all on board already knowing the outcome. An honorable death awaits us." He looked at the young gate guard. "I will make sure the rest know you are in charge per the inquisition knight's orders."

Nakira rode up beside Borgroff and slowly repeated the words Vanya said. "Epic… dwarven… hero. Luthias would be proud. I know I am."

He bowed his head and smiled, "Thank you." He turned to look at the orc commandant. "Get your men ready we ride as quickly as possible. I will fill you all in on your mission once we get there."

Russington rode up beside him. "Uh, dwarf. I wish to remind you I won't be able to protect any of these men. It will be quite the strain on my magic to protect us four."

He looked up with a bit of sadness in his eyes. "They know this is a suicide mission. It's why I told the commandant to be honest with them. But more importantly, they aren't coming with us. I am sending them into the taint from Shadow Pass. They are riding and killing anything they come across until they reach one of two outcomes. Death or Kallinstyne, then whoever shows up, leaves with us, if the taint hasn't corrupted them."

Kaci looked at Borgroff. "A distraction for us and a chance to kill as many demons as possible thereby giving the others more of a chance to evacuate everyone. No more glorious death than death in battle against a demon horde in protection of others."

Borgroff smiled at her comment, "Come on, let's head to the saloon and get a bite to eat and some ale. I need to steady my nerves." He looked over at Nakira. "Now I see why we all follow Luthias. I don't like this leading the pack crap." He smiled, "I'll let him lead while I and my hammers cause the noise in the background."

***

Luthias and Nera followed the river's edge down until he knew they were close to Pantreus. He approached the village seeing the changes the red taint had already made killing everything in its wake. "I wish I had brought Fijandsvarg's blade. Something tells me I may be sorry I left it behind." He looked down at Nera and watched as she stopped and looked around. "What's up girl?" Luthias climbed down from his horse, walked over, and knelt to pet her. "My senses are all over the place and my gut is worthless right now. You are going to have to be my instincts until we get out of this red death cloud."

Before he could continue, Nera growled and jumped forward seemingly snapping at the air. Luthias heard the shriek of a wraith and looked down to see a pool of sticky black liquid form on the ground. He already had a feeling they were all around him, but he didn't know what made her snap and kill that one. He stood up and decided he was tired of the hide-and-seek games. "If you are here and mean me no harm unless your demon master instructs it, appear before me now, or the wolf and I start killing as we go."

Luthias lifted his crossbow and loaded it as Nera began growling and looking all around. He wasn't sure why, but he believed she could see the wraiths despite them still being invisible to him. "At the count of three we start killing at random and the wolf will be guiding my hand, telling me where to shoot my cross bolts." He looked around and saw nothing appearing,

"One." Nera growled and snapped her head to her left quickly. He turned in the direction she turned. He took aim. "Two." Nera continued to stare around her but kept her body facing the same direction. "Three." Luthias fired the cross-bolt and watched it fly straight and dig into a tree about fifty paces away. He heard several shrieks along the bolts path. He looked down, and saw five pools of black liquid appear on the ground in a straight path leading to the tree.

He dropped the crossbow and let it slide back under his jacket. He then pulled his sword out. "This sword may not be the sword known

175

as Fijandsvarg's blade, but it is sharp enough to send you wraiths painfully shrieking back to the demon realm. Despite my warnings to my friends, I know that they are on their way so the more of you I kill the less of you they will need to fight through." He looked down at Nera who had turned slightly left. He slashed his sword out and down sending another shrieking wraith down to the ground in a pool of black liquid.

As the liquid pooled onto the ground, Nera began to growl and bark all around her. He knew that meant they were closing in on him he drew the black obsidian dagger out and kept it in his left hand while keeping his falchion sword in his right. "Okay, let's do this then." He slashed out with his right and then stabbed with his left causing another shrieking pool to form. Out of the corner of his eye, he saw Nera jump forward and heard another shriek. As he did, he felt a set of claws dig into his left shoulder, the same place the hellion had got him years ago and the same place the wraith got him in Kallinstyne, keeping him from shooting Crimson and saving Jadai. He spun around and slashed across his body with the dagger sending the wraith shrieking to the ground.

Luthias slashed out again with the right hand, hearing the shriek of another wraith dying. He heard three more shrieks around him as Nera killed more. Nera then surprised him by walking over and laying down at his feet. He looked around to see five wraiths appear in front of him floating just a few feet away. He wondered what had just transpired but knew he wouldn't get answers from any of them or Nera.

He watched as they parted, making a path between them towards the main square of Pantreus. Luthias walked down the middle of them and stopped. He looked around at the five wraiths and smiled. He raised his weapons and sliced outward with both weapons beside him killing two. He then spun with the sword and dagger straight out and killed two more. He watched Nera chase down, jump and kill the last one.

"That was for making me play hide and seek. I always hated that game as a kid. Hated hiding in the darkness." Nera walked up beside him and sat down. "Are they all dead?" He smiled when she barked and wagged her tail. "Good, but keep your eyes and ears open, from now on we don't play hide and seek. If you see or hear them, we kill them." Nera barked, got up, and spun around in a circle as Luthias laughed and climbed back up onto his horse. "Come on, let's get to Kallinstyne and find this demon."

***

Jadai floated around within the dark red taint filled court square of Kallinstyne. But in her mind, through Zoriyah's eyes, she saw the center square of the bustling city of Blackvale. She could see the city stretching as far as she could see in every direction. She could see the river running through the middle of the city providing beautiful scenery and a natural water source as it ran to empty into the icy waters of the Sea of Souls.

She could see the shops with their ornate architecture lining the streets leading towards the castle. She could see the variety of shoppers; peasants, travelers, and upper-class nobles that came to shop. Even Prince Blackvale would come to the shops just before closing. She could see the houses, from run-down shacks to the upscale houses of the nobles built closer to Castle Blackvale. Suddenly she heard a bark which brought her mind back to reality and to the red taint filled Kallinstyne.

The beautiful river that used to run into the city center is now nothing more than an overgrown forgotten border river dividing two sides that were once one. "This village of Kallinstyne is a pale comparison to the city of Blackvale. With any luck, we will rebuild Blackvale now that Kallinstyne is dead and buried."

She lost so much the night they killed her lover and best friend. He had promised to marry her and make her his queen once he ascended to the throne. It didn't matter to him that she was not of royal blood just like it didn't matter to her what they said about him being a beast fit only to die. She knew their souls were bound to each other for eternity, no matter how many lifetimes it took. They hid him from her for so long, but her patience won out. He was on his way back to her.

The brown terrier in her arms began barking again. "What is it?" She looked up to see a wraith appear in front of her. "Yes, yes what is it?"

"There is an unnatural disturbance in Pantreus. He…is not what we believe. His anger is rising, his mind seems confused. The taint is feeding off his rage. He killed all the wraiths you sent to watch over

177

him. If I may suggest my lady, I would rather you hide and wait within the shadows. Judge when the best time to approach him from within the safety of the mist. The taint is affecting him differently than we believed it would."

"We knew it would affect him and we discussed wraiths would die and be sent back to the realm."

"Yes, my lady, but he is not using Fijandsvarg to kill them. I don't sense it on him."

"Then he is using his crossbow or his blade. It is of no matter. We can retrieve the sword later for the prince to fill with souls."

"But my lady, besides the crossbow and his sword he has taken to using the black obsidian dagger made for the prince."

"No, we don't know what the wraith souls will do to the spell holding the prince's soul." Jadai closed her eyes and concentrated on her surroundings. "Damn it! You're right, something within the taint is off somehow. It seems energized by a dark energy. I can sense his rage breaking free. Tell the other wraiths to keep their distance but watch him. He is already dangerous, if his rage takes over, he will be uncontrollable. I need to know immediately if that happens." With a breeze of air, the wraith before her disappeared. "I need to do some more research how to fix this?" She hastily took off into Kallinstyne castle.

Chapter Twenty-Six

THe group stopped and stared at the burnt and smoldering remains of the bridge leading to Santos Isle and the Royal Palace. Nakira turned and looked at the others. "Looks like Luthias is aware of the danger he is heading into."

Borgroff nodded. "Let's just hope he didn't burn the bridge in front of us to slow us down knowing we weren't going to listen to him." He looked to his left to see the orc ride up beside him. "Well, commandant, I hope you didn't leave anyone alive behind because if you did, they aren't alive now."

The large orc stared at the thick red cloud hovering across the moat of icy water. "It was completely clear after we buried the dead and left for Romnuuski. Some of the men wanted to stay behind to make sure no one disturbed the graves. I'm glad I didn't allow it. If the empress and prince would have been buried here, I would have insisted on someone staying behind."

"I wasn't taking the chance," Vanya said from behind them. "That's why I had their remains taken to the mausoleum underneath Gatesboro's council building. They are resting in peace along with the Traemorra magistrate and his family."

The large orc bowed his head. "I'm glad I didn't have to leave anyone behind to die that way."

Borgroff smirked when he looked at the orc. "Yet, here we are, riding back into it to die that way anyway."

The orc turned to Borgroff and smiled. "Yes, but we are riding into it to die an honorable death. They will sing songs about us for the next hundred years. And we do so in the company of two epic dwarven heroes and a wily roguish heroine." He laughed loud and hard causing his entire body to shake.

Amunique spoke up behind them, "Let's save the hero songs and worship for when we are far away from this dark taint. We need to get these four villages safely aboard the ships and to Traemorra."

They rode for a while and were relieved to find the bridge they needed to cross was still safe and sound. Borgroff looked back at the soldiers. "Okay, I need some soldiers guarding this bridge until the Crosspoint battalion gets here." Two soldiers rode forward. "Good. After they cross, burn this bridge then lead them up the shoreline to Ridgewood. If Ridgewood is empty, then head on to Terra Muse. You all are to find Lady Amunique once you get there." The soldiers saluted.

"The commandant and his men will ride with us along the river's edge a while longer. The others will ride with Amunique and Travon to Shadow Pass and begin the evacuation. Hit the southernmost villages first. This should make Souls Port your final evacuation point. Be mindful of your surroundings. You will encounter demons and wraiths. This trip is a death sentence for some of us but each of us knows every morning could be the last sunrise we wake up to. If you are among the lucky to see another. Then dedicate each one you see to the people we lose."

Amunique rode up to look at Borgroff, Nakira, and Kaci. She reached her hands out taking a hold of Borgroff's and Nakira's while smiling at Kaci. "Luthias would be proud of that speech. I know I am. You two go be the epic dwarven heroes and you my lady rogue, you go be smart and mischievous. I will have all the ale you want waiting for you at the Red Dog." She leaned over to Nakira and hugged her. "Bring them back to me, will you?" She looked at Kaci. "I don't know you yet, but I already know you will be the thing the demon didn't see coming."

Nakira wiped a tear away from her eyes and watched Amunique ride off with the Romnuuski soldiers. She looked at Borgroff who was already looking at her. "What do you say we go save the true hero of this Zjenica Robleus novel and get back to the Red Dog for that ale?"

He watched as she wiped more tears away. He knew she was like Luthias and not much scared her, so he figured the tears were for the only fear she knew, the fear of losing the man she loved. "Let's go kill this demon bitch."

"You got it, boss man," Nakira said making Borgroff shake his head.

They rode along the river's edge until they saw the red wall cloud approaching from the south. "Commandant, I want you and your men to form a line along the leading edge of the darkness. Kill as many demons and wraiths as you can." Borgroff reached out and grabbed the orc's hand. "Fight fiercely. Die honorably."

They watched the orc, and his elite soldiers ride off towards the approaching line of red taint as Russington spoke somberly. "Divine preserve us all."

***

Luthias stopped at the edge of the woods and stared deep into the red tainted darkness all around him. His grandfather helped him learn to appreciate the darkness but the atmosphere within this darkness embodied the eerie feeling Luthias had in Traemorra and Ridgewood ten times over.

"There will come a time when you must embrace the darkness and use it to your advantage." He repeated the words as they bounced around in his mind. The words taking on an eerie meaning within this red taint full of death. With everything that had happened, he now knew there was a deeper meaning to the words than simply not being afraid of the darkness.

Luthias pushed the thoughts to the back of his mind and stared into the red taint towards Kallinstyne. "As darkness spreads, something sinister creeps within." He wasn't sure where the last words came from, but they appeared in his thoughts, and he felt the urge to say them aloud.

He urged his horse forward, taking in the sights around him. The trees were dark gray and withered, as if they were dead from age. Some of the tree limbs reminded him of the old psychic's crippled arthritic fingers and hands. "A little over a day ago these woods were lush, green, and full of colorful life." In his mind, he could still hear the bird's songs in the wind as the insects on the ground joined in with harmony.

He remembered the trees full of green leaves. He looked down at the hard, cracked, gray ground and could remember his horse's hoofs striding on lush green grass kicking up soft brown dirt. In his mind, he could see the yellow, red, pink, and purple wildflowers growing in patches all along the path. The evil red taint left over from the death wraiths and demons has killed all signs of life. Another form of red death taunting his existence. Luthias brought his horse to a

181

halt again as mixed emotions rose to the surface. Sadness that someone could snuff out life so completely. Anger that someone could be so cruel as to want to snuff out life so completely. The rage and sadness boiled over as Luthias let out a scream.

He knew he needed to control his emotions, especially his rage. *"Rage leads to mistakes. Mistakes lead to death...and not always yours."* His grandfather's voice spoke within his thoughts once again. He looked around him and whispered back, "Death and darkness are all that remains of a once beautiful spirited land. That makes the rage feel nearly impossible to control. But I will fight it."

He urged his horse forward once again and headed towards Kallinstyne. He heard a growl and looked around, finally remembering he still had Nera with him. "It's okay girl. We can get through this together." His rage continued to build, the deeper into the darkness and red taint he rode. "But you need to be my anchor to reality." In his mind he could still see the animals running from his approach. Deer and rabbits looking to the brush for cover, squirrels scurrying up trees, and birds taking off in flight from the mortal predator's approach.

But now all that remained were their bones as if they had died years ago. But again, it had only been a little over a day. As the thoughts and images replayed in his mind, he let out another scream that should have sent animals scurrying. But all he saw around him was death, darkness, red taint, and stillness. Nothing scurried, ran, or flew away. "Nothing's left alive to scurry, run, or fly." Luthias raised his head and yelled, "It's only been a day!" His rage showing through in the tone of his voice.

Luthias rode to the main gate and looked towards the barracks. In his mind, he was reliving the madness of that night. He climbed down from his horse and retraced his steps. As he approached the barracks, he swung his sword out and killed a death wraith. Even though the guard and the young men were buried, he could still see them as if they were lying in front of him. He could still see the claw marks across the guard's throat, his longbow gripped tightly in his hand. He could see the chests of the other young men ripped open from the inside. The colors of the demonic blood splayed out on the walls and cots were glowing in the darkness forcing his mind to recall the images. He slashed out with the dagger and killed another wraith. As the thoughts ran through his mind, he put the dagger away and absentmindedly reached back to scratch the wound where the wraith dug its claws into him in Pantreus. He felt a sticky liquid on his hands, he wiped it off onto his armor giving it little thought.

He left the barracks wanting to get the images out of his mind and his emotions back under control. He walked over and leaned against a tree. He tried to slow his breathing, calm his mind, and keep the rage at bay. He heard Nera bark behind him. He drew the black obsidian dagger and spun around slashing the air as he did. A shriek echoed in the dark red atmosphere as another wraith pooled onto the ground. He looked around him slashing and thrusting at random but heard no more shrieks. He heard Nera whine, he turned, dropped to his knee, and petted her. "We'll make it girl. Keep me grounded. Keep me focused."

He could still feel the rage coursing through his body. Nothing he did seemed to calm it down. As he looked back down at Nera, he noticed a purple tinted black dragon scaled skin had replaced the skin on his hands. *"Something sinister creeps within the darkness."* The words replayed in his mind. The taint and darkness was changing him, fighting him for control. Using his rage against him to gain control and transform him into the fiend Koraegin needed. "This taint is not just a dark red cloud settling and spreading death out over the area. It's a living shadow magic entity. Some form of dark demonic energy feeding off my rage, feeding off the darkness and death it leaves behind. Nera, it's changing me girl, we need to get away from this place."

Before he could move, he heard a female's voice speak to him as if someone whispered words in the wind. "Emotions are the key to control, not running away. For the realm of Terra to survive, you must see this through. You need to learn to control your rage along with the sinister beast your rage will feed." Luthias looked around and didn't see anyone or anything but darkness, red taint, and death as the voice spoke to him again on the wind. "Something sinister creeps within the darkness. You."

He looked down at Nera then at himself again. "I'm the sinister beast. I'm Fijandsvarg, the untethered demon." He knelt and petted his wolf. He watched Nera closely and noticed she still had the same calm demeanor she always did. The taint didn't seem to be affecting her mind like it was his.

"This taint doesn't affect her as it does you. Her mind is safe for the time being." He heard the voice whispering to him in the wind once again but still couldn't see anyone else in the dark red taint. But the words the voice said gave him hope this taint wouldn't kill Borgroff or Nakira.

Chapter Twenty-Seven

"Well, we can safely say Luthias came this way," Borgroff said as they rode into Pantreus seeing pools of dead death wraiths all around. "But why would they attack him now?"

"This taint's corrupting effect, maybe?" Russington said as Borgroff, Kaci, and Nakira looked back at him. "This taint will affect him quicker than it will the rest of us including his wolf. Don't get me wrong, this taint will eventually corrupt everything if it touches it long enough. It just takes longer to corrupt mortals than it does demons. The only thing it would affect faster than demons are daemons."

"I don't know about daemons, but considering demons and wraiths are spreading the taint, shouldn't it be more familiar with them than it is with mortals thereby corrupting us quicker?" Kaci asked looking around.

Russington looked at her shaking his head. "You would think so but it is the familiarity with them that causes it to corrupt them quicker. The taint corrupts daemons first, I don't know why. Then it corrupts the most powerful demons since they are the ones who created this red tainted energy in the first place. The wraiths will be among the last to be corrupted before it affects us."

Nakira turned quickly. "Demon! We think Luthias is a demon and Nera is his mortal soul. That is why they don't attack him because they don't see Luthias like we do. We see an elf, but they see the demon within. This means they could be attacking Nera, and he is simply defending her against them."

"Possible but I doubt it, even though she is his mortal soul, they still see her as a part of him. No, this is something else." Russington lowered his head, crossed his left arm across his chest, and rested his right arm on it, scratching his chin.

"What are you thinking, Russ?" Borgroff asked.

He looked up at Borgroff then settled his gaze upon Nakira as she spoke. "I'm not going to like this, am I?" Nakira asked. He shook his head at her. "But I need to hear it all the same. I need to know what we are dealing with when we get to him, man, or beast. I still love him and either way, he is still Luthias."

Russington took a deep breath. "This is only speculation on my part, but I believe his mind is descending into madness. At least, that is what it feels like to him. The demon is taking over and in the chaotic process of the switch it is striking out at the wraiths it sees. He won't see anything or even know why he is doing it. He may even rationalize it in his head as if he is hearing Nera barking or sounding like she is being attacked."

"Darkness leads to chaos." Nakira recited the words from the letter. "Luthias is descending into madness and deeper into darkness within his own mind while the demon fights its way to the surface." Nakira watched Russ nod. "What happens if the demon has full control when we get to him? Is he lost forever?" Nakira asked as Kaci rode closer and grabbed her hand.

"No, but if he is, it makes the acts he must do much harder and it makes it harder for us to reason with him. If we reach him in time, he just needs to merge with Nera absorbing his mortal soul from her. But if he is a demon already, he will have to merge with Jadai first then Nera."

Borgroff sat forward in his saddle when he heard the last part. "Wait, if he merges with Jadai first then he will be two halves of a demon. We already discussed this math, two halves of anything make a whole demon. You're saying you want Luthias to become a full demon."

"In a matter of speaking yes, but what you are forgetting or may not know is Jadai's mortal soul is still intact within Zoriyah. If we get to him before he becomes the demon, Nera will restore the balance within him. Half mortal. Half demon fully under his control."

"But if we are too late, the demon will simply devour the mortal half of Luthias's soul when they are merged. Jadai and Zoriyah will offset the demon and weaken it. Nera will then be able to balance Luthias out." Nakira looked down. "Giving Jadai, or Zoriyah what she wants, to be with Luthias forever."

"My head hurts now. But if…" Borgroff stopped and looked at Nakira. "Sorry, when we are successful. What will he end up looking like? Because even though it's been two thousand years, just like back then, I don't think the world is ready for a werewolf-shaped demon freely walking about the countryside. Even if he is out fighting for justice and righting wrongs."

"All they will see is the beast. Not what's within," Nakira said looking up at Borgroff with tears trailing down her cheek.

"I know. That is a question only time seems to have an answer for and it's not revealing any clues." He watched the others ride ahead. He shook his head and whispered. "An answer none of us may wish to know. Damn her." He shook his head as he rode to catch up. "Let's just hope Amunique and Chief Justice Travon are getting those people out, wraiths and demons are bad enough but if we lose him, no one on this side of Santos will live long at all."

Kaci looked at Nakira. "And if they do, we will all serve him." She watched Nakira nod sadly.

***

"How are we doing?" Amunique looked up to see Brasscoat looking down from the railing of the ship.

"Good, unless you ask the souls, we lost in Shadow Pass. Even with the elite soldiers fighting within the taint to the south, it came up too quickly, but the taint isn't what got them. This taint is full of demons and wraiths. We had to evacuate and leave too many lost screaming souls behind. We heard their screams until all at once it became unnervingly quiet. But we evacuated Ridgewood, Terra Muse, and Orc Point. We just need to get everyone here on the ships and get out of here. The taint is already closing in on us. It has overtaken Ridgewood and most of Terra Muse. Those we don't load up onto the boats may have to fight their way to the river to get across."

Brasscoat looked back onto the ship then back down at her. "I'm coming ashore. This ship is full. I have one more waiting." Brasscoat got to the end of the walkway as the crew pulled it away and the ship prepared to move away from the dock. "The soldiers holding their own with the demons and wraiths?"

"As well as they can. We've lost about half of the soldiers from Romnuuski and half of the soldiers from the local guard units. Lucky for them the soldiers from Crosspoint showed up and gave them

187

some space to breathe. But not much." They both looked at Vanya as she walked up. Amunique looked around. "If you are trying to find Xaika she is helping them hold off the demons and wraiths while we load up. They are holding a line from Terra Muse south to the main path out of Shadow Pass."

Amunique looked from her to Brasscoat, you two get the rest of these people out of here. I'm going to go help with the battle." Before either one could object, she ran off and jumped onto a horse. The soldier holding the reins was surprised but knew better than to object.

It took her a shorter time than she hoped to reach the battle lines. She rode and battled her way through looking for Xaika. Before she spotted her, she heard her voice, "I don't think so, wraith bitch." Amunique looked around and saw her raise a sword and bring it down hard on a wraith who had dug its claws into a soldier.

Amunique rode fast towards her jumping off the horse when she got close. Amunique ran forward and thrust her sword behind Xaika's back killing a purple demon that appeared behind her. "Thanks, but did that demon look like a rabbit to you? Sorry, concentrate. What are you doing here? You need to be helping with the evacuation."

"I am helping with the evacuation. If we don't hold this line here, we lose everyone still on the ground in Souls Port. Brannkaste." She shot fire from her hand killing a flying yellow demon. She looked over at Xaika. "Yes it did and that one looked like a flying vampire squirrel wearing armor."

"The taint is in Orc Point! The taint has taken over Orc Point!" They both heard a rider calling out as he rode passed.

"Damn it." Xaika slashed forward killing a small, lightning-quick green rodent demon as Amunique slashed her sword out killing a wraith. "We need to get out of here." Xaika looked around and grabbed a soldier. "Fight with all you have and lead these troops to the water. Jump in and make your way to the other side."

The soldier nodded and hollered out, "On me! Fight to the river and swim across!"

Amunique looked at Xaika. "What do you have in mind?"

"We need to get to Souls Point and get the ship out of port. Whoever is onshore is going to have to swim to the other side from there. It's our only chance to get them out of here alive. I just hope

Borgroff, and the others are having better luck finding and helping Luthias put an end to all of this.

***

Luthias's horse had more sense than he did, it ran off and disappeared into the darkness back towards the main gate of Kallinstyne. It was getting the hell out of there while it could. He turned back around and focused his sight on the red tainted surroundings. Kallinstyne village. In the distance, Kallinstyne Square and Kallinstyne Castle. His mind took him back to the Festival of Renewal. The decorations, the laughter, the singing, the dancing. He smiled as the pleasant memories replayed. Tears slid down his cheek as the images vanished and the devastation of reality returned.

All around him, he saw the decimated village of Kallinstyne. Sadness and anger replaced the pleasant memories at the sight of the decimated village. Homes damaged, destroyed. Doors ripped off and broken. Kallinstyne looked like a ghost town from the ancient past. But again, it had only been a day.

Luthias walked into Kallinstyne square towards Kallinstyne's castle. In front of him he saw the shape of a female figure hidden within a red mist floating to the side of the water fountain.

"A red mystical demoness floating within this tainted atmosphere of red death. That tells me who is responsible for this evil tainted red death. The taint corrupting my mind, corrupting me into this demonic beast."

She was surprised that Luthias looked like a purple tinted black dragon scaled version of himself instead of the wolfiend. "Transformation has begun, I see." She floated back a little and spoke again. "I'm responsible for so many other things but not for the red taint. My guess is that would be the death wraiths and demons spreading the red taint. None of which are mine. Koraegin's doing. This taint will eventually corrupt everything within it, including me. But the corruption is necessary if we are to rule this realm together for eternity." The red mist around the female form disappeared revealing Jadai's mortal image.

"Jadai? You died! What are you...?" He stopped mid-sentence as he swiped his right arm out in an arc and heard the shriek of a

189

wraith. He looked over to see black liquid dripping off the claws that had replaced his fingers. Something in front of him caught his attention as well, he quickly thrust his left hand forward at arm's length. He squeezed his hand into a tight fist and watched more black liquid drip from his clawed hand as the shriek of another wraith filled the air.

He looked down at his beloved wolf snarling and growling then lunging and killing a small green demon. "The mortal being you possessed was killed by Crimson. Your death wraith made sure I saw it and couldn't interfere. But if any of your angel wraith soul remains, fight the demon. Fight the energy of the red taint. I need to leave and figure out how to stop this red tainted darkness from spreading to the rest of Terra. You can help me end this. I know the angel wraith you used to be is still in there, fight the demon and help me end this."

"Appealing to my better demons are you? You're correct, the mortal soul I possessed named Jadai did die by Crimson's hammer. Her death was a necessary staged dramatic end to my possession of her soul. Her death served the purpose to allow me to do the dark immortal's work undisturbed. I am happy to tell you this tainted darkness has already spread beyond the borders of Blackvale City. As for the distinction between demon or angel wraith, there isn't a distinction between the two anymore. His corruption made sure of that two thousand years ago. For you see, an angel wraith is a spirit with good intentions. A death wraith is a spirit with bad intentions. A demon is just a stronger, more sinfully menacing spirit. A death wraith transformed if you will. So you see, they are all one in the same. My spirit name was Zoriyah by the way. Do you remember the name Zoriyah? Zoriyah Ralinder?"

"I don't recall ever knowing a Zoriyah. I only knew you as Jadai." He shook his head as the darkness took over more of his mind, interrupting his thinking. "This dark red death energy is feeding off my rage making it hard to think. Corrupting my mind. It's not only a tainted cloud but a living shadow magic energized entity. I can feel it getting stronger the longer I'm trapped within it. It's getting harder for me to find the words I need." He looked around at the dark, gloomy, dead red hazy conditions around him. "It's only been a day and this red taint has already corrupted and killed everything that you and Crimson couldn't kill within Kallinstyne. Grass, trees, animals. What have you done demoness?" Luthias swiped his left arm out in an arc and killed one of the large blue demons with a single swipe of his clawed hands. He looked at the glowing blue liquid as it oozed between his fingers and dripped down to the ground.

"What have I done?" She asked sarcastically as she slowly walked over to him and ran her hand down the side of his dragon scale covered face. "Look at your body, my love."

Luthias looked down and saw his armor and jacket was gone. Ripped away by the beast emerging. His body was covered in the purple tinted black dragon scale skin. "Your taint is doing this to me."

"As I said, I'm not powerful enough to have created this." She gestured to the red taint clouds all around them. "Or this," she said gesturing towards his appearance. "You as this fiend version of yourself and this taint are both Koraegin's doing, dark prince. His end result is to take control over you then escape Knarran and rule Terra. I guess he is bored of ruling over the demon realm of Knarran." She leaned closer and whispered in his ear. "I'm not letting him out, though. I have other plans for you and I. Also, this…" She gestured at Luthias's condition. "…is not the result of Fijandsvarg. But this is definitely the figure I remember when you and I were lovers, the first time. Back then you had silver scales over the black skin. Silver claws on your hands and feet. Silver hair. Silver fractured diamond eyes that were reminiscent of a fractured soul. A daemon. Half human. Half demon."

She walked around him running her hands along his smooth dragon scale skin. "Fijandsvarg died during the splitting of Riven's soul. The original council screwed up. The only thing I cared about was the ancient's soul. The living, breathing, untethered ancient soul I desired." She walked around to the front of him running her hand along his body. "Koraegin never found out Fijandsvarg didn't survive because it simply became an inert worthless soulless being that was transferred from mortal to mortal for two-thousand years. He also didn't know that the mortal standing in front of me is also the mortal ancient soul that was Riven." She looked at the wolf. "Your wolf is nothing more than a beast of the wild who became bound to you through the magic spell that caused your rebirth. Somehow between the death of your last identity and the birth of Luthias, you became whole again. Both souls residing in one body.

Mortal and demon back together, which normally would make you a daemonic soul. A soul formed from the union of a demon and a mortal. The union of Koraegin and Queen Viktoria of Blackvale. But since Fijandsvarg is an inert soulless being, you are just a coexisting mortal, immortal being."

She smiled at him, "As for the tainted darkness and red death around us, it was necessary to create the perfect atmosphere to conduct my magic. Well, Koraegin's magic, if I were truly working for him. It also helped to lure you back to Blackvale. Back to where we were supposed to live out our lives. Back to where they tore everything away from me. You, and our beloved city." He watched as she raised her hands signaling the area around them. "Now with Kallinstyne dead, we will rebuild Blackvale City upon its darkened and corrupted corpse. Then you and I will finish the task of ridding the lands of the filthy pretenders that purged the world of our beloved city, our beloved kingdom, and took my love away from me. Riven and I planned to live our lives here. We were going to have children here. Generation after generation of Blackvale royalty would have lived, loved, and ruled here in the Kingdom of Blackvale. By now our kingdom would have spanned all five kingdoms. But gone are the generations of children they killed when they split your soul in two and hid you from me."

She watched his hand snap out and kill a wraith to his left. "The darkness has had a surprising effect on you. The shadow magic energy you feel has strengthened the shadow magic within you. It has brought Riven's beautiful smooth dark dragon scale skin to the surface. You gave the dragon scales a deep purple tint. All the while, the demons and wraiths extend the Kingdom of Blackvale's territory out to its original boundaries. Oceanside to the north. Mountains high to the south. Santos River to the east and what is now called the border river to the west. When we become one as we should've been long ago, everything the taint has touched will be ours to rule together. No one will dare venture into our darkened kingdom."

She walked around behind him, running her hands across his dragon scaled physique. "You and I will be able to live out our lives together like we were supposed to. No one will ever be able to rip us apart from each other again. After we reclaim the boundaries on this side, we will begin working on the Katerran side of the Border River. Renaming the river to its once glorious name, the Riven River."

"I won't…let you possess…my soul," Luthias said struggling to speak as he fought against the corruption.

"Possess?" She giggled at his misunderstanding. "No, I'm not here to possess your soul my love. Well not how you mean anyway. You see, I can't possess your soul. In fact, it's impossible for any demon, wraith or spirit to possess your soul. Not even the divine spirits. What will happen when you and I join our souls together is a magical energy that will transform the both of us. Luthias Blackridge and Zoriyah Ralinder will cease to exist. The resulting energy will bring forth into existence, two new unknown souls. It's the same theory behind each of your rebirths for the last two thousand years. Had the Jegere av Fijandsvarg knew about using the taint as a power source for their magic, then your rebirths could have been easier for them to accomplish. You see this magic won't result in us being sent to the void to be reborn. Instead we will appear here as new grown adult beings. I've spent the last two thousand years researching this magic. Researching Koraegin's taint."

Nera growled grabbing their attention. They watched her snag a demon killing it with her powerful jaws. "Of course, Nera can even live with us. She will be our pet and watch over our children keeping them safe as they play in the countryside."

Luthias watched Nera growling and snapping at the wraiths and demons around her. He walked over and squatted down beside her. His rage took over and he raised both hands. *"Brannkaste!"* With only the thought of the word in his head, Black fire shot out, scorching, roasting, and killing all the demons and wraiths within the fire's reach. Luthias noticed the darkness dissipated everywhere the fire touched. He stayed in the area in the guise of protecting her and immediately sensed a small bit of his mind returning to him. He swiped out with his clawed hands killing another wraith, then used his fire again roasting more demons and wraiths.

"Kill them all if you wish. We will need to eliminate them eventually anyway. The taint will corrupt their minds, twisting their appearance, and causing them to turn against us and each other. We don't want to be caught in the middle of that demonic war. Once people associate these lands with death, demons, and wraiths, there will be no more need for the demons and wraiths." Luthias smiled because she hadn't recognized the thinning of the tainted air, giving his mind a bit of clarity. "I need to go prepare for our joining, you stay and have fun killing the demons and wraiths." She looked back as she whispered to a wraith close by. "Have the wraiths and demons keep him occupied. He is walking a fine line between sanity and insanity, perhaps the fighting will keep his mind intact long enough to finish up the process of Riven's full return. If the shadow magic energy within him overpowers him before that happens, we are done for. The result will be death to this entire continent."

Chapter Twenty-Eight

Quietly and quickly, Borgroff and the others followed Nakira towards Kallinstyne square trying to keep her in their sight within the red tainted darkness. They came across her hiding behind some bushes in the garden area. She was warning them to get down as they approached her. "A large purple tinted black demon is up ahead. It's probably guarding her against Luthias. But I don't see him or Nera anywhere."

Borgroff smiled, "One shot with an arrow will drop that wraith into a black puddle."

"The demon isn't a wraith. It's in mortal form, not mist form," Nakira replied. "The only thing my arrow would do is piss it off and alert it to our presence."

"I fear the chaos I would wreak if anything were to happen to either of you. Know that my heart is always yours and only you can restore my soul from the chaos and darkness." Borgroff looked at Kaci. "Luthias's words not mine." He turned his gaze back to Nakira. "But if you're dead then you can't restore his soul pulling him from the chaos and darkness. He would wreak chaos upon this realm and every living thing without regret."

"Damn!" Kaci said looking from Borgroff to Nakira. "Crimson's chaos times infinity."

Nakira nodded as Russington sat back down after watching the demon and interrupted them. "Jadai's guard, the large purple tinted black mortal demon." Nakira looked at him and nodded. "It isn't watching for Luthias and Nera. I think it is Luthias. It just moved and revealed Nera sitting calmly behind it. Luthias has changed to his beast form, although it doesn't look how legend described it."

Nakira stood up. "Luthias!" She took a step towards him before being pulled back down by Borgroff and Russington.

Kaci held her finger against her own lips telling Nakira to remain quiet while Russ spoke.

Russ shook his head at Nakira. "I know you want to run to him, but we don't know how much of his mind remains within the beast. If any does at all. For all we know there is only the demon left. The path into the darkness leads to the only fate worse than death, eternal imprisonment." As he repeated the words from Luthias's letter Nakira's stare softened with realization. Russ saw that and continued. "We must be careful, but we must also be quick.

The demon is out so we must make sure he kills Jadai first before he kills Nera with Fijandsvarg's blade. If he doesn't we could lose Luthias forever along with everyone in this realm. And for deity's sake, he can't stab Jadai with the daggers."

Borgroff walked up with his battle hammers covered in multiple colors of the sticky liquid from dead demons and wraiths. He took an attack stance as he stared at Russ. "What the hell did you just say? He would gladly kill that demonic traitorous bitch but there is no way he is killing Nera. She's family." He leaned forward. "You'd better explain quickly before I mix some red human blood in with the rainbow of demonic colors."

Russ watched Kaci sling her chained dagger out and heard a demon shriek. He looked at Borgroff then at Nakira and remembered he hadn't told them yet. He signaled Borgroff to get down as he began talking, "Sorry, I forgot I hadn't told you yet. I feared this reaction and death by your hammers," he said looking down. He looked back up into Borgroff's eyes. "He must kill them both with Fijandsvarg's blade. Koraegin forged the sword so that when the Fijandsvarg is killed with it, the wolf fiend's soul is sent to him. This would give Koraegin full control over the wolfiend. The result of which we can only guess allows him full access to this realm somehow. This taint is already making it look like home for him. But the Fijandsvarg fiend absorbs the souls of whatever or whoever he kills with it, not Koraegin. Luthias needs to kill both Nera and Jadai with the sword. It is the only way he can absorb both their souls and rebalance his soul with the demon.

"You should have told us that a long time ago. He has killed wraiths, demons, and others with it not to mention the Bagswell brothers and whoever else during the battle here in Kallinstyne. What does that do to our math of two halves equals a whole demon?"

"No. The lesser demons and wraiths simply dissipate within his demon system strengthening him. It is only the more powerful demons that would change your theoretical math equation. If he were to kill Koraegin with Fijandsvarg, it would take all the souls in Ellehcim to even begin to counter his demonic soul." He looked at their faces and got back on track. "As for the Bagswell brothers they are mortal souls, heinous or not, they should tip the odds in his favor making him more mortal than demon."

"Okay," Nakira said bringing their attention to her. "You said the demons and wraiths wouldn't attack him. If that is true then why is he spinning in circles killing them with his claws and shadow magic fire as they continue towards him?"

Russington looked over the shrubs. "That's impossible. They are lesser demons. They do not attack demons greater in power than they are unless ordered to. Demons and wraiths have an innate ability to detect the strength of other demons and wraiths. If they detect a demon or wraith more powerful, they simply become docile to it." He watched a bit and kept hushing Borgroff when he kept trying to speak.

"Hush me again and I am hushing you with my battle hammers to both of sides of your head. What the hell is happening then? Because as he kills with his claws and fire, they keep showing up dead on the ground."

Russ watched Luthias. "Jadai is keeping him busy and occupied while she finishes whatever dastardly deed she's up to. That could mean he is still hostile towards her for some reason."

Nakira grabbed a hold of Russington. "Fire! It's an element that dissipates the darkened taint. He is using his fire to dissipate the taint around him. I bet it is giving him enough clarity to retain a bit of himself."

Russington looked at Nakira and smiled nodding.

Borgroff tried to step in between them but Kaci reached over and pulled him back as he spoke out loud. "Whatever your thinking, the answer is no."

Nakira held up her hand stopping him. "Whatever you're thinking the answer is yes." She looked at Borgroff smiled and winked. "We are here to save the hero of this Zjenica Robleus novel, remember? If we are going to save him, we are going to need to take risks. If he doesn't kill us, then she will, if neither of them does then the taint and lesser demons will. We might be damned if we do, but we are for sure damned if we don't. I'm determined to turn the end of this

Zjenica Robleus novel into a romance. Guy kills demon, girl gets guy and the long, passionate kiss seals the ending."

Russington smiled, "Then we need to act quickly before Jadai returns."

***

"Captain, take her slow and steady. I'm sorry we had to overload you, but I wasn't leaving anyone on shore to have to swim to safety, not in these icy waters." Amunique watched the sea captain shake Clive's hand and nod. Clive let out a sigh of relief as she approached. "Amunique is everyone okay?"

"Everyone on board is good, Vanya and Xaika are tending to them now. Are you sure we are safe to be this overloaded?"

"Not really, that is why I told the captain of the ship to keep us as close to shore as safely possible. Once we are far enough away, we're going to unload some onto the small boats with some of the soldiers with them." Clive looked up at the captain. "He even delayed his trip to another continent up in the icy cold waters to the north just to help us."

"Luthias would be proud of you for taking the risk and not leaving anyone behind," Amunique said smiling at him.

Clive nodded. "I hope the divine are watching over him. I hope Borgroff and Nakira bring him home safely."

"All we can do is concentrate on saving the ones we are with. Unfortunately, we have no control over the rest. All we can do is pray to the divine that Luthias and the rest make it out alive."

***

Borgroff looked at Nera running beside the horses as they rode away from Kallinstyne. "Why are we taking Nera and leaving him even more alone than when we found him? You all do know there is a hoard of demons and wraiths within this taint, right? My way we all stay in Kallinstyne and help him fight and stay alive. We help him retain what little bit of sanity you said the man has left."

Nakira shook her head. "Once again. He said he believes he is both Riven Blackvale and Fijandsvarg. Not one or the other, both. Nera here is just a wolf who through Russ' father's magic became

198

bound to Luthias but without either soul entering her. He also said that even though he didn't know Jadai's end goal, he does know that she mentioned a large magical explosion of energy." Sadness appeared in her eyes. "He says he thinks our plans told him how to avoid it but he didn't want any of us near the area just in case something went wrong and he couldn't stop it."

"Know that my heart is always yours and only you can restore my tainted soul from the chaos and darkness." Russ repeated the words from the letter Luthias wrote to Nakira. "He somehow knew he would need to be pulled back from whatever is about to happen."

"The hunter?" Borgroff asked looking at Nakira. "Do you think there is a possibility that the ancient hunter theory has been right all along?"

"Could Jadai be working against Koraegin by working with the hunter?" Kaci asked. "Let's at least get out of the taint where we can talk this out safely." She looked at Borgroff. "Then decide when to return and either try and help or find Luthias."

***

Jadai walked out of Kallinstyne's castle naked. She noticed Luthias hadn't fully transformed into the form of Fijandsvarg that she remembered in the later stages when she was with Riven. He still looked like a mortal covered in a purple tinted black dragon scale skin and although he had formed claws on his fingers the fur, the wolf's head, wolf's feet, and wolf's hands hadn't formed. To her he looked like Luthias just in demonic dragon scaled skin, confirming what she believed she knew was true.

The wolfiend's soul was now a worthless entity. Otherwise this living energy taint would have woken it up. She also saw he wasn't battling the wraiths and demons anymore, but she could tell he had just finished because the ground around him was still smoking, smoldering, and scorched black. "Luthias?" The fiend didn't move, just remained squatted on the ground breathing heavily with his pack hanging loosely on his back. She saw Nera wasn't lying beside him anymore.

But she did see drag marks that led off into the darkness. She knew it was only a matter of time until the demons finished the wolf off. "Riven?" She watched his head move slightly but not enough to

199

look at her. "Good, your memory is finally fighting through the taint and Luthias' mind. We can begin, do you have the daggers?" She watched as the fiend in front of her remained still and silent. "In the note I told Luthias to bring the daggers with him, are they in his pack?"

She watched the fiend bring the pack around in front of him, dig through it, then toss the daggers on the ground. "Daggers."

She smiled, "Good, now this next part is important. I need to know that you understand what I'm saying when I say it. I am going to need you to stab me with all three knives in a specific order. Do you understand?"

He looked at the daggers lying on the ground then nodded slowly. "Daggers. Stab. Order."

She smiled as she approached and arranged the daggers by placing the black obsidian dagger on the far left, then one of the two bone-handled daggers beside it, then the final bone handle dagger beside it to the right. "This is the order. You need to stab me in the heart with this black and red dagger first then remove it. Then stab me in the same spot with the two bone handled daggers as I have laid out the daggers. Do you understand?"

She watched him touch the black obsidian dagger and then touch his own heart. She then watched him repeat the pattern with the other two daggers. "Yes, after you stab me with the last dagger," she reached out and placed her own hand over the fiend's heart. "I have a special gift for you that will ensure we are bound together forever. Do you understand?" She watched as he sat there unmoving.

She picked up the first dagger and placed it in his hand. She stood in front of him and watched him pick up the other two daggers. He then stood as she smiled and wrapped her hands around his clawed fist that held the black obsidian dagger. "When you are ready."

A smile appeared on Luthias' face as he lifted his eyes up from the blades in his hands and watched her drop her arms to her side and close her eyes. With brute force, he jabbed all three blades into the dragon skin covering his heart. He made sure all three blades were pushed all the way to their hilts. "Helbrede." He softly whispered as his hands still held the handles of the blades. He could feel the magic working inside him healing his body around the blades.

When she hadn't been stabbed, she opened her eyes to see what the fiend was doing and what was taking so long. Her eyes widened even more at the sight of the dagger handles sticking out of his chest. "No!" she screamed out enraged. "Fiend! What have you done?" Instantly she transformed into the shape of a black and red lace-winged succuba demon. Naked mortal body and head covered in red demonic snakeskin with black dragon scales. Black spiral horns grew from her scalp as her hair changed to a fiery red and her eyes turned black as raven's wings.

Luthias smiled but before he could respond, he heard Nera barking and growling off to the side. He turned quickly and saw his wolf battling with one of the red scorpion she-devils. Even though the taint made it hard for him to think, he knew that meant the others didn't leave like he told them to. Nera's growling brought his mind back to the present. She had the tail in her teeth, gnawing and gnashing, trying to bite it in two while trying to rip the tail off the demon. Before Luthias could turn back around he felt something hit against the handles of the three daggers sticking out of his chest. He looked down and watched the last obsidian dagger fall from her hand and hit the hard ground. "You missed." Luthias growled as he glared into her eyes. "Brannkaste." He shot black fire out of his hands at her.

The succuba demon ducked down then rolled to the side just in time to keep the flames of the fiend from burning her. She screamed out, "All demons and wraiths left within Kallinstyne capture and subdue the fiend for Koraegin." Suddenly, an arrow flew out of the darkness. The succuba screamed as the arrow sunk into the flesh and muscle of her shoulder. She snapped the arrow out of her shoulder as she stared in the direction of the arrow's path.

Chapter Twenty-Nine

Nakira stood at the end of the arrow's path. She was staring and scowling at the demon with another arrow notched. "He's mine, bitch. Hands off." She let the second arrow fly in, catching the succuba in the stomach. The demon screamed and headed towards the castle.

Although glad to have help, he was worried that she stayed instead of leaving like he advised. "Why are you still here?" he yelled as he swiped his claw out and killed two wraiths. "I told you and Nera to leave with others."

As he finished talking a dagger connected to a chain flew in front of Luthias's face killing a yellow armored flying demon. "Yeah, about that," Kaci said yanking her dagger back to her by the chain. "We did leave but didn't stay gone. Borgroff said you wouldn't have left us so we shouldn't either."

"Come here big blue. Let's see who's tougher." Luthias heard Borgroff holler out in the distance.

"Nera, I could use some help. Brannkaste!" Russ's voice filtered in from the darkness as well. "Live or die we are with you, Beastie boy."

Luthias watched Nera run off towards Russ. "Then fight for your right…" he swung his claws out killing a scorpion demon in front of him. "Your right to live. Fight like the lives of everyone in the five kingdoms depend on it. If I scream out run. You fucking run. No second thoughts," Luthias said smiling at Nakira's reaction to his normal speech pattern. "But, Jadai. That bitch is mine. I'm going to rip her traitorous heart out," he said as he hurried towards the castle where he watched the succuba demon version of Jadai disappear.

He entered the castle his eyes easily seeing through the darkened taint clouds. "Where are you hiding? I didn't like hide and seek as a child. Come out and fight me face to face demon bitch." He walked forward into the throne room, *"skjold."* Luthias had simply thought the word but before he could speak it a magic shield formed in his hand. He raised it blocking a black mist that Jadai had breathed out at him. *"Brannkule."* He thought of the word for fireball and a black fireball appeared in his hands replacing the shield. He hurled the fireball, hitting the succuba demon igniting her with black flames. "Burn…bitch!" Luthias closed the distance to her his left hand grabbing her neck. But before he could do anything else, she dug her claws into his face forcing him to let go.

Luthias staggered back grabbing at his eyes barely sidestepping the flames she shot back at him.

"Hide and seek it is then. Come find me lover boy," she said before flying off into the darkness.

Luthias shook his head clearing the confusion out of his mind that the pain had caused. Trying to maintain control over the small portion he had of the beast's mind. But he could feel it slipping from his grasp.

He roared as loud as he could. He wanted to help the others but he needed to kill Jadai before she could enact her plan. He hoped that maybe by killing her the demons and wraiths would stop battling the others. He still had hope that she was lying. He hoped she was the one in control over them after all. "Where did you go, succubitch? When I find you I'm going to rip your heart out!" He looked around inside the throne but she wasn't there. He looked around in the other rooms on the lower floor but still didn't find her. He knew she was hiding and trying to give her wounds time to heal a bit. He just hoped the others were holding their own against her demons and wraiths.

***

Borgroff brought his right hammer over and down squashing a wraith into a black liquid puddle. "Holler out! I wanna hear your voices. Is everyone okay?"

Nakira heard Borgroff and answered first. "I'm okay so far but that she-devil bitch almost stung me. She paid for that decision with her life. I'm heading to you now."

Kaci threw her dagger out catching a big blue jaguar in the neck while Russ blasted it with his fire spell. "Russ, Nera, and I just killed another big blue jaguar. We're heading to you as well. Has anyone seen or heard Luthias?"

Borgroff watched them all walk up to the castle square at once. Borgroff looked towards the castle entrance. "Heard? I believe so if that bestial roar was his. But seen? Not since he took off into the castle chasing that winged version of Jadai. Let's get in there and find them."

Nera ran off into the castle ahead of the group but before the four of them could take more than a step, four red scorpion-tailed she devils and two long-horned big blue jaguar demons appeared and surrounded them. "I got this," Russ smiled at the other three when they turned to stare at him. "Stand in a triangular pattern facing outward with me in the center. Don't let them interrupt me." He started spinning his hands slowly in a circle while chanting. "Syklonvind," he repeated the word over and over. Slowly the wind picked up circling around them, slowing the demon's progress towards them.

Borgroff watched the six demons getting closer to them. "Russ, if you don't wish to be interrupted, put a rush on forming up that imaginary ball of yours or we are in for the fight of our lives. Meaning, we will fight, until the demons take our lives. Right now it's two on one odds in their favor." Just as he finished talking the wind grew stronger, blowing fiercely around them.

Russ shouted out, "Stovdjevelen!" A whirlwind formed a large dust devil storm stopping the demon's approach mere steps away.

The dust devil collected the demons and lifted them into the air above the group. Russ stopped and smiled as he lifted his hands and shouted, "Kjedelyn!" Lightning shot into the air towards the suspended demons. The lightning jumped from demon to demon causing them to explode and shower them in a red and blue mixture of purple demon liquid.

Kaci and Nakira looked at him shaking their heads. "What? I wanted to see why Borgroff liked it so much." He looked at the smiling red, blue, and purple liquid covered dwarf. "I do not see the fascination. This is disgusting. Let's go find Luthias and Nera."

***

"Where… you at, little bitch?" Luthias's speech was actually getting worse this time. Before, he had faked it to fool Jadai. He could use his fire to burn away the taint but that would waste more of his magic and possibly give his position away. He could feel more control over the beast's mind slipping from his grasp. "Find...you...rip your heart out...I will." He entered the room belonging to the magistrate's daughter. His eyes looking back and forth, knowing she could materialize anywhere just like a wraith can.

Just as the thought crossed his mind, claws dug into both shoulders. "I'm right here lover boy. You're good at hide and seek. You found me. I can feel your mind slipping even farther from your grasp. Soon all you'll be is a beast with no moral compass to guide you. You won't even feel a thing when you rip your girlfriend apart. Let me finish my work and you can avoid that end."

The claws retracted from his shoulder as he spun with his own claws out but she disappeared before he could grab her. "Bitch...scared." He let out a guttural roar as his anger and rage increased. "Fight...me!" He smiled as he barely sensed her appear behind him once again. He spun around and grabbed her by the throat squeezing and digging his claws into her neck. He saw her thrust a blade towards him. He knocked the blade out of her hands then thrust his clawed hand straight into her chest. "You missed...again, but I didn't."

She watched the beast's smile widen as she felt its claws dig deeper into her chest. She could feel his hand ripping through skin, tearing muscle, and breaking bones to get to his ultimate goal. Her heart. She watched his smile widen as he pulled her blackened demonic heart from her body. "Your heart...is in my." A sinister look appeared on the fiend's face. "Hand." The blackened heart sprayed blood only once as he squeezed his fist, crushing her heart.

Black demonic liquid ran through his claws as she shrieked. "Brannkaste." He shot fire burning her as she collapsed into a puddle of the same black demonic liquid. "No love match today...Succubitch!" He quickly grabbed her dagger off the ground and slid it into the small dagger sheath built into the outer part of his pack. He then pulled the other daggers out of his chest, noticing the tips of all three had broken off inside him. He placed his hand over the wounds. "Helbrede." He watched the holes scar over as he dropped the broken daggers inside his pack.

Luthias heard Nera yelp behind him. He spun around and saw a blood red scorpion she-devil headed towards him. Its eyes glaring at him. A look none of the other demons have had. Emotion. An evil glare of pure hatred. The taint was corrupting the lesser demons now. Her face was disfigured with corruption. Behind the approaching red she-devil, he saw Nera had ran in to help him but had been caught by the she-devil. She was now lying on the ground. Motionless.

Her own red blood mixing with the blood of the demons she'd killed. He knew the scorpion had stung her. Sensing his distraction and his eyes on the wolf, the scorpion she-devil swung its tail out stabbing him in the side. Luthias recoiled in pain from the stab of the scorpion's stinger. He let out a guttural roar as he drew Fijandsvarg's blade and swung it across his body, cutting the demon's tail off. The she-devil screamed an ear-splitting shriek as Luthias pulled the stinger tail from his body.

The she-devil's poison pumped through his blood stream and dropped him to his knees. Fijandsvarg's blade dropped from his hands as he fell forward to catch himself. The palm of his hand landed on the hilt of the sword. He tried hard to rise back up but felt the demonic poison spreading through him fast. Its paralyzing effects taking over his body, making it harder for him to move. The she-devil swung her hand out and dug her claws into the middle of his back. She slid her hand up his back, tearing through the dragon scale skin, muscle, and bones.

He gritted his teeth against the pain of her claws tearing through his skin and muscle. His scream sounded like the roar of a beast as he thrust one of his taloned hands out ripping into the she-devil's leg. "Drop...to my level?" He tore at skin, muscle, and bone until she dropped shrieking in front of him as her claws dislodged from his back. "Like...Jadai...you fail."

Before Luthias could shove his claws out and kill it, he saw a big blue long horned jaguar demon walking up behind the still shrieking she-devil. With a swipe of its claws, the jaguar sent the she-devil collapsing into a red demonic liquid. The jaguar demon stood towering over Luthias who was still on his knees, bent over, one hand lying on the hilt of Fijandsvarg's blade. Luthias noticed his other hand close to Jadai's unused dagger in the sheath of his pack hanging off his shoulder. Luthias grabbed the blade and shoved it into the jaguar. "Enjoy Jadai's company."

The jaguar demon looked at the dagger sticking out of his stomach and smiled as he dug his claws into the claw marks in Luthias's back. The jaguar dragged his claws upward through Luthias' body following the scorpion's path, digging deeper. The demon smiled as his claws ripped through more skin and muscle. "You…can't win!" The beast's gritty dark sinister voice stated. "I will have your soul and control over the ancient's shadow void magic." Luthias knew in that moment that Jadai had taken over control of the beast.

Luthias roared as pain racked his body. He tried hard to get up. Tried hard to force the cat's claws out of his back, but he struggled because of the demonic poison of now both beasts. Their paralyzing effects taking over his body, making it harder for him to move and causing even more pain to shoot through his body.

Luthias used all his strength while the jaguar focused on his face. Finally, Luthias grabbed hold of the hilt of Fijandsvarg's blade. He smiled up at the towering jaguar demon. "No…you won't!" he screamed in a bestial roar as he brought Fijandsvarg's blade straight up between the jaguar's legs. Using all the strength he could, Luthias stood bringing the blade upwards splitting the jaguar in half from its crotch to the middle of its chest.

The cat roared in pain as Luthias lost his strength and fell. He expected the jaguar demon to drop into a blue demonic puddle of liquid. But instead, the demon seemed to vanish directly into the blade as it dropped and clanged onto the hard ground. He watched Fijandsvarg's blade glow blue then purple as more pain ravaged his body even worse. His body felt like someone was not only ripping it from his soul but was ripping his arms and legs from his body as well. A brief thought of the pain Riven must have felt crossed Luthias' mind. But the sound of lightning coming from outside the castle brought his attention back to the circumstances surrounding him.

Out of the corner of his eye he watched a white wraith floating towards him. He watched it bend over and pick up the purple glowing blade. The wraith slowly floated towards him with the blade. He watched the wraith's taloned finger trace over the tip of the blade. He knew it was tracing the runes. Luthias had learned them and their locations on the blade. "Chaos. Harvest. Legacy," he said as the wraiths slender fingers traced each rune, nodding its head as he spoke.

He was powerless to defend himself. After defeating countless demons and wraiths. After defeating Jadai and the last two corrupted demons, it was going to be a simple wraith who would succeed where more powerful demons had failed and died by his hands. A simple wraith, a white witch, would be the one to send control over his fiend form and the realm of Terra to Koraegin. He watched the wraith raise the purple glowing blade above Luthias's heart.

The wraith hesitated a second then thrust the purple blade hard into Luthias' chest. He felt the wraith's cold fingers wrap his hand around the hilt of the blade and heard a whisper reach his ear from the wraith's true form within the white mist. "Absorb all the souls you have killed with Fijandsvarg's blade. The mortal souls you killed will strengthen the mortal half of your daemonic soul. The souls of the spirits you killed will give new life and strengthen the spiritual half of your daemonic soul. Absorb the demon cat's magic. Absorb the scorpion she-devil's venomous magic. Their magic is yours to command. Use their magic and strength to defeat Koraegin's forces. More will come. Fijandsvarg is not a worthless soulless demon." He watched the wraith turn and look at his motionless wolf. "It is just not yours to control."

"You, however, do have full use of Fijandsvarg's blade. Every being you kill with it from this point forward, mortal or spirit, will now strengthen your magic and both sides of your soul. As a shadow warrior, it is the darkness within you as well as around you that you must fully embrace and use to your advantage. More darkness is coming to the realm of Terra, Luthias. You must be equally dark. I will be watching from within the shadows."

Luthias felt a surge of dark energy shoot through his body, then up through his heart, and out through the sword. Luthias roared in agony as the purple light grew in intensity, blinding him, and blasting the wraith with pure magical energy causing it to dissipate. After a minute or two, his vision returned. He noticed the sword had been removed from his chest and lay beside him. It now had a permanent purplish tint. He also noticed that while he was still in pain, the wounds he could see on the front of him were now healed.

He turned his head to where Nera lay. Motionless. He hurried over to her and cut her with the purple tinted sword. "Helbrede." He healed the cut immediately after cutting her. "Let's hope she is right and you are the one to control the Fijandsvarg fiend and its powers."

Chapter Thirty

Borgroff looked at the demon liquid covering him then smiled at Russ, "Hell, I'm glad we stayed and helped after all. Especially now knowing Russie-boy can perform magic like that." Borgroff patted Russ on the back before heading off towards the castle. "Let's go find Luthias and Nera."

They hurried towards the castle. Hoping to hear the sounds of battle echoing around, but all they heard was the eerie sound of silence. Nakira was worried they hadn't arrived in time to help. As they entered the castle doors, they stopped to listen, hoping to hear sounds of movement. But the night air blowing around them was all they heard. Suddenly, a bright purple light lit up the darkness from inside the castle. Blinding them.

"What the hell was that?" Borgroff asked as he looked around trying to get his eyes to focus just in case demons and wraiths were around. "Throne room. Largest room in the castle. Lots of room to move."

They stayed close together keeping their weapons ready for any demons to show up as they eased forward. Nakira shook her head. "I'm not liking this. It's too quiet."

"The path into the darkness leads to the only fate worse than death, eternal imprisonment." Borgroff whispered then sighed heavily. "Eternal Imprisonment. Trapped inside the hellish realm of Knarran?" he asked rhetorically. "Trapped inside his own mind while Jadai or Koraegin acts as his demonic puppeteer?"

"Definitely strings attached to that relationship," Russ said as he stared off into the darkened tainted castle throne room.

"Got that right," Borgroff grunted out. Before he could finish talking, a noise like someone collapsing and something metal landing on the floor echoed from upstairs. "Towards the back of the castle, upstairs."

Nakira peeked into the magistrate's room then shook her head at the rest indicating no demons, Luthias, or Nera. Nakira hurried to the next room. She saw Luthias kneeling over Nera who was lying on the floor motionless. Luthias was still covered in the fiendish deep purple dragon scales on top of his black demon skin. He had deep claw marks dug into him from the middle of his back to his neck. But somehow they had been healed already and scarred over. She rushed to kneel beside him. "Luthias, are you okay."

"Yes," the dark venomous voice surprised her a bit. "Come on Nera, respond to the magic. Feel Fijandsvarg's magic coursing through your body. Use the taint's energy." Suddenly he thought about what had just happened to him. He quickly turned to the others all standing around him. "Step back out and close the door just in case another energy blast like the one that coursed through me happens again." Nakira looked at him worried. "Don't worry. It won't affect me. Don't ask me how I know."

They hurried out into the hallway and closed the door to await something to happen. After waiting for a few minutes, a bright purple blast of energy escaped from all sides of the closed door. When the brightness faded Nakira opened the door to see Nera sitting herself up while Luthias helped her.

Nakira ran forward, embracing Luthias and knocking him to the floor. She wrapped her arms around him. "I thought I lost you."

He chuckled, "I did too." He held her tight loving the warmth of her body against his.

"Luthias Blackridge, that is you right?" Borgroff asked laughing. "If not Nakira is already a goner. No helping her now. Nera, girl!" Nera ran up to him almost knocking the dwarf down. "I'm glad to see you back up and active girl. But what's with the shift in color. You're purple like Luthias' eyes." She barked and shifted into a large demon hound with black demonic skin and deep purple dragon scales.

Luthias and Nakira stood up. "She is Fijandsvarg now." He looked at Russ. "According to what I've learned from within this taint. Fijandsvarg was rendered useless to mortals when they split Riven into two souls. The beast was always supposed to be the beast."

Russ nodded. "The mortal was always supposed to be the mortal. So that means you have Riven's soul inside you and she now has Fijandsvarg."

Luthias nodded. "Up until I gave her Fijandsvarg's soul I had both souls. I say we find me something to wear that will hopefully cover me completely until I figure out how to switch back to my normal self.

Kaci chuckled as she walked in carrying a mage's robe. "Here. I saw this in a room a couple of doors down while we were searching the rooms to find you and Nera." Luthias threw the robe over his head and slid it on. "Now I can look at you without feeling guilty while being around your girlfriend and my boyfriend." She nudged Borgroff with her hip as Borgroff laughed.

Nakira pulled at the sleeve of the mage's robes. "I was so excited to see you two up and alive that I didn't even care once I saw you." She saw the claw marks on his face and stab wounds on his chest underneath the partially opened robe. "But how are we going to get you into Crosspoint without someone seeing you looking like some dark fiend from their nightmares?"

Luthias looked at Russ. "It's dark outside still so once we gather everything up and get to the horses, Russ will use a teleport spell to get us outside of Crosspoint. Then we will ride in with me covered as much as possible until I get into a room." He looked at Nakira. "Yes, I will get checked out head to toe once I change back to normal," Luthias said as Nakira nodded smiling.

Luthias looked from Russ to Borgroff and Kaci. "You two go grab the horses and bring them to the castle square. Nera go with them and protect them. We will meet you down there once we gather everything." Borgroff and Kaci rushed off down the stairs.

Nakira wrapped her arms around him gently hugging him. "I was so worried about what we would find."

Luthias hugged her back. "I know, but somehow this taint has an energy that somehow helped both me and Nera to heal up. I have the fractured daggers," he bent over and picked Jadai's dagger up off the floor. "And now Jadai's dagger." He smiled, I sent her back to Knarran within a jaguar demon's soul. They are all in my bag. The rest will be best explained when Vanya, Etherika, Amunique, and Russ are there to decipher as I explain. I say we get out of this taint and stay in Crosspoint tonight. Tomorrow we can head to Traemorra and have Amunique call everyone together for a meeting to discuss what happened." Luthias pulled her back in to a tight hug and kissed her. "I'm just happy as hell to be leaving this taint alive and still in this realm. Hunter and Koraegin be damned. The short version, I ripped Jadai's heart out of her chest in time for her to watch me crush it. Then of course as I said, I sent her into a jaguar demon and sent them both back to Koraegin after I cut the jaguar balls to sternum." He looked at Nakira. "Since you all killed the few other demons I could feel, the demons and wraiths around Kallinstyne are gone. The only ones I feel now are well north of us. Probably up by the northern shoreline. We can kill them later. Right now, I need sleep and to sleep on something other than the ground."

"Wait." Nakira pulled him to a stop. "If Nera has Fijandsvarg, why are you still covered in the demonic skin?"

"According to Jadai, Zoriyah whoever she claimed to be in the end, this is Riven's skin you're seeing. But I also have the jaguar demon and scorpion demon's magic inside me. Although a different demon, you are still dating an immortal demon."

Nakira smiled, "Now in bed, I get to be the demon hunter. Let's go before we energize this tainted energy with some sexual energy of our own."

Luthias laughed as he and Nakira exited then climbed up onto her horse. "Let's hurry and get all of us out of this taint. I will fill everyone in once we get back to Traemorra. They should already know. I've had one of Amunique's wraith ravens on my tail this whole time. She wanted to help physically but the taint was too dangerous for her to venture into. Russ, get us out of here."

***

Luthias didn't rest well during the night in Crosspoint. At times, he watched Nakira sleep by his side snuggled up against him, always in contact. Scared of a replay of the last time they slept together. Scared she'd wake up again to find him gone.

Like maybe if she was in contact with him while they slept, he couldn't disappear this time. Most of the night though, he tossed and turned through a dream. A nightmare. Even though he'd lost Fijandsvarg to Nera, he could still feel the jaguar and scorpion demon dwelling deep inside him. Lurking just beyond his reach, beyond his ability to understand how to utilize them. Luckily, at some point in the night, he switched back to normal mortal looks but with a slight difference. He was now slimmer than his orc size that he was before losing Fijandsvarg.

In the early morning darkness, he could feel the demons stirring inside him. Waiting to be released onto the Realm of Terra. How to use and control them both, he didn't know. For once in his life he was scared of what dwelled within him. He had lost the wolfiend. He'd been stabbed with Fijandsvarg's blade but somehow the wraith allowed the wolfiend to be transferred into Nera. Legend says once he was stabbed with the sword the wolfiend would return to Koraegin.

Starting the beginning of a darkness that would be accompanied by a demon apocalypse led by Koraegin, the dark lord of the demons. He shook the thoughts out of his mind. Hopefully, Amunique, Vanya, and Etherika could help him understand what had happened and how to get control over what was stirring inside him. He cuddled up to Nakira. Kissed her lips. Held her body close to his. All of which he never imagined he'd get to do again. She smiled a sleepy smile as her eyes fluttered open. "Morning handsome. I'm glad you decided to stick around in bed this time."

He smiled back, "Figured it was safer to wake up with you than disappear back into the taint once again." He leaned in and kissed her once again. "I love you. I have a question for you?"

She snuggled in close, her face only a breath away from his. "I love you too and I have an answer for you."

He smiled, "Hopefully it's the right answer." He sighed, "I know I should have taken you all with me. I shouldn't have sent you away from me when you showed up. Even though I did both to keep you all safe from her and possibly myself, it wasn't fair to you all."

"This sounds more like a whole lot of guilty conscience instead of a question." She giggled when he rolled his eyes. "Sorry, continue."

"I'm glad you all defied me and stayed close. I nearly died battling Jadai's demons and wraiths. I survived stabbing myself in the heart with three daggers. I survived the taint corrupting my body and mind. A corruption that transformed me into the demon we were trying to find. The demon I thought she was. Fijandsvarg. My armor and jacket got shredded and ripped away from my body as the beast took over. I lost my faithful wolf to the demon's poison. But somehow she was brought back to me through the magic of a wraith and Fijandsvarg's magic. Both of which gave her a demonic soul since she is now a demon hound. I'm glad I didn't end up doing all this alone, on my own. A Knight Hunter uses the troops at his beck and call in the best way he sees fit. A Knight Inquisitor does not act on his own behalf, he must do what is necessary and use the kingdom's forces as best he can."

She rolled her eyes and kissed him shutting him up. "Will you ask me to marry you already," She rolled him over and slid on top of him straddling his mid-section. "So I can say... oh hell yes."

He laughed as he stared at her. "Rambling?"

"Shut up and enjoy the victory over the forces of darkness. However, we all made it happened." She ground her hips in a circle over his. She smiled seductively as she stared into his eyes and whispered, "Are you ready to enjoy your treasure before going to get a complete check over by the doc?"

Chapter Thirty-One

The next morning, Luthias and Nakira bought him a black tunic, black britches, and a black gambeson to wear instead of the mage's robe. Afterwards, they walked over to the hospital to get Luthias checked out. After an hour, the doctor walked out and told Nakira, Russ, Borgroff, and Kaci that they were going to take him into the surgery center to repair the scarred tissue over his many wounds.

While they waited, everyone else surprised them by showing up and joining them to wait for him to come out of surgery. After several hours, the doctor walked out to greet the now much larger group waiting for news.

The group waited while the doctor looked over them for a minute. "Those that entered with him this morning knows Luthias walked in on his own but I will say, on the inside, he was still in bad shape. Us normal mortals would not have been moving let alone walking. We would've been declared dead and buried on the battle field." He smiled hoping to ease their tension a bit. "But I've dealt with Knight Hunter Blackridge and enough of his injuries to know better than to ever count his stubborn ass down and out. His most serious injury was that he was stabbed at least four times in the heart. Again, a normal mortal without his healing ability is dead right then. We found the tips of three blades left embedded and fused together in a triangular pattern inside his heart. Whatever fused the blade pieces together also fused them into his heart. No way we could remove them without killing him. The injuries to his heart will heal around the fused blade pieces, but it will take longer than usual for him. Usually, we can increase the patient's healing strength magically, but whatever magic was being used is too strong for us to counteract. But, again, his heart is healing on its own. It will keep him inactive until its healed. The scorpion sting and claw marks he sustained throughout his body were healed using some sort of powerful force enhancing his healing ability. I'm not asking for an explanation for his injuries or this powerful force. I know he just came out of the tainted lands. With Luthias, I know there is some sort of magic going on around and within him all the time. The three blade tips were rune engraved so we know some of the magic stems from them. He is being sutured up as we speak. He should be out of surgery in an hour or so. He will recover fully, after a few months or so of downtime. I want to determine the amount of damage from the demon poison before I say anything definitive. For now, I plan on keeping him here for a day or two for observation." He smiled, "Or until his stubborn ass decides he's tired of lying around and doing nothing."

Borgroff chuckled, "So Knight Hunter Blackridge will be walking out of here today then."

Luthias's mom smiled shaking her head, "No, because the girls and I are staying by his side and he's not leaving until the doc says he is cleared to do so. I almost lost my son and all of you all. I'll be hovering around you all like a hawk every time any of you are near me."

Xaika crossed her arms and smiled, "And after that only when Nakira and his mom says he can leave. Unless he's willing to hit a girl in front of his dad and mom." She winked at his parents. "I can play the part of an injured female if I need to."

The doctor smiled at the group, "He won't be allowed visitors until this afternoon. I have him heavily sedated so we won't know anything about him until he wakes up. I suspect that will be this afternoon or evening."

As the doctor walked off, Vanya looked at the group. "Since we know he's okay, I'll be of more use working with my staff on these daggers. I want to find out what magic Jadai had coursing through them. You all keep me updated through Amunique's wraith ravens. Soon as my staff and I know anything you all will know." Vanya kept the obsidian blade, then handed a bone blade to Russ and Etherika.

Russ nodded. "Same here. If you don't mind me using a teleport spell to get you there, I will get you to Gatesboro faster. Tyra and I will work together."

"If you'd like, you can use the resources in the council's research chamber. I'll even make sure everyone knows you're in charge of the project. I also have two rooms there right in the research area for you two to stay in. It would certainly make me feel better having both blade types being researched in the same facility," Vanya said looking at Russ. Russ nodded.

Etherika handed her blade back to Vanya. "Study all the blades there. I will send a few mages to assist the research effort."

Vanya nodded then pointed at Xaika. "Stay with him until Nakira or Braelyn sends you away." She winked at Nakira as they said their goodbyes then left.

Nakira informed the staff they'd all be at the Crosspoint Cafe if the staff had news. They sat around eating and telling stories of an adventure or other times they had with Luthias. It is said that laughter is the best medicine for an aching heart, but their minds still ached to see Luthias walk into the cafe. At one point or another, each one of them looked over at the door as it opened. They anticipated him walking through the door smiling while pretending to be insulted, he wasn't invited.

As they were all still sitting and talking, the doctor walked in and greeted the group. "Luthias is resting well. We've already taken him off the sedation, but the demon poison in his system should make him sleep into or maybe even through the night. You all may go see him in groups of three or less." He looked at Nera. "Sorry girl, groups of four or less. I know you'll be in there regardless of what I say and I'm not going to argue with a demonized wolf hound." He reached down and petted her head as the group laughed.

Nakira, and Luthias' parents, Demir and Braelyn were the first three to stand. Amunique smiled, "You all go ahead. The council is picking up the tab." Amunique looked at the doctor. "Chief Justice Travon told me to thank the medical staff. She said to tell you your food is paid for as well."

The doctor nodded. "I will gather up a list from my staff and come back then."

"I'll wait here and help you bring it back," Clive said as he smiled at the doctor. "It's the least we could do for you all."

Nakira, Braelyn, and Demir walked quickly into Luthias's room and saw him lying looking helpless in bed. "This is your son's new look. Slimmer with more defined elven features."

Nakira sat down on one side of the bed staring at him as his parents sat down on the opposite side. "I'm so glad he made it out of there alive." She laid her head down onto the bed against his arm as she held his hand.

His parents sat quietly for a while watching their son, thankful he survived. Fearful of what might be coming after their son next. Braelyn being a priestess for the Church of the Divine Spirits knew this all had to do with the dark lords' council of the demon realm. She knew dark lord Koraegin had his filthy claws in this somehow. She looked over and nudged Demir seeing Nakira had gone to sleep.

The rest of the evening they all took turns in the room with Luthias. Once night set in Nakira stayed in the room sleeping off and on in the chair by his bed. Never letting go of his hand the entire time.

As the sun rose, shining its early morning reddish orange hue through the window, Nakira felt Luthias's hand grip hers a second then release it. She opened her eyes and saw him moving around. But his eyes remained closed, and the movement stopped. She slipped her hand out and walked out to see if anyone else was awake. She walked out and saw Braelyn and Amunique awake and talking. Both smiled at her. She waved them both to come with her. "I think he's waking up. He squeezed my hand and moved."

Nakira stepped forward as Luthias opened his eyes and saw her, his mom, and Amunique staring down at him. "What's going on?" he asked as he raised his head and looked around. He sat up and cautiously scooted himself back against the wall. He looked down and lifted the covers off his legs. He smiled when he saw his own mortal skin, mortal fingers, mortal legs, and feet still. "No black demonic skin. No deep purple dragon scales." Nakira picked up the mirror and gave it to Luthias. He took the mirror and looked at the reflection. "Wait, what? Silver hair and goatee? Silver fractured eyes? He lowered the mirror. Nakira took the mirror from him, laid it down, and hugged him. Luthias squeezed her tight. "Did I come out of surgery with this look? How long has it been?"

Amunique smiled at him. "Yes, this is the look we got greeted with out of surgery. Slimmer body. Silver hair. Fractured diamond like silver eyes. We'll hold off on answering anything else until after the doctors take a look at you," Amunique said as she patted his foot.

The doctor walked in and rushed everyone out. "I'll let you all back in here after we're done."

It wasn't long before the doctor walked out to address the group. "He is looking extremely well considering what he just went through. He'll be free to head out this evening, but he'll need to remain under doctor's care. Of course, with the guidance of no fighting or strenuous activities for another few months. Oh, and I've told Luthias this already but I'm sure he'll need to be reminded since he told me not to tell you all." He laughed when Braelyn and Amunique rolled their eyes. "No ale for at least this next month either. I'll give you a great blend of tea that will help his heart to heal better and stronger, not quicker. You all can go see him together since he just woke up. I'll start his release papers and give them to him when you all clear him."

When they walked in, Luthias looked up surprised. "Wow, almost everyone's here. I might need a bigger room." He smiled at everyone as Nera jumped onto the bed and laid down by his leg. "The Red Dog will be big enough." Luthias chuckled when he saw his mother shaking her head.

"After your release papers are finished and signed. Then and only then with your promise of following the doctor's orders along with mine and Nakira's orders. I will be staying in Traemorra to help with the refugees anyway. Your dad and I are sleeping in the room next to yours in the Red Dog Saloon."

Luthias nodded his head. "I promise. I'm guessing you all want to know what happened to me in the taint. First information I know everyone is wondering about, yes Nera has Fijandsvarg now. Vanya told me something while we were at her estate. As you search for answers, remember not all is as it seems."

Amunique looked at him. "I could tell in my visions that the darkness was hiding something from me."

"It was hiding the truth." Luthias looked up at everyone. "Hiding the truth right before our eyes Nera was only ever a natural wolf. I was both the Fijandsvarg wolfiend, in an inert useless state and Riven Blackvale hidden beneath the demon's disguise." He gestured to his new looks and size. "This, I'm assuming is Riven Blackvale's appearance and my new appearance from here on out. By the way Jadai took an express ride with a jaguar demon back into the demon realm. After I ripped her heart out, crushed it, then stabbed the jaguar with her blade. But I believe something else was supposed to happen with Jadai's daggers. I believe he needs my soul, Riven's soul as well as Fijandsvarg's soul for some reason. We need to figure out why and how we can stop him. More dark forces will come after us and with Jadai's treachery and failure, you can bet they will be more loyal to Koraegin and more dangerous to this realm."

"I doubt the next demon will be in a planning stage for the next two thousand years," Amunique said drawing a halfhearted laughter from the group.

Luthias smiled and nodded as he looked at Etherika and Syneris Rein. "You two ornery Rein women with us for the foreseeable future? We could sure use more support."

"Especially since Knight Hunter Blackridge will be working from the Red Dog saloon for the foreseeable future," Nakira said winking at them then kissing Luthias.

"Yeah, yeah," he said laughing as he looked passed the group out the window while he petted Nera.

Outside near a tree he watched a white ring of mist form on the ground then rise as it spiraled in a circle. Inside the mist he saw a feminine figure standing and looking his direction. He knew it was the wraith that stabbed him with Fijandsvarg's blade. He watched the figure lift and place a finger to where her lips would be, as an angelic voice whispered directly into his mind.

"darkness doesn't always refer to the absence of light. Sometimes, it refers to the absence of morality. It is this darkness that must be the fuel used to create the dark, vengeful savior the realm of Terra needs. shadow clouds form in the distance. A dark storm is brewing. A tempest is coming to this realm. A tempest the likes this realm hasn't seen in four thousand years. You must be fully prepared. Mentally. Physically. Magically. Nera is indeed the wolfiend, Fijandsvarg. Even though the Fijandsvarg beast went to her, Fijandsvarg's magic stayed within you. You are now what's called the triad prism of two magical factors. First is demonic magic. Fijandsvarg, a jaguar demon, and a reaper scorpion demon. All three feeding the darkness within you. The darkness and turmoil you feel lurking just beyond your grasp. The second magical factor is more dangerous than that even. Three ancient shadow magic souls converged to one point, into one being. You. We will get into that bit of magic later once you have recovered. For now concentrate on healing."

Luthias watched the figure within the mist bow then disappear. Her angelic voice whispered the words of his grandfather, *"There will come a time when you must embrace the darkness and use it to your advantage."*

The End.

Epilogue

In the depths of Knarran, a feminine shaped blue jaguar demon paced around the red ash covered black igneous rock terrain. She stopped and stared at the eternal fires burning in the pits around her. "I should have been in control of the wolfiend. I would have been laying waste to that damned realm. But instead, he ripped my heart out and somehow trapped me inside the form of this infernal lower-class demon. Damn it! How could he have retained access to his own mind? The taint should've empowered the daggers magic bringing Riven to the forefront of the beast's mind."

She looked around when she heard slithering noises coming from all around the caverns. "Oblivion." She whispered. A large dark ash gray snake slithered up to her and raised its head and upper body, matching her height. Its diamond shaped saffron eyes glaring at her, its reddish black tongue flicking just barely out of reach of her lips. Jadai gulped noticeably, knowing what the snake's presence meant.

An ethereal voice broke the silence booming and echoing throughout the caverns all around her, "You should have followed my instructions." Jadai knew the ethereal voice meant Koraegin was close by in person. She could feel him painfully probing around in her mind. "Had you done so, you would have had full control of the wolfiend's soul within the realm of Terra. Which in turn meant I could have switched places and gained access to the mortal realm again. I would have been in control of the ancient's soul and powerful shadow void magic. Which Luthias now controls thanks to your deceit."

The snake slithered around her. "Should have, would have, and could have are worthless words. Words that lead only to pitiful excuses of why my minions fail to complete their missions. Accomplish the task I give you however you can. That is all I ask of my minions. Demon, mortal, or daemon. Mortal souls who fail get trapped in the middle of a pit of flames, burning for eternity. Demons who fail get swallowed up by the darkness of oblivion painfully ceasing to exist over hundreds of years. Daemon's get ripped apart and endure both. You failed!" the ethereal voice shouted. "Luthias now has the only three souls known to ever exist with the ancient form of shadow void magic within him. Not to mention, three different powerful demon magics as well. I need the ancient's soul. Riven Blackvale. I need that shadow void magic."

The snake slithered around behind her and flicked its tongue against her ear as the ethereal voice whispered. "My wraiths tainted and darkened the lands of the old Blackvale kingdom increasing my chances of entering the mortal realm. You ruined that chance."

A shimmering red haze appeared in front of her. She watched a red dragon scaled version of the wolfiend she expected Luthias to look like appear and approach her. Koraegin walked around behind her looking at her in disgust. "A female jaguar. I didn't use them as demons for a very specific reason. I don't even feel the presence of any of the wolfiend within you. Meaning, besides accomplishing getting all three void souls into one body, you failed me completely."

Jadai bowed her head. "I will make sure the mortal mage pays for the blades failure to complete their task of penetrating his dragon skin and allowing my soul entry."

Koraegin walked around in front of her as he laughed, "All three points of triad's prism have converged into Luthias's soul. If he dies, they are all dispersed once again. Each soul finding a new body to be reborn in." He watched the snake slither behind him and await its meal. Koraegin smiled at Jadai. "You were told to accomplish three simple tasks, collect and disperse the two other void souls within Luthias under your demonic control. They were dispersed into him but not under your demonic control." He leaned forward. "You failed. Secondly, you were to gain control of the wolfiend's demonic soul. Which you also failed." Koraegin stepped aside as Oblivion slithered back up to stand mere inches away from her face. "Your third task was to give me access to the mortal realm and the shadow void magic through the ancient void souls. Through Luthias." He looked around at the igneous rock around him. "Which you failed as well, or you would've been in control down here. You would have been Mistress of Knarran. That was your boon for succeeding. Oblivion is your punishment for failing."

Oblivion opened its mouth wide then unhinged its jaws to open it even wider. Koraegin walked away running his hand down the snake's head. "Enjoy your meal, my pet. Make sure she is released into the seventh descent of the fiery caves to finish dying. The major demons down there have all but lost their minds. They will shred her to pieces," Jadai screamed in protest. Her echoing screams instantly quieted into a deathly silence. "The sound of sudden and utter silence. Now I can concentrate," Koraegin said as he watched the snake devour Jadai and the blue jaguar.

Koraegin roared out in anger as he struck a rock wall and sent igneous rock flying across the caverns. "Damn it! I need the wolfiend's magic. I need the ancient void souls. I need their ancient magic. I felt when the three souls of the foretold triad prism converged within him. I felt the dark energy burst that should have sent me the power to escape Knarran and enter the realm of Terra through their void souls. How the hell did she fuck this up again?" He closed his eyes and concentrated as hard as he could. His eyes suddenly popped open as his lips snarled and he looked at the snake devouring her meal. "Although she was traitorous, she didn't fuck the plans up. Someone interfered. The ancient soul's mysterious protector. Whoever she is. Damn it!" He swung again knocking more rock loose sending it bouncing across the cavern. He looked over at the eternal flame burning in one of the many fire pits throughout the cavern system. "Whoever is meddling will burn for eternity, screaming in torment."

He ran his hand along the snake's head pondering his next move. "Spiders, spin me up a large chrysalis. I have a special demon in mind. This soul will be brought up from the seventh descent of Knarran's caverns and reformed. A soul I trapped eons ago."

'Of Shadows, Sins, & Saviors'
Book 2 is coming soon!

Words used within OS³ novel with an explanation for better understanding.

<u>Fijandsvarg;</u> Two old language words combined to bring about one. Fijands, old Gothic, meaning fiend or enemy. Varg is old Norse meaning wolf, evildoer, outlaw.

<u>Jegere av Fijandsvarg;</u> Jegere av is Norwegian for hunters of... Hunters of the Wolfiend.

<u>Wolfiend;</u> Wolf and fiend combined as one word.

<u>Futuo;</u> Latin verb form of 'fuck.'

"All magic has a cost." Spells below depend on mage strength, level of learning, as well as amount of magic within them. Even if a mage has an enormous amount of magic within them, it they cast a spell over their ability to control and understand, it can still kill them. Thank you to the Norwegian language for the use and loose interpretation of the following words.

<u>Kjedelyn = Chained lightning</u> (A lightning spell sending a bolt at one or several enemies.)

<u>Brannkaste = Fire throw</u> (A fire spell like a flame thrower.)

<u>Brannkule = Fireball</u> (A spell that creates a fireball that the mage can throw at an enemy.)

<u>Skjold = Shield</u> (Brings up a magical shield blocking incoming damage, magical or otherwise. Amount and strength depend on mages skill level and amount of magic.)

<u>Syklonvind = Cyclone wind</u> (A spell that creates a strong circular wind where the user desires. Distance and strength depend on mage's ability and amount of magic.)

<u>Stovdjevelen = Dust devil</u> (A spell creating a dust devil tornado collecting enemies and suspending or throwing them. Distance and strength depend on mage's ability and amount of magic.)

<u>Jage Brannpil = Chase fire arrow</u> (A spell that ignites the arrow and sends it back after the archer. Must be a shadow magic user of immense strength to perform.)

<u>Dra = Pull</u> (A spell pulling an item or individual towards the mage.

Item weight and size along with mages level are factors on what can be moved.)

Helbrede = Heal (A spell that heals the being wherever the mage is touching, including himself. The amount of healing and the degree of healing is determined by the mage's strength of magic.)

About the Author

B G Ridge is a retired father of six. Who's he kidding, you never retire from being a parent, no matter the kid's age. He lives in Oklahoma with his wife and dog. He graduated from the school of hard living and bad choices. Every bad choice turned into good experiences for scenes to plague the protagonists and antagonists of his books. He loves reading and writing medieval and sci-fi fantasy novels along with spending time with all six of his kids and his many wonderful grandchildren.